Mystery Hun
Hunt, James Patrick, 1964-
The reckoning

THE RECKONING

THE RECKONING

JAMES PATRICK HUNT

FIVE STAR
A part of Gale, Cengage Learning

GALE
CENGAGE Learning·

Farmington Hills, Mich • San Francisco • New York • Waterville, Maine
Meriden, Conn • Mason, Ohio • Chicago

GALE
CENGAGE Learning

LIBRARY OF CONGRESS CATALOGING-IN-PUBLICATION DATA

Hunt, James Patrick, 1964–
   The reckoning / by James Patrick Hunt. — First edition.
      pages ; cm
   ISBN 978-1-4328-2913-1 (hardcover) — ISBN 1-4328-2913-0 (hardcover)
   1. Hostages—Fiction. 2. Families—Fiction. 3. Domestic fiction. I. Title.
PS3608.U577R43 2014
813'.6—dc23   2014027363

First Edition. First Printing: December 2014
Find us on Facebook– https://www.facebook.com/FiveStarCengage
Visit our website– http://www.gale.cengage.com/fivestar/
Contact Five Star™ Publishing at FiveStar@cengage.com

Printed in the United States of America
1 2 3 4 5 6 7 18 17 16 15 14

THE RECKONING

ONE

They heard the vehicle before they saw the glare of its headlights. Coming from the south, louder as it came towards them on the narrow country road. Three men were lying on their stomachs and elbows in the wet spring grass, feeling the chill. The man at the end, whose name was Richard Billie, lifted his hand, gesturing for them to remain where they were.

The vehicle was closer now and they could see that it was a white Ford pickup truck. A newer model with four doors, long as a high-end fishing boat. Richard Billie liked that it had four doors. The truck slowed and made a left turn into the parking lot of the convenience store and bait shop that was on the other side of the road. They heard country music coming from the truck before the driver turned off the ignition and walked inside.

Amos said, "Let's go."

Richard Billie said, "No."

Amos Denton was a big man. Fat and blubbery and about a hundred pounds heavier than Richard Billie. His breathing became audible when he had to climb stairs. He had kept up with them though. Now he was shivering in the night, thinking if he had stayed back at the prison, at least he'd be warm.

"It's cold," Amos said.

"Shut up," Richard said.

"We got to keep moving—"

"I said shut up."

Richard Billie was aware of the third man with them. Javier

Sandoval. Pretty boy with smooth skin and curly hair. Javier was letting Amos speak for him, seeing if Richard knew what he was doing. If he could get them out of this county. They could stay out in the cold for a day, maybe even three days, before they were caught by the prison guards or the local police. Or died of exposure or starvation. It would all be a waste of time if they didn't get out of the county soon. Richard Billie was thinking these things through and he knew Javier was too.

Richard said, "We try to take the truck now, we'll be seen by the cashier inside."

"So what?" Amos said. "We can snuff him along with the driver. No witnesses."

Richard shook his head. He was aware that Javier was considering the logic of Amos's suggestion. Richard was the one with the gun. The gun they had taken from the prison guard. A Glock .40 caliber. After overpowering the guard, Amos strangled him so they wouldn't have to use the gun and make a lot of noise.

Richard said, "There's probably a video camera somewhere in there. We'll be seen. Then they'll know what vehicle to look for."

The convenience store sat on the northwest corner of a four-way stop. It was called Bessie's Fuel Point. There were no other businesses around. No homes or other people.

Now Richard looked at Amos and then at Javier. Looking at Javier, he said, "Wait here."

Richard Billie stood up and walked out of the ditch. He ran across the road and crouched down behind two trash receptacles near the exit of the parking lot. He remained there when the driver of the truck came out of the store. The motor came to life and then the truck rolled to the exit. When it stopped at the edge of the lot, Richard hurried to the passenger door and climbed in.

The driver looked over to the pony-tailed, dark-faced man pointing a gun at him.

Richard said, "Yeah," affirming that it was happening. Richard said, "Turn right and then stop when I tell you."

The driver was a man of about sixty. He took in Richard Billie's orange jumpsuit and knew that he was in the presence of an escaped convict. Richard let him comprehend it and said, "You'll get to go home alive so long as you cooperate. Okay?"

"Okay."

"Now pull over here."

The driver saw two shapes rise out of the field and run towards the truck. Two more men in orange jumpsuits, and it seemed unreal. One of them was a Mexican and the other a massive white fellah. His heart was pounding and the men opened the back doors of the truck and then they were in too. The driver could hear the fat one breathing hard behind him.

"Get moving," Richard said.

They had driven about four miles when Richard Billie told the driver to pull over. Richard reached over and turned the ignition off and took the keys. He told the driver to get out. Richard followed him out the driver's door, taking the keys to the truck with him.

In the back seat, Javier Sandoval smiled. *He doesn't trust me,* Javier thought. *Thinks I'll drive off with the truck while he's gone. Well . . . I might have.*

Javier watched as Richard led the driver off into a field, keeping the driver in front of him. They kept walking and soon they were no longer visible, fading out in the dark or having gone over a rise. Javier wondered if there were any cigarettes in the truck.

Amos said, "Getting cold in here again. He could have left it running."

Javier shook his head to himself. Fool, he thought.

Another minute passed and then they heard two faint pops coming through the night. A few minutes later Richard Billie came back from the dark wearing the driver's boots and coat.

Two

Tracy told John she didn't have time to make him eggs. He said that he liked eggs and toast for breakfast, putting a *but* into the statement as children will—"But I like them."

Tracy, getting short, said, "What did I just tell you? There isn't time."

John didn't respond to that one. He stared up at her. She looked back at him for a moment and then took the Frosted Flakes out of the larder and set it on the table in front of him. Then she provided him with a bowl and a spoon and milk.

As she did these things, she said, "You're eight years old now. You're not a baby. I shouldn't have to do everything for you all the time."

"Okay."

"Every morning we go through this—this thing where I have to wake you up three times and then you're late for school and I'm late for work."

"Okay."

He poured milk over the flakes and started working on them. Quietly. But she could see that she had wounded him. Shit, she thought. Is it his fault that he's eight? She wondered, not for the first time, if her expectations of him were unrealistic. She wondered if her sniping at him had anything to do with expectations.

In a softer voice, she said, "Okay. You don't have to eat it like you're a German shepherd. We'll make it." He looked at her and she smiled at him. A mother's apology.

Tracy said, "Do you have your soccer stuff ready?"

"Yes," he said. He pointed to a knapsack at his feet.

"Okay," she said, "Aunt Katy will pick you up from school and take you there. When you finish, I'll pick you up."

"Okay."

"Don't go home with someone else. I'll be there."

"I know, Mom. I'm not stupid."

"No one called you stupid," Tracy said.

Tracy walked John to the door at the school and kissed him goodbye. John's teacher gave her a wave, and Tracy waved back and returned to her car. Some of the other kids' mothers lingered in the parking lot to chat, but Tracy kept moving. She got into her Jeep Cherokee and put the schoolyard noises behind her. Then she drove to the hospital in midtown Tulsa where she worked as a registered nurse.

It was around eleven o'clock when her friend Karen came by her workstation. Karen Rudnick was a paramedic. She and her partner had brought in a patient with a massive coronary. The hospital staff gave the patient anticoagulants and sedation for anxiety and kept him alive. Karen asked Tracy if she had time for a cup of coffee in the cafeteria and Tracy said she did.

In time, Tracy came to tell her about her breakfast with John and wondered aloud if she had behaved badly.

Karen Rudnick said, "God, Tracy. You barked at him a little bit. Did he cry?"

"No."

"Then so what? You're not abusing him. You're just a little impatient. I think you're thinking too much."

Tracy said, "Maybe."

"No. No maybe," Karen said. "Is this so hard to figure out? Really?"

"What?"

"You've been a single mom now for, what, six months?"

Tracy looked at the table. "I don't know if single is the right word."

"Sorry," Karen said. "I wasn't trying to be . . . you know what I meant."

"I know what you meant."

"What I'm saying is, it's not like you to second-guess yourself. Everyone knows you're a good mom. And that you're doing the best that you can."

Tracy made a face.

Karen said, "You're not—you're not taking anything, are you?"

"You mean antidepressants?"

"Yeah."

"No. Just a couple of glasses of wine. At night. Sometimes at lunch too."

"Don't kid about that," Karen said. "It worries me."

"Don't worry about me. I don't like people worrying about me."

"But we *do* worry."

Tracy said, "I'm not drinking too much. I'm not having a breakdown. I'm just grieving, okay?"

"I know that." Karen Rudnick sighed. "Maybe you should take some time off."

"That would just make it worse. Stewing in it."

"Stewing in it? Christ, it's not like you're upset at being left by a boyfriend. You lost your husband. How can you not stew over that?"

"It's better that I work. It's been six months and I can't just spend my life being a . . . I don't know. A professional mourner."

"I don't understand you."

"It's hard to explain," Tracy said. She paused and looked at her friend. Maybe she would be one of the few who could understand it. Tracy said, "Sometimes, I get angry at people for not being sympathetic. Wait, that's not the right word. I mean, sensitive to it. You know, overhearing someone talk about casualties in Iraq as if they were just statistics. Not men or people. But then other times, I get upset at people for giving me too much attention. When he was killed, I had people putting teddy bears at my door. Teddy bears."

"They meant well."

"I know they did. But . . . don't you see? It's not *their* grief. There's something wrong with that."

"Something wrong with feeling pity?"

"I told you it was hard to explain." Tracy said, "Sometimes, I think it would be better if we lived in a place where people didn't know about it."

"Are you thinking of moving?"

Tracy shrugged.

"Oh," Karen said. "Don't do that, Tracy. You've got family here."

"His family," Tracy said.

Karen Rudnick regarded her friend.

Tracy Coughlin. Thirty-two years old. Cute, dark haired and creamy skinned. Five six in heels, though not looking petite or frail. Rarely wears make up. A serious, weighted expression that seems to fit in at a hospital, but can light up with a lovely smile and warmth when she thinks something is funny. A woman who works hard at her job and family and hasn't asked too much from life. A woman who lost a husband she loved very much to a car bomb in the Anbar Province, Iraq. Like many nurses, she is not one to wallow in sentiment or self-pity. But she's pissed off now at fate and George Bush and maybe at some other people who don't necessarily deserve it. Maybe even Drew . . .

Karen said, "They've been supportive."

Tracy looked away. After a moment, she said, "I have to get back to work."

THREE

Mike Prather usually got out of bed at 6:00 A.M. He grew up on a farm in northern Michigan—hunting country—and he had formed the habit of early bedding and early rising in his youth and it had stayed with him. He was now a special agent with the Kansas Bureau of Investigation (KBI), stationed in their Wichita office.

His path to a career in law enforcement had not been direct. He was the youngest of four boys. His parents had been strict Presbyterians, intolerant of foul language and filthy habits. Intolerant, too, of failing to use the gifts that God had given them. Much was expected of the Prather children.

And, to a point, much was returned. Mike's oldest brother had become a successful doctor, an ob-gyn with a thriving practice in Grand Rapids. The second son was a lawyer in Chicago. The third, a fighter pilot in the Navy, now holding the rank of captain and commanding the Strike Air Test Directorate at the Naval Air Station at Patuxent River, Maryland.

After their father had died, Mike's mother had sold the house in northern Michigan and moved to a condominium in Grand Rapids to be close to her son the doctor and her grandchildren. The condominium was located in a community of many retired people in their seventies and eighties. Mrs. Prather had made new friends and had joined a bridge club and, once a week, would lunch with friends at the local Chili's.

Mike Prather had not suggested that she move to Wichita.

Like his brothers, Mike Prather had married young. At twenty, he wed his high school sweetheart, a willowy brown-haired girl whose name was Betty Hochheim. Betty was nineteen at the time. They were both students at Michigan State. Mike graduated with a degree in business administration and got a job with a well-known telephone company in Kansas City. The salary offer was more than he had hoped for and the benefits seemed almost generous. He discussed it with Betty and she agreed that she could transfer to the University of Missouri, Kansas City and get her accounting degree there.

They left for Kansas City a young, hopeful, happy couple, optimistic about their futures and their marriage.

A year went by. Betty graduated college and began studying for the Certified Public Accountant Exam. She was a smart, studious young woman and Mike was not surprised when she passed the exam on the first try. After that, she secured a position with a large corporate accounting firm. With their futures seemingly intact, they decided they were ready to start a family.

Despite the pregnancy and workload of their respective careers, Betty still encouraged Mike to go to night school to get a master's in business administration. She said there was no reason not to since Mike's company would pay for it. Mike agreed.

It was at night school that Mike met a classmate who was a police officer with the Kansas City Police Department. They became friends. The policeman was relatively young and had not yet become cynical or wary of civilians. He told Mike Prather funny stories about police work. Busting gay guys trying to solicit action at parks and movie theaters, settling domestic disputes that could be situation comedies. And so forth. Mike said the work sounded fascinating. The cop asked if he would like to go on a ride along.

Mike said he would. He rode in the back seat of the patrol

car, his classmate and his classmate's partner in the front, the partner doing the driving. During the patrol, they got a dispatch saying there was a shooting at a small hotel near Bush Creek Park. The officers responded gleefully, turning on lights and siren and pressing the accelerator to the floor, the cop driving crying out, "Yeah! Fuck yeah!"

And instead of being repelled or even frightened, Mike Prather felt the rush himself. In that moment, he knew he had more in common with these cowboy cops than he would ever have with any of his coworkers at the telephone company. He knew that he envied them. That he, too, wanted a career in law enforcement.

But a month later, his wife gave birth to their daughter, and Mike Prather told himself that he needed to be realistic. He had a lovely wife and a child and his life was not simply his own. Betty told him that after a year, she would want to return to work. Mike said that was okay with him (even if his parents would disapprove). He kept his personal ambitions and dissatisfaction to himself.

So he continued to drive to work every morning with a certain resignation. At times, he would think about his place in the family. Brother doctor, brother lawyer, brother soldier, brother . . . what? Corporate stud? Corporate climber? Or corporate cog?

When he got his MBA, he knew that the next logical step would be a position in management. At work, he was competent and he got along well with others. And he was not surprised when his supervisor called him in one morning and told him he was being considered for a position in human relations.

Mike asked what it was and learned that the job basically would require him to fire middle managers around the country. A hatchet man.

At that time, Mike Prather was twenty-seven years old.

Understandably, he was surprised that they would offer such a position to someone his age. He was told that his youth was an asset. As was his inherent likeability. Mike had trouble understanding that.

He was also told the job would not be permanent. He would have to do it for about a year at most. A sort of rite of passage.

Mike said he wanted to sleep on it. The supervisor said that was fine with him, but his manner made it very clear that Mike should take what was offered if he expected to have any future at the company.

Mike Prather had never been unfaithful to his wife. He doubted he had ever even lusted after another woman. Yet he felt a guilt not unlike that of a philanderer's when he confessed to his wife that night that he wanted to resign from the company. She tried to persuade him to take the promotion, pointing out that if he didn't take the position, someone else surely would. The people would still be laid off.

Mike had said, "But that's not the point. I'd be the one doing it."

He would remember her next remark. "It has to be done. It's not inhumane."

That was when he told her that perhaps it was a sign. He had been considering a career in law enforcement for some time now . . . and his buddy had said the KCK (Kansas City, Kansas) Police Department was taking new applicants and that there would be a place for him.

This didn't go over too well with his wife. She had returned to work at the accounting firm and was making a salary at least equal to his. Perhaps understandably, she was not willing to see her husband take a considerable cut in pay. But money aside, she had by then become accustomed to a certain class structure. Her friends and peers were white-collar people. Lawyers, bankers, accountants. Having a cop for a husband would be a difficult fit, statuswise. Betty Prather foresaw conflict.

But she was not unaware that her husband had been unhappy for some time in the corporate world. And she was persuaded by his argument that he would eventually fail in a corporate career.

Mike Prather secured a slot in the Kansas City, Kansas Police Department Training Unit and resigned from his job at the telephone company. Three years later, he had had enough of the patrolman's rush. He had enjoyed the work and enjoyed being part of the cop tribe, but busting drunks and dopers and breaking up fighting spouses can only thrill for so long and he wanted to use his head more than his baton. For reasons almost forgotten, he had once gotten in a pissing contest with the KCK PD's captain of detectives. He wanted to be a detective but he suspected, with reason, that the captain of detectives would prevent him from getting the post. Or succeed in undermining him if he did. That was why Prather applied for the investigator's position at the Overland Park station of the KBI.

Mike Prather was a good law enforcement officer and a more than competent investigator. His instincts were sound, and beneath the quiet farm-boy appearance, he was a pretty tough customer. He was respected by his peers and generally liked. Those who knew him best could not imagine him in any other career than law enforcement. He fit the cop's mustache.

But he was smooth faced and young when he married Betty. They had both been young. Kids, really, who grew up and went in different directions. By their midthirties, they realized they hardly knew each other anymore. And when their daughter left for college, the house they shared became very lonely and empty.

It wasn't so much that, apart from their daughter, they had nothing in common. It was that they really didn't know each other anymore. With Julie gone, they were forced to acknowledge it. They weren't lovers. They weren't even really friends. Mike wasn't surprised the day Betty said, "We need to talk."

After the divorce, Mike Prather had taken the senior investigator's position at the Wichita station. He had not remarried. Betty had, though, to a financial planner. Mike hoped she was happy.

Now in his midforties and living alone, Mike was still sleeping when his cellular phone rang shortly before seven A.M.

He got it on the second ring.

"Prather."

"Mike, it's Arland."

Arland Johnson, the assistant director of the KBI. He ran the Wichita branch.

Prather said, "Yes, sir."

"You up?"

"No. I was going to take a vacation day today. The hearing didn't end until nine o'clock last night."

"Hearing?" Arland said. "Oh, the Billingsley thing?"

Prather rolled his eyes. The Hennessey thing had only been discussed with Arland about a hundred times. It had been on the front page of the *Wichita Eagle* at least three times. Three cops at the Hennessey Police Department had been charged with having sexual relations with a prostitute who worked part time at a convenience store. One of them had been caught in the back room, flagrante delicto, by the store manager. The cop had been in uniform, partly, and was on duty. The chief of the Hennessey PD had tried to dismiss it after the outcry, saying basically that boys will be boys, but the mayor and the town council didn't share this worldview, noting that there was evidence that the young lady in question was mentally unstable and that all three of the cops named had been on duty.

An independent investigation was requested and the KBI was sent in. The case was assigned to Special Agent Prather. As a KBI agent, Prather had investigated plenty of police misconduct.

He was well aware that young cops tend to be sexually reckless, but as he continued his investigation, he learned that the young lady had been involved not only in some prostitution but also a little drug dealing. Prather also found out that the three young cops were aware of this. Armed with what they knew about her, they could arrest her or they could get her to give them blow jobs. So it wasn't just a matter of boys being boys, after all. It was law enforcement officers using their authority to pressure a girl to have sex with them. Arguably, it was rape.

That was how Mike Prather summed it up in his report. And that was how Agent Prather testified at the officers' termination hearing. And how he intended to testify at the criminal grand jury proceedings.

The termination hearing had been exhausting. The three cops were represented by the same lawyer. The lawyer had been tenacious and had cross-examined Prather for three hours. Prather never got upset or lost his cool, even when the lawyer talked smack to him and tried to goad him into losing his temper, saying things that would get him decked if he were in a bar rather than a courtroom.

The attorney for the city asked him a few questions on redirect and then the investigatory panel let him off the seat. It was past midnight when he got home.

Now Prather remembered that he had called Arland on the way home and told him he would need the day off tomorrow. Which was now today.

Arland said, "Oh, that's right. You told me last night, didn't you?"

"Yeah," Prather said. "Don't worry about it. What's up?"

"We got a jail break in Elk County. Three escapees. Two of them murderers."

Prather said, "Anyone killed?"

"Yeah. They killed a guard. Strangulation, we think."

Without thinking about it too much, Prather said, "Are you going out there?"

"Well . . . I've got the board meeting this afternoon. Can you go?"

Prather was aware that manhunts attract large numbers of police officers. Some are there to genuinely help. Others are there to be seen. By other officers or by television cameras. Mike Prather was an investigator who didn't mind spending hours interrogating a suspect, befriending him at the beginning, talking to him as he would a normal person, establishing a relationship and eventually extracting a confession. But Prather liked to hunt too. He was not, by nature, an executioner. Either for the corporation or for the state. He believed, for example, that the Hennessey cops should not be cops anymore and that they probably belonged in prison. But he did not enjoy seeing them break down and cry when they realized they were finished. For Prather, the fun was in the hunting, the pursuit. He was forty-six years old and he had not yet tired of it.

Prather liked Arland even though he knew Arland was lazy and disinterested in the nuts and bolts of police work. He knew that any state agency needed its share of bureaucrats like Arland Johnson. Prather didn't mind going to Elk County even though Arland's motive in asking him to go was chiefly to benefit Arland. Arland did not see, at this time, a profit in being seen at the scene of the crime. But, by gum, he would send his "best man."

Prather said, "Yeah, I'll go."

Arland said, "Call me if you need anything."

For a moment, Prather almost thought he meant it.

FOUR

Dr. Pasu had asked for her assistance. The patient was a black male in his late fifties, thin and frail. There was no odor of alcohol about him but his eyes were watery and unfocused. He was sedated but his groaning could still be heard in the hall. His shirt was covered with blood.

They had him in one of the X-ray suites. Raj Pasu was a surgery resident, a few years younger than Tracy. With the patient and Dr. Pasu was a male LPN named Jerry.

The patient was still bleeding.

Tracy said, "What is it?"

Dr. Pasu said, "A bleeding tooth socket. He pulled his own tooth with a pair of pliers." The young doctor was trying to affect an ER nonchalance, but the patient was bleeding profusely and Tracy could hear the fear in the doctor's voice. To have a patient bleed to death because of a pulled tooth . . .

Dr. Pasu was intelligent and competent, but it was also his first year in residence. Tracy had found no reason to dislike him.

She decided to go right to it. She looked at the young doctor and said, "Have you dealt with this sort of thing before?"

"No," the resident said. A near plea in his eyes, hoping for a lifeline. "Have you?"

"Yes," Tracy said. There was no victory in her reply. She did not seek victories with physicians. Not unless they had it coming. She moved next to the doctor and the patient.

Tracy said, "Have you got any sort of clot?"

"Yes," the doctor said. "But I think it's beneath the socket in the molar."

"Oh," Tracy said. "Well then it's probably not formed tightly enough. If the pressure's not on the bleeding point, the bleeding's not going to stop."

The doctor looked at her. He wanted to avoid panic, yet he was reluctant to cede what little authority he had to the nurse. A moment passed and he couldn't help saying, "It's not?"

"No," Tracy said, "it's not. You're going to have to remove the clot that's there and start again."

". . . remove it?"

Christ, Tracy thought. He's a kid. "Yes. Here," she said, reaching for the forceps.

The doctor stood back and Tracy used the forceps to remove the clot from the socket. The wound gushed, flowing even more blood than before. The LPN helped Tracy clean the wound with sterile swabs. The LPN reached for Gelfoam to pack the wound and Tracy said, "No, that won't work. Get me a tea bag."

The doctor and the male LPN looked at her.

"A tea bag?" the LPN said.

"Yes," Tracy said. "*Now*. Please."

"Get it," the doctor said and the LPN rushed out of the room.

The patient continued groaning and Tracy said, "Sir, don't worry. We're going to get you taken care of."

The moan softened, a muted expression of gratitude somewhere in there.

Tracy said, "Pulled your own tooth, did you?" Her voice a mixture of comfort and mocking scold.

The patient said something and Tracy said, "What?" And then he managed to convey that a friend had helped him pull it.

Tracy nodded her head and said, "You need to go to the dentist next time."

"You *have* done this before," the doctor said.

"Yeah," Tracy said. "Gelfoam won't work."

"But a teabag will?" The doctor seemed to forget the patient could hear what he was saying.

The LPN returned with a tea bag. Tracy asked the patient to clamp down on it and he did. They stayed with him for the next thirty minutes. After that, they removed the bag and the bleeding had stopped. The patient was smiling.

In the hall, Dr. Pasu said, "How?"

"It's the tannic acid in the tea," Tracy said. "It contracts tissue and checks the discharge of blood. You could have done the same thing with silver nitrate. But I'm not comfortable putting silver nitrate in the mouth."

"You really saved my bacon back there."

Tracy kept her smile to herself. The doctor thinking about his bacon as opposed to the patient's. But his placement of priorities was not uncommon in the medical profession. Doctors and nurses learned to be dispassionate. She said, "Don't worry about it."

But the doctor was still feeling sorry for himself.

Tracy wanted to roll her eyes. Instead, she said, "Raj? Despite what you may think, there are very few geniuses in medicine. It's mostly experience. I've handled that sort of thing before. Now you have too."

She left him with that.

FIVE

There was a Loretta Lynn song playing on the radio. Something about having one kid needin' uh spankin' and another needin' uh huggin' and another one on the way. It was set on this station when they picked up the truck. The farmer must have been a country music fan. Classic country.

Javier hated country music. He didn't much like country people either. Particularly not these country people. He suspected that Richard Billie was playing the music to irritate him. Let him know that he was in charge. Javier thought of the look Richard had on his face when he came back from killing the farmer. Tough and cold, but Javier thought he was performing a little too. Richie liked having the stage.

The sun was up now. Richard Billie had the farmer's coat on. But all three of them were still in the orange jumpsuits branding them state prisoners. Javier had said—once—that they were going to have to get some clothes soon even if the police didn't find the farmer's body. Richard Billie nodded his head but didn't say anything else about it. And Javier knew Billie wanted him to say, "But what are we going to do? What are we going to do?" Show a little panic so the redneck could feel superior. And Billie would say, "Getting worried, boy?" Or something like it, the piece a shit. Well, fuck him. Javier wasn't going to give him that.

Richard slowed the truck as the sign appeared telling them they were entering Sedan, Kansas, population 1093. They stopped at a traffic light then turned south. There were houses for only a couple of blocks before the town's neighborhood was behind them. They made another turn onto a dirt road and soon they parked in front of a small house with white paint peeling off the sides.

There were two cars parked on the grass in front. One was a red Ford Escort. The other was a 1970 Ford Mustang, white with a black vinyl top.

Richard Billie opened the door and said, "Come on" to Javier. Giving him an order. Javier took his time, pretending he didn't hear it and was planning on going in the house anyway.

He followed Richard and Amos into the house. They didn't knock on the front door. They just walked in.

Christ, it was disgusting. Dog shit on the floor and the faint acetate smell often associated with methamphetamine. There was a pizza box on the coffee table with a couple of slices of pepperoni left. A couple of pornographic DVDs on top of the television. Hillbillies, Javier thought.

An Asian man of slight build came out of the bedroom. He was wearing sweats and a T-shirt. His name was Doan Nguyen.

Javier saw alarm in his eyes.

Richard said, "Hey, Doan. What's going on?"

Doan Nguyen took in the sight of three men wearing prison fatigues.

"Hey, Richard," he said, his voice covering a tremor. Just.

Amos walked over to the coffee table and picked up a slice of pizza.

Richard said, "Where's Russell?"

"Russell? Er, he violated his probation."

"Yeah? Flunk a piss test?"

"Yeah. They revoked his parole. He should be out next month. What are you guys doing here?"

"Amos," Richard said. Amos looked to him and Richard

gestured with his head to the bedroom. Amos walked to the bedroom.

Doan said, "It's just Terry. You know her. She's cool."

"Yeah, I know," Richard said. Richard smiled. "Hey, man, you think I'm going to give your woman to Amos? We're not fucking animals."

Amos brought Terry out. She was taller than her boyfriend and wider in the hips. Pale skinned and large breasted with hair dyed black. She wore a blue T-shirt and underpants.

"Hey, guys," she said.

And for a moment, Javier wondered if she had had something going with Richard. Maybe in the past. Her tone sleepy and nonchalant.

She said, "Oh, shit. You guys break out?"

"Yes, ma'am, we did," Richard said.

Doan looked from Richard to Terry and then to Amos. Briefly, he looked at Javier. Then he said, "Look, man, Russell's not here. What do you want?"

Richard smiled and said, "Take it easy, dude. We ain't going to stay the night. We just need some food and a change of clothes."

"But Russell's not here," Doan said.

"We're friends too," Richard said. He pointed to another doorway. "Russell still sleep there?"

"Yeah."

Amos went into Russell's room. Javier followed him. Javier would feel better when they had changed clothes.

In the living room, Richard said to Doan and his girlfriend, "Come here."

Doan made a face and Richard said, "*Come on.* I'm not going to hurt you. Come on. Let's go into the kitchen. Catch up."

In the kitchen, Richard said to Doan, "Sit down at the table there. Just sit down."

Doan took a seat at the kitchen table. Terry leaned up against the kitchen counter, her thighs were visible, large and pale but smooth.

Richard said, "I know what you're thinking. You're worried about Amos. Well don't worry, all right? I'll tell you what, you loan us some money, we'll get right the fuck out of here. You guys probably got to get to work, anyway, huh?"

"I'm off today. Terry's got the eleven to seven shift tonight at the Kwik Stop."

Richard said, "You got any weapons in the house?"

"No. Russell's on parole. Probation officer comes by and checks for that. There's no guns here, Richard."

Richard stared at him from across the table. "You sure?" he said.

"I swear, Richard."

"We don't," Terry added.

"What about money?"

Terry said, "We—"

"*I'm asking him*," Richard said, his voice raised.

It stilled the room. Terry was no longer trying to pretend she wasn't scared. Doan kept his hands on top of the table. The couple had met Richard and Amos only twice before. Russell had brought them by and Doan had thought then, *trouble*. Hardcore losers. Mad dogs that you'd never want to turn your back on. Russell was fun to party with, but Christ he could be so fucking stupid.

Doan said, "I've got a couple hundred bucks in the house. That's it. You can have it."

"Bullshit. You guys are fucking crank dealers. You got at least a couple thousand in here."

"No. I swear to you. We don't."

Richard took the Glock out of his belt and set it on the table. He heard Terry gasp and he turned the barrel towards Doan.

"We don't," Doan said. "We don't do that anymore. Russell's on probation, for Christ's sake. We got parole officers coming through here checking shit."

Amos and Javier came out of the bedroom wearing Russell's clothes. Tight on Amos, very loose on Javier.

Javier looked around the living room again. His eyes went first to the last slice of pizza in the box. Then they moved and rested on a set of car keys on top of the coffee table.

In the kitchen, Richard kept his eyes on Doan as he said, "Terry?"

"Yes."

"You know where that money is?"

"Yes."

"Go get it. Amos, go with her."

Terry walked out of the kitchen and Richard said, "Hey, just watch her, okay? We don't have time for you to get laid."

On the other side of the table, Doan trembled.

Richard looked at him and thought, *no.* He won't try. Richard said to him, "Take it easy."

Terry came back with Amos. She handed a wad of bills to Richard, her hand shaking.

Richard riffled through it and sighed. "Shit," he said. "This isn't enough to buy us dinner."

"I'm sorry, Richard," Doan said.

"Never mind," Richard said. "All right. I'm sorry, but we're going to have to take you out to the back barn. Don't *worry.* We're just going to tie you up so you can't call the police after we leave."

"Rich—"

"Come on."

Doan said, "But we'll be cold out there."

"Amos'll bring you a blanket. Come on."

They went out through the back door. Doan shaking, Terry

31

crying. Doan saying, "It's going to be okay, baby. It's going to be okay." The small man comforting the large woman.

The structure behind the house was not so much a barn as it was an extended garage. It had four bays. Two of them were occupied by an old fishing boat and a riding lawn mower. Richard and Amos directed them to the back of one of the empty bays. Terry was about to ask what they would tie them with when Richard raised the pistol and shot Doan twice in the back of the head. Then he turned and shot her in the chest. She flipped over on her back and he walked over and shot her through the forehead.

"Well," Richard said, "that takes care of that. There any clothes left for me?"

"Yeah," Amos said. "There's more."

Richard looked at Amos for a moment.

Then he said, "Where's Javier?"

Javier tried both of the Ford keys on the Escort but neither one would unlock the car. *Christ. They don't lock the front door to their house but they lock the doors to an eight-hundred-dollar car.* He hurried over to the Mustang. It was unlocked. He got in and sat behind the wheel.

And saw a large hole in the floor where the gearshift was supposed to be. Trying to steal a car that didn't have a transmission.

Javier managed to laugh at it as Richard Billie walked up to the car.

Richard said, "Going somewhere?"

Javier got out of the car and shut the door behind him. No way was he going to apologize to this hick. Javier smiled and said, "I'm ready when you are."

Six

Dr. Schell was the hospital's assistant administrator and though he had his own office, he did not have a secretary. His office had a window with a view of Woodward Park but was otherwise small and modest. Tracy knocked on the door and he called out, "Come in."

Tracy stepped in, closing the door behind her.

Dr. William Schell was about sixty. Tall and slim, with his hair swept back, he looked a bit like Peter Fonda.

Tracy said, "You wanted to see me?"

"Yes," Dr. Schell said.

Tracy thought, *If he asks about the Houston job, I'll tell him the truth. I've been offered a position, but I haven't made a decision yet.* Tracy did not consider Bill Schell a friend. He was not exactly a warm man. But he had always treated her professionally and with respect. She would not want to lie to him.

Dr. Schell looked up from his papers and observed her through his glasses.

He said, "We've been sued."

"Oh," Tracy said. It was not unusual for the hospital to be sued. She said, "Is it something having to do with me?"

"Perhaps," Dr. Schell said. "Did you assist Dr. Hernandez on or about . . . let me see here . . ." He picked up a copy of a legal petition, filed and stamped at the Tulsa County Courthouse. "On or about April 30, 2006?"

"I don't remember. I've assisted him more than once."

"It was an MVA. The patient's name was Curtis Van Gelder, white male of seventeen years of age, intoxicated, blood alcohol level of two-three, a passenger in a car driven by his friend, riding on the Broken Arrow Expressway. The driver lost control and the car left the highway and rolled over several times. The driver was killed. Van Gelder was brought by EMSA to this hospital where he was operated on by—"

"I remember now."

Dr. Schell took his eyes off the petition.

"So you were there?"

"Yes. I assisted. Nothing went wrong."

Dr. Schell lifted a hand. "Let's not go into all of that now. The hospital's attorney will want to discuss it with you."

"Okay," Tracy said.

Dr. Schell regarded her for a moment. Then he said, "But you did say nothing went wrong."

"Well, the boy died. Yes. But, procedurally, Dr. Hernandez did nothing negligent or improper."

"The petition says Dr. Hernandez severed his innominate artery."

"That's not what happened."

"What was the cause of death?"

"His aorta was ruptured. We have an arteriogram that showed that before the surgery. So Jeff—Dr. Hernandez—knew about the risk of surgery and explained it to the kid's mother. I know he did that."

"You *saw* him do it?"

"Well, no, I didn't see him do it. But he always does. And he faced the mother too after the boy died in surgery. He was the one who told her."

"Was there an autopsy?"

"Yes. The autopsy confirmed the ruptured aorta."

Dr. Schell sighed. "Well, then we really don't have much to

worry about."

Dr. Schell and Tracy Coughlin were not callous people. But like many in the medical profession, they were unsentimental when dealing with matters of life and death. It was, to them, a job. And they could not be good at it without being at least a little cold-eyed and unemotional. They were hard shelled, but they were not jaded.

Also, Tracy was no cheerleader for doctors. She knew there were physicians who were incompetent and had no business being near an operating room. But she did not think Dr. Hernandez was one of them.

Tracy said, "Will I have to testify in a deposition?" She had done it before.

"I don't know," Dr. Schell said. "Once the plaintiff's lawyer reviews the autopsy report, he may withdraw the suit. Or ask for a ten-thousand-dollar settlement, to go away. Which we would give him."

"It *was* sad," Tracy said. "He was just a boy. But his friend was the one that killed him. He was drunk and driving, the dumb shit." Tracy spat out the last words involuntarily. They sounded harsh, even to her.

"I know," Dr. Schell said. "And I'm sure the family sued him. But how much money can a dead teenager have?"

"Not as much as a hospital." Her words still sharp.

Dr. Schell raised an eyebrow.

"Ah, don't be too hard on her, Tracy. It may have nothing to do with money."

Tracy reddened. She had not expected such a reaction from the doctor. His tone was partly a scold, partly counsel.

"Well," Tracy said, "I didn't mean . . ."

"Grief manifests itself in different ways. The boy's mother could be greedy, yes. But if you're going to be in medicine, you're going to have to realize it makes no sense to get mad at people who sue us. We can't know what they feel. It isn't really our business to know, if you can understand that."

"I know. I—"

"Let me finish. Sometimes, relatives of the victims, they want some sort of closure. Or, rather, what they *think* is closure. But closure is an illusionary concept. You don't get closure for something like that, even if you pop a hospital for millions of dollars. This woman is grieving the loss of her child. On top of everything else, she's probably very angry. I'm sure Dr. Hernandez did everything he could, but he's here and her son's not. You can't expect her to be rational. Can you understand that?"

Tracy looked away from him and said, "Yes, sir, I can."

Dr. Schell looked at her for a few moments, his blunder dawning on him.

"I'm sorry, Tracy. I wasn't thinking."

"It's all right," she said. "If that's all, sir, I'd like to get back to work."

SEVEN

Historically, most hospitals in the United States have been established either by nonprofit institutions or by state and local governments. The nonprofit institutions were often founded by a Catholic order and named accordingly. Sometimes, the nonprofit hospitals were founded by people with great wealth who wanted to give something back to their communities. However, in recent years there has been an increase in private, physician-owned hospitals. These are for-profit enterprises. This trend was a natural result of a free-market economy. Physicians on staff at the nonprofit hospitals saw that the hospitals were collecting millions of dollars in revenues for providing surgical specialties like orthopedics, cardiac surgery, and transplant surgery. More and more, the physicians conducting those surgeries came to believe that they were entitled to a bigger share of that revenue. The hospitals (and their lobbyists) disagreed, arguing that the surgery revenues helped compensate for the areas in which the hospitals undoubtedly *lost* money; specifically, maintaining emergency room services and providing Medicaid.

Herbert Bock, M.D. was one of the surgeons who took the side of free enterprise. At least for himself. He had resigned from the staff of St. Jude's a year earlier to take a position at a physician-owned hospital in Houston, Texas. Once there, he realized he wanted to invest in the hospital himself. In the meantime, he was informed by his superiors that the physician-owned hospital was in need of an experienced scrub nurse. Immediately he thought of Tracy Coughlin.

He had called her and told her the job was hers if she wanted it.

Tracy had worked with Herb for over a year. He was heavy and a little goofy but, she thought, he was a competent and ethical doctor and probably a good man. And he could make her laugh, even lately. Herb Bock was married and didn't have kids and he had never come onto Tracy or said anything vulgar or unpleasant around her. He respected her professionally and he would never offer her a job out of pity. Nor did he have any romantic designs on her.

After she left Dr. Schell's office, Tracy checked her cell phone and saw that Herb had called her again and left a message. She checked it and heard his familiar, nasally voice telling her to give him a call back today.

Shit. He'd probably want an answer today. He had called her last week and told her they'd pay for her flight to Houston just to meet her. He had said she should at least check the place out. He had said, "No pressure." Herb liked saying "no pressure."

But there was. More money, sure. But a move to Houston would mean finding a new place to live. Selling her house in Tulsa. The house she and Drew had bought together. A move to Houston would mean putting John in a new school. Uprooting him and her too. There was no downplaying it. It would be a big change..

Who would John know in Houston? Who would *she* know in Houston? Apart from Herb Bock, she wouldn't know anybody. And some maternal voice told her, *but you'll make new friends.* And Tracy smiled at the thought of that. She didn't really have many friends here. She considered Karen Rudnick a good friend, and once in a while she would confide in her sister-in-law, Katy. Yet she knew that she and Katy would probably have never formed a friendship if she hadn't been married to Katy's brother. Katy was . . . different. Sweet and generous, but not the most perceptive woman in the world. She didn't get the jokes or observations that Drew did. Drew could make you laugh sometimes just by cocking his eye. Drew.

He was like Tracy but not like her. Where Tracy would be content avoiding a party and people, Drew would persuade her to socialize. And once Tracy got to the party or barbeque, she would actually enjoy herself. Drink a glass of wine and laugh and sometimes even watch a quarter or two of a football game. Drew had been good with people. Easy and comfortable, a natural leader. Quiet Tracy and sociable Drew. They complemented each other.

Tracy once read a short story for a college course about an unhappy man who looked through married couples' windows at night. He did this not for the purpose of seeing them naked, but to see what the couples were like behind closed doors. He peeped through lives and he invaded and he saw a series of contrasts and false fronts. A couple who made a point of touching each other affectionately at social events never laid a hand on each other in their own homes. Another seemingly happy couple living separately at home, the wife putting curlers in her hair and going to bed at ten o'clock, the husband staying up alone and watching television. Putting on a display for parties, trying to earn approval from people they probably wished were dead.

It was a depressing story. Tracy had been around twenty when she read it so she didn't give it much thought. But after she married, she sometimes thought about it. Sometimes after parties with Drew's friends, she would think about it. It interested her, this notion of people performing for their friends. And though she knew it was unseemly and uncharitable, she liked to look for the deceptions.

Still, she knew that she and Drew had not tried to deceive anyone. They were as happy in the home as they were outside of it. Sometimes during the blackest depths of her grief, she wondered if she would have been better off if their marriage had been a fraud. When it got bad, very bad, she actually contemplated trading the good times they had had to relieve the horrible one she was having now. She wondered if it would be better to feel guilt over the relief that her husband was dead and gone. Maybe that would be better than feeling this god-awful loss and pain. This fear that it was more than she could bear. That one morning she would not want to get out of bed anymore, and she would just sink into darkness. But then the feeling would pass and she would feel ashamed for nursing despair, knowing she had betrayed Drew in some way by entertaining such an idea, wondering if he would forgive her if he knew.

Her profession hardened her to death and loss. But not her own. No profession could do that. In the workplace, they saw her as a tough nurse. A good nurse who knew how to keep her head and didn't lose control. But they didn't see her at home. They weren't looking through her windows at night. They didn't see her snapping at a little boy who really didn't deserve to be snapped at. They didn't see her reaction when the television news programs aired those stupid, maudlin pieces where the soldier came home from Iraq and embraced his child. Keep the cameras rolling Deborah Norville because we all know what a father-child reunion can do for the ratings. But it would never happen for her son. Never.

EIGHT

They were laying the groundwork for a new housing subdivision northeast of the city. Engines grunted and rumbled; massive yellow machines pushing and moving dirt. Excavators, off-highway trucks, loader backhoes. Digging holes and laying trenches for utility lines, sewage and telecommunications. Pulling the beginnings of a neighborhood out of a field. A vast amount of ground to work.

Off to the side of the site were two men standing by a white pickup with a sign on the door that read Coughlin Excavating.

At sixty-three years of age, Lee Coughlin remained an imposing figure. Tall and broad of shoulder. The men on his crew called him sir, if not Lee. When angered, he was known to call an inexperienced man out of the cab of a backhoe and climb in and do the job himself. Showing them how to do it right. He would come out later and say to the man, "Got it now?"

Now he stood next to his truck with Frank Hall, a real-estate developer whom he had worked with before. Frank had driven over in his new Mercedes to see what Lee was talking about and how it concerned him.

Lee made a gesture out to the site that months earlier had been an unworked field. He was pointing to all the dirt that had been dug up. Frank Hall knew what was coming. Hall tried to get to the bad news first, saying, "Our surveyors said there'd be a cut of twenty-five, thirty thousand yards. How wrong were they?"

Lee said, "It's at least double that. I think it's going to be about eighty-five thousand yards."

"Ah, shit."

"Better to know now."

"Hell."

Lee said, "Frank, I didn't draw the plans. We're just doing the excavating."

"I know, I know." Frank Hall wasn't going to argue with him over the details of their bid. He knew Lee Coughlin was very careful about the terms of his agreements. Frank Hall's surveyors had provided the dirt estimates and they had undershot. Now they had all this goddamn dirt. It was something you had to deal with in this business. They called it "balancing." You don't want to buy the dirt because there's not enough, and you don't want to have to pay to have it hauled away when there's too much of it.

Frank said, "You know anyone who needs the fill?"

"Not offhand," Lee said. "That's not part of our agreement."

"I know. I'm just asking."

"It's not my dirt."

"I know, Lee. Assuming I don't have anyone close by who wants it, what are we talking about?"

Lee Coughlin looked out at the site again. He said, "I can call Harold Sykes over at Bulldog Trucking. Short haul, I think it might be around two to three dollars a yard."

"Oh, shit. Come on, Lee."

"You asked me."

Frank Hall sighed. "Listen, I'm not going to ask you for any favors, okay? But can you give me a couple of days to see if I can find someone who'll take it?"

"Sure."

"Thanks, Lee."

Frank Hall shook his hand and then walked back to his Mercedes. He got in and turned it around. Lee could see the red mud streaks on the lower part of the chassis. He believed Frank would get it washed off as soon as he got back into town.

Lee looked up at the sky above the site. Overcast now, grey with some hints of black in the clouds. It was going to rain. They could continue the job in the rain. So long as they could see. His crew would be safe and warm in their cabs.

He remembered working construction when he first got back from the war. Building homes in south Tulsa. He had been a young Vietnam veteran at the time with nothing more than a high school education. Long hours in the summer, men passing out in the afternoon from the August sun. Six-day work weeks, twelve-hour days. And when the heavy rain came along one morning and shut down the workday, men actually cheered with relief.

He had married Susie that fall, one of his friend's girlfriends from high school. He had run into her after he finished his tour and learned that she and the boyfriend were through. That night he took her to a drive-in at the Skyway Drive-In—the movie was *Five Easy Pieces*. Three months later, he persuaded her to marry him.

A couple of months after they married, Susie found out from one of his friends that he had been awarded the Silver Star for bravery in combat.

She asked him about it later.

"Why didn't you tell me about that?"

"Why should I have?"

"It makes you a hero," she said. She was smiling.

He didn't smile back. He shrugged and said, "They have to give those things out. Political reasons."

"Ronnie said you saved the lives of your fellow marines."

He shrugged again. "Some of them saved me. At other times." He turned to her and said, "I'm not ashamed of it. I'm not saying that. It's just that . . . there were other guys there too who deserved it just as much. More, probably."

"Some of them didn't come back."

Lee had rolled his eyes then. Not out of contempt, but more a soldier's cynical weariness. You got in the field and the first thing to go was any sense of bogus romanticism about war. *Some of them didn't come back.* Well, no. But that was not the sort of thing you liked to hear from a civilian. Even your wife.

Susie meant well, though. She was more or less uninterested in politics. She had not protested against the war. Had not suggested he was a baby killer. She was in love with him.

And he with her. For Lee, Susan was something of a gift. Someone he had come home to. He was not a religious person, but he felt a gratitude that he had been spared from the war. Not maimed or killed. He felt a . . . luck in it. A fortune. He believed it was something he should capitalize on.

When Susie's parents died, they left her a small parcel of land in West Tulsa. Susie said it wasn't worth that much, but Lee did some research and learned that the land was very close to a newly constructed highway. He persuaded her to hold on to it.

Using the skills he had learned in construction, he helped build a small hotel. Susie helped until she became pregnant with their first child. The hotel was finished when their daughter, Katy, was still in diapers. Susie helped Lee run it and they managed to make a small profit. They had almost ten thousand dollars saved by the time Drew was born and that was when Lee bought his first backhoe. He made a bid on a job for the city and two years later they sold the hotel.

The years passed while he built up his excavation business. His crew grew from two men to fifteen and he purchased more equipment, buying most of it used to keep the costs down.

Katy was in her second year of college at Oklahoma State

when Susie was diagnosed with leukemia. Four months later, she was dead.

Lee had not remarried. He didn't even date. Women liked him and approached him, but he showed no interest. He focused on his work and Katy and Drew and his grandchildren.

Now his cell phone rang. He answered it.

"Dad?"

"Hello, Katy. What's up?"

"I'm supposed to pick up John from school and take him to soccer practice. But I can't."

"What's the matter?"

"Anna has to be in Bixby for a dance class and I can't get her there and pick up John at the same time."

Lee sighed. He said, "Didn't you know about this conflict before?"

"Well, they rescheduled Anna's class. So . . ."

"You want me to pick up John."

"Could you? It would really help me out a lot. I've already called Tracy and she said it's okay with her."

Lee thought, why would it not be okay with Tracy? He said, "Okay."

"Just pick him up and then take him to soccer practice. Tracy will pick him up after that. It should only take about a half hour."

"All right."

"Are you sure it's all right?"

"He's my grandson, isn't he?"

"Yeah. Of course. Okay. Thanks, Dad."

"Bye."

Lee clicked off the phone. He was not especially surprised. He loved Katy, but she had always been a little scatterbrained. Forgetting to cook dinners or show up for appointments, etc. When she finished college, she hinted that maybe she could come to work for him. Without hurting her feelings, he persuaded her that she wouldn't be happy there.

In contrast, he thought that Drew could have been happy working for the company. He saw in Drew an ability to handle the jobs as well as the ability to lead. But Drew had told him he didn't want to drive bulldozers and dig holes for a living. He became a firefighter instead.

Lee's instincts had proved correct though, to a degree. Within two years with the fire department, Drew was promoted to shift captain. Drew wanted to lead, he could see. But he didn't want to do it at his daddy's company. Lee was proud of him, to be sure. But he had hoped then that, as the boy had proved himself in another venue, maybe then he would consider coming back to Coughlin Excavating. Ultimately, Lee wanted Drew to take over the business.

After he graduated from high school, Drew enlisted in the marines. He went to boot camp at Parris Island and did tours in Okinawa and Twentynine Palms, California. His last eighteen months of regular duty was at the Marine Corps Air Station in Yuma, Arizona and he said he never wanted to see that place again. He did his four-year stretch and came out when he was twenty-two, having achieved the rank of staff sergeant.

Two years later, he enlisted in the marine reserves. The marines found that he was proficient at training and gave him a nice billet. As a reserve, he got a monthly stipend and was required to give back one weekend a month and a couple of weeks active duty for the year. Drew didn't really need the money. The truth was, he liked the reserves. He liked being a part-time marine. It meant something to him. It was part of his identity.

Along with most of the people in the country, Lee watched in stunned horror as the planes struck the towers on 9/11. But his anxiety increased in the following months as politicians and talk-radio warriors spoke of the need for preemptive military action and retribution. Lee had done his military service and gotten out. He had never had any interest in being a soldier again. He had never contemplated being an army reserve or even being in the National Guard. He had seen enough. But Lee knew the drill. Military reserves could treat service almost as a break away from the tedium of a civilian life—a weekend camping trip away from home. But when the country went to war, they could activate your unit and you would go too, no buts about it. It wouldn't matter whether or not you were married and had a family. Having a family, in itself, would not count as a hardship exemption. That was the agreement Drew and thousands of other men and women in the military reserves had made.

Lee believed in keeping agreements. He believed that Drew had made an agreement with his country and that he had to abide by that agreement. Still, when war began to seem inevitable, Lee had wanted to go to his son and ask him if there was a way he could get out of it. Lee had thought about doing this even though he knew it would be wrong.

Can a man be objective about war when his own family is involved? Can he support a war that might cost him his own son? His only son? Lee had tried to be objective. Lee Coughlin had an old soldier's pacifism. He had been trained to kill and he had killed. He had seen combat up close, had been there and done it. He knew it was something that should only be done as a last resort, not as a mission of misplaced vengeance. He believed that he would have opposed the Iraq venture even if Drew were exempt from service.

But it didn't make any difference now. He had not tried to persuade Drew to get out of his obligation. Drew's unit was called up and eight months later he was killed.

Lee had kept his letters and copies of his e-mail dispatches.

He hadn't had the courage to reread them since Drew had been killed.

Lee's phone rang again.

"Daddy?"

It was Katy.

"Yes."

"I forgot to tell you something. I think it's important."

"What is it?"

"Tracy's thinking of moving."

"What?"

"She told me that she might take a job in Houston," Katy said. "And I'm not supposed to tell you that . . ."

Lee closed his eyes. Opened them. "I'm glad you did," he said.

Katy said, "Now don't say anything to her."

"I'll try," Lee said.

NINE

Tracy told him she wouldn't have time for lunch, but that she could steal away from the hospital for about twenty minutes if he wanted to meet for coffee. She hoped that that would put him off. It didn't, though, and Lee said coffee would be fine.

They agreed to meet at the Starbucks in Utica Square, near the hospital. Tracy walked the two blocks, a tan mackintosh over her green scrubs. She saw him through the window. A tall man, still handsome and slim. Drew had inherited Lee's lean figure and pose, but not the hard looks. Drew was softer.

Lee touched her on the arm. It was his way of showing affection. He had never been physically demonstrative. When she married Drew, Lee had not raised his glass for a toast to the bride and groom. Drew later told her that his father would have been too shy to do that. Tracy said, "Him?"

Lee said, "Thanks for coming. Can I get you something?"

Tracy didn't want to be rude. "Just a small coffee," she said. Though she was more or less coffeed out for the day. She would sip a bit of it while they talked and he told her what he wanted to see her about. Though she was pretty sure she knew . . .

She went to a small table and sat down. From there she watched him stand in line. God. Lee Coughlin in a Starbucks. He was a contrast with the other people sharing the line. Behind him, a short fellow in his thirties with a protruding stomach, wearing a backpack. In front of him, a large lady wearing a rather loud Coca-Cola sweatshirt. They seemed ridiculous next to this figure from another time. This hard-looking man who looked like he'd done stunt work on westerns in the sixties. Who looked like he could still break a horse.

Tracy believed she was not intimidated by her father-in-law. That she never really had been. When she had first met Drew, she thought him to be one of the strongest people she had ever known. Drew had not been afraid of people. Had not been shy. Drew had liked to joke dryly with his friends, cut up in a deadpan tone. But Drew became another person with his father. Calling him sir more often than he called him Dad.

Hell, she thought. *What difference does it make now?*

Lee came over. He set the coffees down and sat across from her.

She could say to him, "Bet you thought you'd never come here, huh?" See if that would make him smile or put him at ease. Say, "How have you been?" She could say those things to him if he were a normal person or if she wasn't his daughter-in-law.

But then he looked across the table at her and she knew it would be best to go straight to it.

"I think I know why you wanted to see me," she said.

Lee said, "Yes?"

"Is it about Houston?"

"Yeah. Katy tells me you're thinking of taking a job there."

"I'm just looking into it now. I don't know what'll happen."

After a moment, Lee said, "Is it a better job?"

"I would be a scrub nurse. That's a nurse that helps the doctors during surgery. It would mean more regular hours. A little better pay."

"Cost of living's higher in Houston."

"Not so much," Tracy said.

"Couldn't you find work as a scrub nurse here?"

"Maybe," Tracy said. She didn't see a point in lying.

Lee said, "Why move then?"

Tracy didn't avoid his eyes. It was best to address Lee directly. She said, "Maybe a change would be good for us."

"You and John?"

"Yes."

"But you don't have any family in Houston."

She was about to say she didn't have any family here either. She was from Kansas City originally. She had come to Oklahoma to attend nursing school. She could tell him that, but it wouldn't be fair. Not even to this man.

She said, "I know that. But I . . ."

"Then why do you want to move there?"

She gave him a sharp look. "Am I obliged to explain it to you?"

"I didn't say that. It's just that, well, he has family here."

"John?"

"Yeah. Who else would I be talking about?"

"I don't know. Listen, Lee. I don't need your permission."

Lee Coughlin looked away from the table for a moment. Three people nearby were trying to have a business meeting, using words like "paradigm" and "proactive." He wondered why anyone would take the time and money to discuss business here.

Lee said, "I think you misunderstand me."

"Yeah?" Tracy said, her tone not too friendly.

"I'm not trying to tell you what to do. Where you can live . . . but we're a family here. John's cousins are here. His Aunt Katy and Uncle Mark. They consider him one of their own."

"And you?"

"He means something to me too."

"Oh. Well, that's nice."

He seemed to feel the sting of that. He said, "He means a lot to me."

Tracy said, "You trying to atone for something?"

Lee mentally rolled his eyes, the girl getting emotional on him. He said, "I don't know what you mean. I'm only saying that you would be taking him away from people who care about him. People who want to be a part of his life. It would be hard on them too."

Tracy gave him a bitter smile. "Hard on them," she said.

"Yes."

Tracy said, "So, I'm being selfish. Is that it?"

"No. I'm not saying that." He paused. "What is it? Are you wanting to meet someone else?"

He had not meant to offend with the question. Lee Coughlin was a hard man, but not a cruel one. Still, he was a man and was not able to see things the way a woman would. He was ignorant and insensitive in the way that the most decent man could be.

Tracy said, "Jesus Christ. Is that what you think?"

"I—"

"You think I want to move to Houston for a boyfriend?"

"No. I don't—"

"What do you think I am?"

"Now—"

"I can't believe you said that."

"That's not what I meant. I'm sorry." He said, "The truth is, I'm afraid you're moving away for the wrong reasons."

"And what would those reasons be? Maybe I want to get a new start. Are you saying I'm running away?"

"I don't know if you're running away. I think you're angry."

"Yes. Wouldn't you be?"

"At what? The war? What?"

She stared at him. A young lady staring at him without fear. Staring at him with a mixture of anger and curiosity.

Finally she said, "You really don't know, do you?"

He didn't answer.

Tracy stood up and walked out, leaving the coffee untouched.

TEN

She tried to hold on to the anger as she walked past the shops—
the trendy restaurant, the Spray's Jewelers, the high-dollar candy
store—her hands in the pockets of her raincoat, determined to
hold on to her bile, her irrational fury at the man back there in
the coffee shop. *That* man. That jerk. That clueless son of a
bitch. But then the stores were behind her and the hospital
loomed up before her a block away and she broke into sobs.
Crying now. Crying like a little girl.

No, no, no, no.

God, he would have loved to have seen this. Awww. Little
lady crying. It's okay, honey. It's okay. Let me get you some tissue. The bastard.

*I lost my husband, you prick. My husband. My son no longer has
his daddy. That's it. It's permanent. You dare to suggest that I should
stay in this fucking town. For you? So . . . what? So you can have
the relationship with John you didn't have with Drew? For you, you
son of a bitch? Tough, remote daddy wants to be the soft-hearted
grandpa? That's supposed to make up for it?*

Back there, she had almost lost it. She had almost unloaded
on him. They should have left years ago. They should have left
Tulsa after they had gotten married. Right after. Moved to
Kansas City or Chicago or Dallas, somewhere far away from
the dad. It would have been different then. Drew might be alive
if they had done that.

But they hadn't. They had stayed while Drew got his EMT

license so he could become a firefighter. Stayed while she became pregnant with John, and after he was born, the family circled around and babysat and watched and gave him gifts on birthdays and Christmas and that was that.

They weren't bad people. She knew that, even now. Katy was a little off, but goodhearted and loving. Mark, her husband, was dependable and droll and a good father to his own two children. And Lee was quiet and really not intrusive, but always there. Always a presence. And that was the problem.

It could have been different if they left. Maybe it would have been different. It would have been okay if it were just Katy and Mark and their two children pitching in to help. Maybe it would have been different if it were just them. Or maybe it would have been the same even if they had moved away. If there was not the presence of Lee, there would have always been the specter.

The Old Man. Dad. *Him.* All his life, Drew had tried to measure up to Him. Lee the businessman, who built himself up from nothing. Lee the father, who always took care of his family and never betrayed his wife. Lee the soldier, who went to Vietnam and came back with the Silver Star medal. Lee the rotten bastard who did nothing—*nothing*—when his idiot son enlisted in the reserves so he could be a tough guy like his dad.

Jesus Christ! This was the twenty-first century. This was modern times. Where did these guys come from? Who were they? Had they watched too many movies about honor and truth and duty when they were kids? Did they not realize that John Wayne dodged the draft and never once saw action at Iwo Jima? Dumb-ass Okies with their "right is right" notions. Why did she have to fall in love with one of them? Why did she have to fall in love with this one's son?

Before the president had said Saddam had twenty-four hours to get out of town, Tracy had asked Drew if he could get out of the reserves.

Drew had said, "I can't."

"Why not? You have a wife and son."

"That doesn't qualify me for an exemption. They're sending reserves that are fifty-five years old."

"You can't leave us."

"I don't want to leave you or John. But I signed on . . . before all this . . . shit. Besides, even if I could get a hardship exemption, I couldn't do that to the other guys in my unit."

"Couldn't do what?"

"Stay here while they went off. I'd never be able to forgive myself."

"You'd never be able to forgive yourself. Jesus Christ."

"You don't understand."

"No, I guess I don't. You seem to be more worried about what your buddies would think of you than your wife and kid."

"Oh, shit, I don't even know why I told you that because it doesn't make any goddamn difference. I'm telling you, it doesn't matter because I cannot get a hardship exemption. They will not do that."

"You can't get one if you don't try."

"I'm not going to try because it'll be a waste of time."

"You're not going to try because you're afraid your asshole buddies will find out about it."

Drew hadn't responded to that.

It was no use. And when Drew talked, it was Lee she heard. Lee speaking of duty and country and unwarranted attacks. Not that she had ever actually heard Lee say those things. He didn't say much in general. He didn't preach, didn't boast. But it wasn't what he said. It was his existence that spoke. The existence that Drew tried to live up to.

She should have spoken to Drew about it. She should have told him that he didn't have to apologize to anyone. She should have told him that *she* was fiercely proud of him. That he had nothing to prove to her or to John.

Would it have done any good? Would it have done any good to tell Drew that he was already a hero, already a man? Lee, you bastard. What is it about you that made him feel he had to prove himself? Did you withhold approval? Did you show him disappointment? Was your approval more important to him than the love of his wife and child? More important than their needs? Did Drew finally get that approval, that respect, by dying? Dying for what?

ELEVEN

By midmorning the manhunt was in full swing. A command center had been set up at the Elk County Sheriff's Office and the early daylight hours brought helicopters and planes from Kansas Highway Patrol buzzing over fields and wooded areas, using their heat-seeking devices to find men hiding in the brush, their body temperatures higher than the damp spring earth.

Deputies, local town officers, Kansas Bureau of Investigation (KBI) agents and state police swarmed the county and surrounding areas. Lot of windshield time, stopping at places of businesses and homes and doing knock and talks. Photos of the fugitives were distributed to all the media outlets.

It was sometime between ten and eleven in the morning when one of KHP's helicopters spotted a body lying in a field. Circling back to investigate it, they came down to land on ground the pilot hoped wasn't too soft. The patrol officers crouched beneath the slowing rotor blades as they came out of the copter and they feared they were approaching a dead man before they reached him.

There was no identification on the body, and the state officers called local deputies to the field. It wasn't until then that they confirmed that the deceased was a local farmer named Ben Hagermann.

Sheriff Don Edwards later told the senior supervising KBI agent, Prather, that Ben Hagermann's wife had called the station the night before to say that he was missing.

Agent Prather said, "She called your dispatch last night?"

"Around midnight," the sheriff said.

Prather said, "Didn't you think then that there could be a connection?"

The sheriff sighed. "I don't know. I wasn't advised of it until this morning."

"And now they've got his vehicle," the agent said.

The sheriff made a gesture, suggesting they were trying as best they could. While thinking, Lord God, it slipped through the cracks. Two men dead now. A prison guard who got jumped by three guys armed with a makeshift knife, probably melted down from a section of a plastic cafeteria tray. They took his gun away from him and then strangled him to death. No mercy. They used the gun later to kill Ben Hagermann. A man who'd never done a lick of harm to anyone.

Prather said, "Do we have their DOC files?"

"Yes. I was thinking we should have a briefing at noon."

"Okay," Prather nodded. "Before we do that, can you tell me what you think?"

Sheriff Edwards understood where the agent was coming from. Prather wanted to know his thoughts behind closed doors, rather than in front of a room full of law enforcement officers.

"About what?" the sheriff said.

"About why two yokels would be escaping with a highly ranked member of the Tijeras Cartel."

"You mean the Mexican?"

"Yeah. As I understand it, he was prosecuted by the U.S. Attorney's office on federal narcotics trafficking charges. Why was he at Elk County?"

"I should ask you. It's a state facility in our county. Doesn't make it a county facility."

"Okay," Agent Prather said. "I confess, I don't know either."

"I reviewed Sandoval's file," the sheriff said. "He had a state assault-and-battery charge in addition to the federal counts. Maybe the feds wanted to stick him here awhile to make him feel like he wasn't such a big shot. But your guess is as good as mine."

"Okay. What about the other two?"

"Now them I'm familiar with. Richard Billie and Amos Denton were convicted in 2004 for the slaying of Chrissy Anne Poteet. A sixteen-year-old girl. They abducted her and took her out to a field, raped her and killed her. Both got life sentences with no possibility of parole. They're turds, both of them. Been running around together since they were kids. Always been in trouble. They're wicked men, especially Richard. Sadistic and mean. Hard-core shitpokes."

"What were they doing with Sandoval?"

"I don't know. I have no knowledge of him being linked with them. Not apart from this."

"Relatives?"

"Amos's mother is in Longton. I've had two deputies interview her. She says she hasn't seen or heard from him. I've got two men posted near the residence in case they attempt a visit. He's got a sister in Kansas City. She says she hasn't heard from him since he got sent up. She says she cut him out of her life years before that. But KCPD is keeping an eye on her residence as well."

"And Billie?"

"He's got an ex-wife and kid in Elk City. No sign of him there."

"Your deputies have spoken to her?"

"One of them."

"I'd like to have a couple of my agents interview her, if you don't mind."

"I don't mind."

"Have you had a chance to go over the inmates' visiting lists?"

"No. Not yet." The sheriff would not admit aloud that he hadn't thought of it.

Agent Prather said, "Can I see the files?"

"Help yourself."

TWELVE

They crossed the state line on a dirt road that was not on the state map. South into Oklahoma and now in the Osage Hills. It made Javier nervous, not seeing any highway signs or familiar conveniences. How did Billie know they weren't lost, maybe driving one of these twisty back roads back into Kansas? The boy said he had grown up on these roads and knew his way around. Richard Billie insisted on driving and keeping the gun too.

Richard Billie seemed to hear what Javier was thinking and he said, "You think we're driving this thing to Dallas, you're crazy."

Javier looked across Amos Denton's girth to acknowledge him. Gave him a glance and looked back out the windshield.

Javier said, "We had an agreement."

"Fucking A we did. I agreed to get you out. I didn't agree to take you to Dallas. And if we're going to be talking about fucking agreements, my man, what about that shit you tried to pull back there?"

Javier smiled.

"Huh?" Richard said. "You were trying to shag out on us."

Javier shrugged.

Richard said, "Say the car had been right, were you planning to send me the fifty grand in the mail?"

Javier said, "You'd have done the same thing."

"Bullshit. I don't leave men behind."

Christ, Javier thought. *I don't leave men behind.* Like he'd been in the fucking military or something. Javier said, "The deal was, you help me bust out, I'd pay you some money. I didn't say I wanted to go on a goddamn crime spree with you."

"Dude, we needed clothes and we needed traveling money and I didn't see you getting them for us. I was getting things done."

"You didn't have to shoot 'em."

"Shit," Richard said, grinning. "Come on, man. What the fuck am I supposed to do, leave them alive so they can call the cops? You knew that was gonna happen the minute we walked in."

Javier shrugged again. Like he didn't care, which he didn't. "They were your friends," he said.

Richard Billie chuckled. "Yeah, well," he said, "you do what you have to do. But I don't see you doing a fucking thing. We needed transportation, I got it. We needed clothes and some traveling money, and I got that too. Meanwhile, you're sitting on your nuts second-guessing me."

"You get me to Dallas, I'll pay you."

Richard Billie spoke to the Mexican like he was a young child. "Javier," he said, "how long do you think we can drive this truck, huh? We have to get gas and something to eat. Use the farmer's credit card to pay for it and maybe we'll be swarmed by cops before we can fill the tank. We fugitives, boy."

"Get another car, then."

"Do that and I gotta use the gun again. I've only got so much ammo."

"That's not my problem."

"It is your problem."

"All right. Pull over and let me out."

Richard Billie laughed. "What?"

"We split up. End the partnership."

"Partnership? What fucking partnership is that? What have you been doing? You go to a restaurant and eat the meal, you don't ask for your money back afterwards. I got you out. You promised you'd pay me fifty thousand for that."

"Get me to Dallas and I'll pay you."

"Javier, for a supposed big shot in the Tijuana Cartel or whatever you call it, you ain't too goddamn bright. How am I going to get you to Dallas without all three of us getting busted? They know our names. They know our faces. And here we are all together. Three Amigos."

"That's what I'm telling you. It's better we split up."

"Right. *After* I get my money. Then you can go wherever you like. And we'll go wherever we like."

Amos said, "You guys are giving me a fucking headache. Why didn't you talk about this before?"

"Shut up," Richard said. To Javier he said, "Listen, we're better off than we were twelve hours ago. Right? But we have to keep cool and think things out or we're all going to get caught. You told me you can get me fifty thousand dollars. Now I'm wondering: was that legit or were you just talking shit?"

Javier saw the cold menace in Richard Billie's eye, the gun still in his hand. Javier said, "I didn't lie to you."

"Yeah? Let's hope not. How were you planning to get it?"

"My people will get it to me."

"Your people." Richard Billie smiled. "How? You call ahead and tell them to bring their MAC-10's, dispose of a couple of white boys?"

"Come on, man."

" 'Say hello to my lil' fren',' " Amos said, as Richard kept smiling.

"We're just kidding you, Javier," Richard said. "Here's the shit: There's no way we're going to make it to Dallas. We're on borrowed time as it is now. Here's what we'll do. We'll be in

Tulsa in about an hour. We hole up there, hide this truck. It's a big enough city to hide in. You get in touch with 'your people,' have them bring the money to *us*. Get cleaned up, fed, and rested and then we settle up our debts. Then you can go wherever you want. How's that sound?"

Javier regarded Richard again. Took in the blue-eyed stare and the pistol again and realized the man wasn't asking a question.

THIRTEEN

It was not Lee's first time to pick John up from school. He had done it before when Drew had been around. Tracy worked full-time at the hospital and Drew had had the typical shifts at the fire stations. Twenty-four on, forty-eight off. There were times when other members of the family would pitch in and help out. It had never been a problem. Gratitude was expressed, but not overly so. It was expected. They were family. Tracy had been okay with it then.

She was okay with it now, Lee thought. She had asked Katy to pick up the boy. So . . . was she okay with Katy but mad at him? What had he done?

Was it just grief? Could he expect her to be rational? He wasn't sure. Apart from his relationship with his wife and his daughter, he had not had much experience dealing with women. Not relating to them. His world had been such that most of his contact was with men. The marines, construction work, running the hotel, and then the excavation business. He had never thought in terms of whether or not he was a chauvinist, a dinosaur. He believed he was fair with everyone.

As he sat in his truck waiting for the children to come out of the school, he thought about the first time he met Tracy. Drew brought her over to dinner at Katy's house. It was the first time he'd ever brought a girl to a family dinner and Lee knew then he was going to marry her.

And this was okay with him. He'd thought then that she was

bright and that she had her stuff together. She was polite but she didn't kiss up to him either. And he liked that. After the engagement was announced to the family, he stood in the same room with them and had an irrational fear that the girl would approach him alone and ask him if he missed his own wife or some other sentimental thing that was none of her business. She didn't, though, and he was greatly relieved. Later, he wondered why he had been afraid that she would ask him such a thing. Because she's a young woman? Young and getting married and wrapped up with emotions? No. That wasn't her. She wasn't silly.

After that, he felt better about her. He wasn't quite sure why. But it seemed that she had demonstrated a sort of maturity and strength. And though she was a couple of years younger than Drew, Lee started to think of her as being a little older. As if she would be taking care of him.

They had never really talked with each other. Not intimately. It was as if they both recognized that such things were not quite their style. Not even a shared glance, for that would have been false and forced as well.

She's not mad at you, he thought. *She's lost her husband. She's lost my son. It's the grief. She's a young widow.*

Lee remembered his wife's parents. His father-in-law dying of cancer, lying in a hospital bed, hurt and angry as hell and yelling at Susie's mom over something meaningless and making her cry. Susie yelling back at him not to treat her mom that way. Soon everyone in the room was crying, except Lee.

Lee was no psychologist. But even he could see that Susie's dad just wasn't himself. He had never known the man to mistreat his wife. He was frightened and angry. And he was taking it out on the woman closest to him.

She's taking it out on you, Lee thought. But he still didn't understand why.

He heard the school bell ring. He got out of his truck and approached the school exits. Within a couple of minutes, he saw John. The boy saw him and gave him a welcoming smile.

Lee felt a wrench of fear. And he knew why he felt it. *I'm sixty-three years old,* he thought. *Maybe I've got ten more good years. Ten more years to spend with John. Fishing, camping, talking. Ten years to spend with the boy as he grows into a young man. Ten years—slower years—to relax and not think and move so much. Maybe sell the business. Get rid of all that time worrying about utility lines and excavation sites and surveyors who don't know their head from their ass.*

Ten years of that. Just a few years of that, please. Don't take him away.

"Hi, Poppa."

"Hello, John. I'm to take you to soccer practice." Like he was under orders.

"There is no soccer practice."

"Why not?"

"Coach said the field's too wet and muddy from the rain yesterday."

"Oh. Well, you want to come over to the house? I can fix you some toast."

"I know how to make toast."

"French toast."

The boy's face lit up. Young enough to get excited by the foods he liked. Lee felt another wrench, softer this time. "Yeah?" John said.

"Yeah. Let's go."

John was sitting at the kitchen table, telling him about the guys on the soccer team. Complaining about the strikers who ran at the ball and didn't stop to think about where to put it or how to get it around the opposing team. John said he "was losing his temper" over it. Lee smiled at the boy's words; he'd probably learned them from his mother. The boy sat at the table while Lee mixed the batter to dip the bread into and then laid the slices in the iron skillet.

John was like this with him. Chatty. Free of self-consciousness and hesitation in a way that Drew had not been. Drew had so often been quiet around him. He had cooked for Drew too, hadn't he? It was hard to remember. It had been different when Drew was eight. Everything so rushed then. Busy. Back then, they had had to live modestly, worrying about bills, worrying about whether he could make the loan payments on the massive machinery that was necessary to run an excavation business. Men of Lee Coughlin's generation did not take off work to watch their children's school pageants. And he was of the belief that the children wouldn't mind if he missed that sort of thing anyway. When he was a kid himself, he would've been humiliated if his father had indulged in such things. He tended to think other men felt the same way.

Lee finished preparing the after-school snack and set it before John. He placed the bottle of syrup before him. Lee let John have the table to himself as he leaned against the kitchen counter and sipped his coffee and read the newspaper.

"Hmmm," John said. "That's good."

"Thanks."

"Where'd you learn how to cook?"

"I worked sometimes as a short-order cook when your grandmother and I owned a hotel."

"You cooked?"

"We had to do just about everything."

"Maybe I could buy a hotel when I grow up."

Lee grunted in skepticism. He was just a boy, thinking such a life would be easy. But grown men and women had said much the same thing. *I should do that.* Own a hotel. Like it would have been a nice, leisurely life. Bob Newhart standing behind a desk with a cute wife twenty years younger than him. Unaware that staff has to be paid and until you can afford to do that, you're going to be doing everything yourself. Cooking, cleaning, bookkeeping, manning the desk. Eighteen-hour days, typically, for him and Susan. And that had been early in their marriage. He would not have been able to do it without her. Clichéd as it was, those had been his and Susan's happiest days. They worked and they saved and they prospered and they moved on.

They had bought this house after they sold the hotel. A modest two-story, four-bedroom house in midtown with a built-in two-car garage. It was located at the end of a tree-lined road in a midtown neighborhood. The house was not particularly special, but it had a big lot and a lot of privacy. After Susan had died, Lee had plenty of money to move to a tonier neighborhood. But he hadn't wanted to. His children and his wife were gone and the house meant something to him. Besides, though he had never been intimidated by anyone, he felt uncomfortable socializing with people of wealth. He didn't like golf. He had never joined a country club.

He set the newspaper down when he heard the doorbell ring. He wondered if he had locked the front door after he got home. If it were Katy, she would have just let herself in. He opened the door without looking through the window.

It was a man in his twenties. Dark hair pulled back in a ponytail and a tattoo on his neck. Immediately Lee sensed danger.

"Excuse me, sir," Richard Billie said. "Is this by chance the Wilson residence?"

"No," Lee said.

At that moment, he heard a sound coming from the kitchen. The back door closing? Then the boy cried out. "Poppa!" Lee turned his head back.

Then Richard had stepped in the front door, closing it behind him. He pointed the Glock at Lee's midsection.

"Step back, old man," Richard said.

This isn't happening, Lee thought. *It's so quick. So immediate. This isn't happening.* He turned around at the approaching sound. John with two men behind him. A Hispanic and a large, fat man with slits for eyes. The big one had his hand on John's shoulders.

"Poppa!" John said, and broke away and ran to him. Lee caught him in his arms. Holding the boy, Lee turned back to gunman.

"All right," Lee said. "Let's remain calm."

"I am calm, old-timer."

"What do you want? If it's money, I'll give it to you, no problem."

"Shit, I *know* that."

"We're going to cooperate with you. Okay? So there's no need to hurt anyone."

"I know you're going to cooperate. Amos, go lock all the doors and close all the shades. Javier, check to see if anyone else is in the house."

The Hispanic one seemed to look at the long-haired guy before he moved. The fat one did as he was told right away. Lee felt his heart sink. They were using each other's names, indifferent to whether or not he heard them. And that wasn't good. That wasn't good at all.

Richard gestured to the couch with the gun. "Sit down."

Lee walked John over to the couch and sat him down next to him. Lee kept his back straight.

Richard said, "Put your hands on your knees. I said, put your hands on your knees."

Lee said to John, "Do as he says. It's all right."

Richard said, "What's your name?"

"Coughlin."

"First name."

"Lee."

"Lee Coughlin. You seem pretty well off. This your boy?"

"My grandson."

"Awww. Where are his parents?"

"His mother's at work. His father's not around."

"Where is he?"

"He died. He was killed in Iraq."

"Well," Richard said. A grin on his face. "Ain't that a shit sandwich."

Lee felt his chest tighten, his hands flinching on his knees.

Richard said, "Hold on, old-timer. You take a swing at me, you're going to get yourself and the boy killed. Understand?"

Lee said, "What do you want?"

The Mexican came back down the stairs. He nodded his head to Richard Billie. Then Amos was in the living room with them.

Lee said, "If you tell me what you want, I'll be in a better position to cooperate with you."

Richard Billie smiled again. Like the old man was being cocky with him. He looked from Amos back to the old man.

"You're a tough one, aren't you?" Richard said.

"No," Lee said. "I'm not that. I want to give what you want and get you and your men out of here." Lee was giving him something there. Telling him that he was the leader.

"Right," Richard said. "Well, old man, I don't see much here I want to take."

"Take whatever you like. Just go."

"We'll go when I say. You understand that? I asked if you understand that."

"I understand."

Richard Billie was sensing something from this man. A sure-

ness and an authority. He had worked for people like this before.
It never lasted. People like this were never happy unless they
were giving men like him shit.

Richard said, "What's your story?"

Lee said, "Excuse me?"

"What do you do? How do you make ends meet?"

"I work in excavation."

"Exca*v*ation? What's that?"

"Digging trenches. Holes. It's . . . nothing."

"Yeah? But you're the boss, huh?"

"In a way."

"Used to telling people what to do?"

Lee said, "Not so much."

Richard was smiling again. "Yeah," he said, "you are. The big
fucking boss man. Use convict labor?"

Lee didn't answer.

"Do you?"

"No," Lee said.

"This must be eating your lunch, huh. Couple of fucking
dirtbags come into your house and start telling *you* what to do.
How's it feel to be on the receiving end, boss?"

"Listen to me: I've got nothing personal against you. Or
them. I don't even know you," Lee said. "Why don't you tell me
what you want."

It was a risk and Lee knew it. Telling the punk to get on with
it. Lee was sensing this young man. A loser and a troublemaker,
violent and looking for a way to bring it out. He had made the
mistake of hiring one or two of these in his time. The sort that
show up to the job site and the senses tell you right away there's
going to be trouble. Losers and squirrels. But no one had ever
pointed a gun at him. Or at one of his grandchildren.

Richard stared at Lee for a moment, wondering if he should
just raise the gun and put one in his chest now. Teach him to

watch his mouth. Then he'd have to do the kid.

And then what? Maybe one of the neighbors down the street would hear the gunfire and call the cops. The stolen pickup in the driveway. And they would probably need the old prick to get them out of here. At a minimum, they would need his car.

The boy, Richard thought. *The old prick wants to protect the kid.* He's not going to endanger the boy. So long as we have the boy, the old man will do whatever we want. If not for the boy, they'd probably have to kill the old man now. 'Cause he seemed like the sort that didn't like to be pushed around.

Richard said, "First off, we need the keys to your garage."

Lee reached into his pocket and took out a set of keys attached to a ring. On the ring was a small automatic garage door switch. Lee stopped himself from chucking the keys at Richard Billie's feet. He was fairly certain that sign of disrespect would get him shot.

With his head, Richard gestured to Amos. "Give 'em to him."

To Amos, Richard said, "Put the truck in the garage. Make sure that door is closed."

Amos started to do it. But Richard stopped him.

"Wait a minute," he said. "Check the old man's truck. The glove compartments, etc. Something tells me he's got a gun in there." Richard trained the pistol back on Lee. "Am I right?" he said.

After a moment, Lee said, "You're right. It's in the glove box."

"What is?"

Lee sighed. "A revolver."

Richard brightened. "Okay, then," he said. He said to Amos, "Check the rest of the vehicle too. Make sure there's not another one he's not telling us about."

Amos left and Richard said, "What about in the house? Any more guns?"

"No."

"Don't lie to us, Lee. We're going to check, and if we find one, we'll break the boy's arm."

"I'm not lying."

"We're going to check anyway. Here's the thing, old man: I know you better than you think. You think you're pretty tough and you think you're smarter than me. But you're not. You lie to me, I'll know it and it'll be him that pays for it. You try to fuck with me, I'll kill the boy first. Do you understand that?"

"I haven't lied to you."

"Don't."

"I haven't lied to you," Lee said again. And now his arm was on John's shoulder, steadying him. "If it keeps us alive and safe, I will do whatever you want. But you haven't told me what you want."

Richard said, "We just need a place to stay for a while. We'll let you live if you cooperate with us. Just don't you fucking think about trying to outsmart me. Now. Does the boy live with you?"

". . . No."

"With his mother?"

"Yes."

Amos returned through the back door. He showed Richard the revolver, a .38 snubnose. Richard asked him if he put the truck in the garage and Amos said he did. Then Richard asked if the garage door was closed and Amos said, yes, he had done that too. Amos said, man, he was fucking starved and he was going to go in the kitchen and get some food. Richard told him to go ahead.

Javier remained in the living room with the rest of them.

Richard said to Lee, "Where is she? Where's his mama?"

"I told you. She's at work."

"Where does she work?"

"She works at a hospital. She's a nurse."

"What time does she get off?"

"Usually at five thirty, I think."

"Don't you know?"

John said, "It's five thirty." Lee could feel the boy trembling. Lee said, "I don't often—it's five thirty."

Richard Billie said, "So what was the plan? Were you going to take him back to her place, or is she coming here?"

"I was going to call her and offer to bring him to her house," Lee said. "Why don't you let him go? I'll stay with you and do whatever you want."

"What are you, stupid?"

"I'll pay you for it. I have some money. I'll pay you to let him go. I'll stay with you. You'll still have a hostage."

"No deal, pop. First of all, I let him go, he'll tell his mama on us. Also, with him around I think you're more liable to behave yourself. You got a cell phone?"

"Yes. In my jacket."

"Where's that?"

"Over there."

Richard called out for Amos. He called out again and Amos came out of the kitchen holding a sandwich.

Richard said, "Amos, get the cell phone out of his jacket. Hold on to it." To Lee, Richard said, "Here's what you're going to do: you're going to call the kid's mom, tell her to come here and get the boy."

Lee stared up at the man with the gun. He said, "I can't do that."

"You're going to do that."

Lee felt his heart quickening. The punk was giving him a hard, fierce look. The face of a loser suddenly in power. Half his age if that, but if he didn't have the gun, Lee was fairly certain he could beat the punk senseless. Rush him and knock his head against a wall . . .

But he *did* have a gun. And two other men with him.

With effort, Lee managed to remove the desperation and fear from his voice. He said, "There's no need to bring her into this. She doesn't know about you or them. Why don't you leave her out of it?"

"She's his mother. You think she's just going to forget about him?"

"She wasn't planning to pick him up until tomorrow anyway."

"Pop, what did I just tell you about trying to outsmart me? Do you remember what I told you?"

"I remember. Listen, it's easier for you, it's easier for all of us if there's less people here. Let me call her. I'll tell her he's not feeling well and that he's going to spend the night here. That's one less person you have to worry about. One less person to keep an eye on."

Richard Billie was smiling again, performing for the other two. Lee was beginning to see that he enjoyed performing.

Richard said, "It'd be one less for you to worry about too. Wouldn't it?"

"Please," Lee said, the word escaping him before he could think about it.

"No deal," Richard said. "We have to operate like nothing's wrong. See? You call her and say he's sick, she's going to know you're full of shit. She gets suspicious, maybe thinks you want to do something—well, you know."

Behind them, Javier made a face registering his disgust. "Billie," he said.

"What?"

Javier was staring at him. A prison stare. It held for a moment and then Javier said, "Just get on with it."

Richard stared back at the Mexican. Giving him his badass convict look for the required three seconds, letting him know he wasn't backing down.

Richard said, "The point is, you call her and try to talk her out of getting the boy, she's going to smell something."

"She—"

"Don't argue with me. She's going to know something's wrong. Maybe she'll show up here with a lawyer. Maybe she'll show up here with a cop. And if that happens, the boy dies. And you die."

"I—"

"Let me explain something to you: me, Amos, we're serving life sentences. For murder. We got nothing to lose. Nothing. We see cops outside, we'll kill the boy. And then we'll kill you. No negotiation, no standoff. Just bam and then bam."

Richard pointed his gun first at John's head and then at Lee's as he said this. Pantomiming it.

Richard said, "The cops find out we're here, they'll be more interested in catching us than protecting you. That's how it works. We're fugitives." Richard said that part with pride. "So you don't want them to know we're here. All that's going to do is get you and the boy killed."

Lee said, "I told you before, I'm going to cooperate with you. Now I meant that. You've explained to me what you're up against. Now that I know, I have no interest—no interest—in getting in your way. But there's no need for the boy's mother—"

Richard Billie pointed the gun at John. "Discussion's over," he said. "Do it now."

FOURTEEN

"Hello?"

"Tracy. It's Lee. I've got John here at my home."

"Oh. No practice?"

"No. Apparently the field was too wet."

Lee was sitting in the chair across from the couch where Richard Billie was sitting next to John. Billie still had the gun, pointed casually at the boy.

Lee said, "Can you come get him?"

"Sure. It'll be twenty minutes."

"Okay. Bye."

"Bye."

She was gone. And he thought he should have said something else. He should've said he would have him waiting at the door. Have him waiting at the door, shove him out when she got there and then slam the door behind and rush the son of a bitch while telling Tracy and John to run. He could have said something to her.

But the man was sitting on the couch next to John. Sitting next to the child. Lee knew wickedness and hatred and anger. He'd seen it in men. He'd seen it in enemies. He wanted to believe this man with a ponytail was a poser and a punk and nothing more. But he knew that wasn't true. He knew that this was the sort of man who would shoot a child.

It was good he hadn't said anything unusual on the phone. Because Richard Billie would have known it. The way an untrustworthy person never trusts anyone else. Billie would have known.

Richard Billie said, "You trying to cook something up, pop?"

"No. I've done you what you want." Lee got to his feet. "Why don't you move away from him now?"

"Ooh. You trying to tell me what to do?"

"You're getting what you want," Lee said. "But if you think I'm going to stand by while you abuse him, you're wrong."

"Abuse him? What do you think I am?"

"I don't know," Lee said, giving it a hard meaning.

Richard Billie stood up and moved toward Lee. Behind him, Amos tensed with the revolver. Amos feared that the old man might try to rush Richard then.

"Hmmm?" Richard said. "You saying I got short eyes?"

Lee didn't answer. Instead he looked dead into the convict's eyes, letting him know in that moment just how little he thought of him.

Richard slapped Lee across the face.

John cried out. He got to his feet.

"Stay where you are," Lee said. "John. Just stay where you are. Sit down. Sit down."

Richard kept his prison stare on Lee. "Huh?" he said. "Is that what you think I am?"

It was the Mexican who spoke then. Not because he was disgusted by violence. He'd seen plenty of that. Much worse, in fact. But he had the masculine distaste for cowardice.

Javier said, "Hey. Richie."

"What?" Richard said.

"Give it a rest, huh?"

Richard Billie turned to him. "Who says?" he said.

Jesus Christ, Javier thought. Little *cono* smacking around an old man, threatening a kid. Thinking it made him tough. It was embarrassing. Javier walked over to him. Standing nearby, he said in a low voice, "You want to kill the guy, do it. But don't try to get him to make you do it."

Richard Billie gave him a sharp look then.

Javier said, "I mean, what's the point?"

"You trying to tell me what to do, amigo?"

"It's your show, Richie. But I don't see what you proving here." The Mexican was smiling at him now.

Richard looked at the Mexican looking back at him, holding that smile. And Javier knew that Richie was thinking about turning that gun on him. But he couldn't do it. Because he needed the money Javier had promised him.

Richard looked back at the old man. "Get on the couch," he said.

Lee did so. He knew the slap hadn't drawn blood, but he could still feel its sting. His heart was beating. He had never been slapped like that in his life. Not even as a child. It had been a struggle to stand there while it happened. To stand there after it happened. He wanted to rush the punk then. He was close enough to do it. Maybe a one in five chance of reaching the man's gun before he could use it to shoot.

But if he failed, he would be killed. If not by Richard, then by the fat one behind him. Maybe killed with his own gun. And then John would be alone. Not just John, but Tracy too. When she came.

Christ. Tracy. He had called her on the telephone and led her into this trap. This nightmare. Tracy the mother, Tracy his son's wife, Tracy the nice girl who'd never harmed anyone. He had placed the call that would bring her to these men. They had used her son to make him place that call. Used blood against blood.

He remembered reading that the Nazis used to do things like this at the concentration camps. A couple of prisoners would assault a guard, perhaps in an attempt to escape. Upon being caught, the condemned men would have to select *another inmate* to share in their execution. This would be done in front of all the prisoners. To send a message. That had just been one of their tricks.

Knowing that, you began to understand why it was stupid for people to ask why the victims could be so passive.

On the couch now, he could feel John's shame. Like Drew, John had always worshipped him. A figure of strength and toughness and calm demeanor. Standing there while a man slapped him across the face. Being a boy, it would be that image that would resonate with John. But what about the real transgression? Calling John's mother on the phone and bringing her to this? Could he ever be forgiven for that?

Stop it, he thought. *Stop this shit.* There's no time to feel self-pity. If he let himself get caught up in it, he would be finished. They would all be finished.

When Tracy got here, he would have to figure some way out of getting John to the door. Pushing him out there with Tracy, and then shutting the door after them. Maybe they could get away then while he stalled these monsters.

. . . maybe.

Or maybe it would get them all killed.

FIFTEEN

Prather knew Cullen from the Union City job a couple of years ago. They had a corrupt chief there running a department where pretty much all the cops were crooks. The chief and the assistant chief were taking payoffs from the local meth dealers, one of whom was the assistant chief's brother. They killed a rival dealer and his girlfriend and tried to kill the girlfriend's sister when she came to town and asked too many questions. The sister somehow found a couple of men to help her out and several gunshots were exchanged before it was all over.

KBI had sent Prather there after the chief was arrested. Will Cullen, a new agent at the time, had helped Prather conduct the investigation and together they gathered enough evidence to send the crooked chief away for twenty-five years. Cullen said that he couldn't believe an entire police department could be crooked. Even if it was small and in someplace as isolated as western Kansas. Prather thought about the New York Police Department, circa 1970, but kept that to himself.

Prather knew that Sheriff Don Edwards was not like the chief in Union City. Edwards was an honest cop but he was old and he was tired. Three convicts escaped from prison and two people were dead and there would probably be more before they were caught. This reality did not thrill him to the hunt. It deflated and depressed him. Sheriff Edwards probably wasn't at fault, but his was a political position and he would almost certainly catch some blame for it.

Prather shared his thoughts about Sheriff Edwards with Agent Cullen. He said that Edwards was a good man and that he would probably be glad to cede authority to KBI on this matter but that the KBI was not to make Edwards feel unimportant or unappreciated because it wouldn't do Edwards or them any good.

Prather said, "The sheriff said he already sent a deputy to interview Richard Billie's ex-wife, but maybe they didn't ask as many questions as they should have."

Cullen said, "We can bring her and the kid here." They were still at the command center that had been set up at the Elk County Sheriff's Office. Cullen said, "That way, she'll feel safe."

"That's good thinking," Prather said. "But if we go to her house and sort of . . . take a look at it, maybe we'll hit on something."

The KBI agents were in a blue Crown Victoria. Agent Cullen pulled it up behind the state police car that was parked in front of Cara Bracknell's house. Prather gave a wave to the state troopers who were looking at them in their rearview mirror.

The troopers got out of their car and the four law enforcement officers met in the street. One of the troopers brought a shotgun out with him, as if the fugitives might come down the road any minute. Then he decided against it and put the shotgun through the open window of the patrol car. The troopers said they hadn't seen anything. That they hoped the turds would come here so they could just shoot them and be done with it. They said if that didn't happen they were liable to shoot Cara Bracknell's boyfriend because he had a big fucking mouth.

Prather said, "She lives with a guy?"

A trooper said, "Yeah, some asshole calls himself 'Bear.' Comes out here with his shirt off, the faggot, prancing around, bowing up, trying to tell us we don't need to be here because *he's* got it under control."

Cullen said, "What's his story?"

"Ah," the trooper said, "he's just a punk. His real name is Steve Beaufort. Acts like he's a badass, but he's had a couple of DUI's and nothing much more."

Prather said, "Has he got a gun?"

The trooper said, "He didn't *say* he did. But he might." The trooper shrugged. "There's no violation of law there."

Prather said, "He threaten you?"

"No," the trooper said. "I threatened his ass, though. I told him we were conducting a stakeout and it was not a good idea to interfere with us and to get back in the house. He argued with me a little, and then went back inside."

Prather said, "You mind going up the front steps with me? I'm not wearing a uniform, and he might be pointing a gun at the door."

The trooper said, "You think he's scared?"

"Wouldn't you be?" Prather said.

The agents walked alongside the uniformed trooper and went up the steps of the small, shabby house. The trooper called out to Bear Beaufort and Beaufort came to the door.

Sure enough, he did look scared.

Prather gave him a quick look and said, "Are you Bear?"

"Yeah," the boy said. "Who are you?"

"Special Agent Prather. I need to speak with Cara."

"She already talked with the cops."

"I understand that," Prather said and stepped into the house. Bear Beaufort had to step back to avoid being bumped by the agent. Prather wasn't going to ask for permission.

He saw a woman of about thirty sitting on a couch with a blanket thrown over it. She was holding a baby. On the floor was a ten-year-old boy, sitting cross-legged and playing a video game.

"Well come on in," Bear said. Trying to get something back.

"Will," Prather said, "would you talk with him please? In the kitchen."

"What did I do?" Bear said.

"Nothing," Agent Cullen said. "I just want to ask you a few questions, okay? Come on."

Cullen led the boyfriend away, leaving Cara Bracknell with Prather.

The boy looked up at Prather, acknowledging him briefly, then returned his attention to his game. It was that quick, and Prather hoped his gut feeling that the boy was cold and unfeeling was wrong.

Cara Bracknell wore a tank top that revealed large, droopy breasts set far apart. There seemed to be a small dent in her chest between. Her face was shiny and ceramic looking and unattractive. She looked like a stripper. Her expression was tired and worn out and when she spoke it seemed like she was used to dealing with law enforcement.

"I already told the deputies I haven't heard from him."

"I know that," Prather said. "Do you mind if I sit down?"

"Go ahead."

Prather sat and gestured to the boy on the floor. In a quiet voice he said, "Is he Richard's?"

"Yeah. Travis. We call him Travis Beaufort. Not Billie."

"Oh. Did Bear adopt him?"

"No."

Prather was not going to ask any more about that. It was not unusual for women to name their children after their current boyfriends, trying to patch together a family.

Cara said, "I'm still Bracknell, legally. But me and Bear are going to get married sometime this year and then I'll be Beaufort. But we're calling him Beaufort now just cause."

"Bear's going to adopt him?"

"He *can't*. Richard won't relinquish paternal rights. We have to have his permission before Bear can adopt Travis. Not that Richard gives a shit about him. He just wants to have something he can use against me."

"To get money?"

"Yeah, or trade it for something. You know, that son of a bitch once tried to get child support from *me*. Can you believe it?"

"I can," Prather said. He looked at the boy who didn't seem to be hearing a word of it. Prather said, "Do you mind if we talk over there?"

Cara Bracknell looked at the boy and figured out what the cop's concern was. She shrugged and said, "Sure."

They moved out of the boy's earshot and Prather said, "You told the deputies you haven't seen or heard from Richard."

"Yes."

"And you were truthful about that?"

"Yeah. I wouldn't help his ass."

"Does Bear have a gun? Come on, you can tell me."

"Yeah, he does. He's scared. I am too."

"Do you think Richard will come here?"

"I don't know. I don't think he's into me or anything. I haven't had anything to do with him since he went to jail. We were broken up before that. But he knows where I live. And that's bad enough."

"You think he'd harm the boy to spite you?"

"He'd do it to spite the boy. You're not from here, are you?"

"No. I'm based in Wichita."

"Let me tell you what he once did. When we were divorced, he did shit for Travis. Shit. And then I got hooked up with Tim. Tim Bracknell, my second husband? Richard calls up here to yell at me about something, something about child custody, and Tim got on the phone with him to defend me. They get into it.

Richard hangs up the phone and comes over here and starts fighting with Tim. He bit Tim's nose off."

"That's terrible. Was he arrested?"

"Yeah. But he got a lawyer and they argued mutual combat or some shit and Richard got a suspended sentence. Tim had a record too, though nothing like Richard's. Tim didn't want much to do with me after that. I didn't blame him. I mean, who needs that shit?"

Agent Prather did not reply.

Cara Bracknell said, "I got to tell you something: when he and Amos killed that girl, I was relieved. Isn't that terrible? I always knew that he'd kill someone, and I was always afraid it'd be me or Travis. Or maybe Bear or Tim. He killed that girl and they got him and put him away and I didn't have to worry about him anymore. You have no idea what it's like to be scared all the time."

"We'll find him."

Richard Billie's ex-wife sighed and for a long moment didn't say anything. Then, "Yeah, I imagine you will, eventually. He's wily but his luck never holds out. But by the time you find him, he'll have damaged a lot more people. What's he killed since he broke out, two?"

"Yes. Two."

"He's got nothing else."

Sixteen

Tracy parked in the driveway of Lee's house. She got out of her car and looked up at the sky. Grey now, maybe a threat of rain. Dreary, almost oppressive. Then she put her sights on the house and thought, *shit*. Last time she had seen Lee, she had given him heat. Now he had John with him. She did not worry that Lee would harm John. She had never worried about that. But now Lee might think she would want to apologize to him or something. Or, worse, ask her if she wanted to talk some more about it. Finish what she had started. He could be direct like that when he wanted to. *Get it over with*, she thought. *Get John, thank him for his help, and go.*

She walked onto the porch and rang the doorbell.

She would not have done that if Drew were still around. If Drew were here, they would have opened the door and walked right in. Drew had his own key.

Richard snapped his fingers at Amos.

"Take the boy and get in the back of the house. *Now.*"

Amos moved toward John. Lee started forward, but then Richard Billie was pointing the gun at him.

"Hold it, pop," Richard said. "Amos, you hear a shout, a warning, anything, you shoot the boy." To Lee, he said, "Now you're going to the answer that door. And remember, that boy's life is in your hands. Go."

Lee looked toward John, now in the hold of the enormous

Amos. Amos started to pull John away.

Lee said to the boy, "It's okay. Everything's going to be okay."

"Move," Richard said.

The doorbell rang a second time. Lee moved toward the door. *God,* he thought. *God forgive me.* His plans for escape were destroyed.

Richard Billie stepped out of the view of the doorway. Javier remained in the dining room.

Lee opened the door.

Tracy looked at him with an expression that was neither angry nor friendly. Businesslike, if anything.

"Hey," she said.

"Hi," Lee said. "Come on in."

She stepped in and then past him.

Richard Billie was the one that slammed the door shut. Tracy's eyes went wide as she took him in, Richard not saying anything as he stepped forward and pulled her bag off her shoulder and threw it on the floor.

"What the—"

But then Lee took her by the shoulders and pulled her towards him, out of the reach of the fiend who he thought might just hit her.

"All right," Richard said. He was now pointing the gun at both of them. "Let's everybody be calm."

She knew, yet she didn't know. They called it home invasion. Predators breaking into a person's home and holding the occupants hostage. You heard about it on television. But it was in the bad neighborhoods. It happened to drug dealers being ripped off by crooks knowing there would be easy money there. But *here?*

A Mexican man came into the room. Soft eyed and smooth skinned. Almost pretty, but alien to this home.

"Oh my God," Tracy said.

"It's all right," Lee said. Though he knew it wasn't.

"Where's John?"

"He's okay." Lee looked at Richard Billie. "Show her the boy."

Richard gave Lee another hard look. But Lee didn't drop it.

"Show her the boy, for Christ's sake. You want her to start screaming?"

"Amos!" Richard said. "Bring the kid out."

They came out of the back room and John broke out of the big man's grip and ran into his mother's arms.

Lee could feel his daughter-in-law trembling with fear. He was about to speak, but was surprised to hear Tracy speak first.

Looking right at her lead captor, she said, "What are you doing here?" Her voice controlled.

Richard did a sort of mock double take. Lady talking shit to him, huh? He smiled again, though not in the same way he had at Lee.

"Pardon me?" Richard said.

Tracy said, "What do you want?"

"Ma'am," Richard said. "We are fugitives from the law. And we have decided to be your guests for a while."

Lee started to intervene. But Tracy was speaking again.

"Are you on the run?" she said.

"I think I just told you that," Richard said.

Tracy said, "Why don't you lock us in a room? Take the keys to my car and go." She said it like it was a directive. This from a cute little thing wearing a nurse's scrubs.

Richard Billie stared at her for a moment. He looked over at the Mexican and then at Amos. Then he looked back at the woman and laughed.

"Get on the couch," Richard said. "All of you."

Tracy felt her father-in-law pull gently at her shoulders.

"Come on," Lee said.

Richard directed Amos to keep the revolver trained on them while he went through Tracy's bag. He pulled out a cell phone and kept that. Then he went through her purse. There was eighty-seven dollars in there and he took that too. He put her car keys in his pocket and then he threw her bag aside.

Looking only at her, Richard said, "Who knows you're here?"

"No one."

"What about your husband?"

"My husband's dead."

"How?"

"He was killed in Iraq."

Richard nodded his head slowly at that. Another nasty grin on his face. "Yeah," he said, "I heard about that."

Tracy said, "Then why ask me?"

"To make sure your daddy ain't lying to us."

"He's not my father. He's my husband's father."

"Oh. Right." Richard was grinning at her again.

Lee didn't like what he was seeing. It was bad before. Bad when they had him and the boy hostage. But now . . . Tracy had no makeup on and was wearing her work clothes. But there was no hiding that she was a very attractive young lady. This crocodile of a man was noticing it too. Looking at her and grinning and sizing her up . . .

And she was looking right back at him. Doing her best to hide her inner terror, and doing a pretty good job of it too. She must have been trained, Lee thought. Trained to know that creatures like Richard Billie feed off fear. Are emboldened by it.

But, good Christ, he hoped she knew what she was doing.

"All right," Lee said. "You've got all three of us now. So that should make things easier for you."

And now Billie was looking at him instead. That was better.

Lee said, "You don't have to worry anymore about whether or not someone's going to show up here or come looking for us.

So why don't you take what you need and go. You can lock us in the basement. Or in one of the rooms upstairs."

Richard was about to speak, but Lee continued.

"I'm not trying to tell you what to do," Lee said. "You're the one in charge here. I'm just trying to work with you so you get what you want and I get what I want."

"What *you* want," Richard said.

"All I want is for the three of us to stay safe," Lee said. "You can have money. You can take the car. You can lock us up so we won't be able to escape."

"And when someone comes here to set you free, then what?"

"By then, you'll be long gone," Lee said. "I don't care what happens to you as long as you're gone."

Richard gave him a look.

And Lee said, "You know what I mean by that. It's of no consequence to me whether or not you're caught. Just so long as you're gone."

After a moment, Richard said, "The basement, huh?"

"Yes," Lee said.

"How do we know you don't have a gun hidden down there?"

"I don't. Have one of your men check."

Richard turned his gaze toward Tracy. "How about you? No gun in your bag. Do you have one in your car?"

"No," Tracy said.

"You sure? Your husband was a soldier."

"I'm sure," Tracy said. "No gun. I hate guns."

Richard smirked again. "We're going to check anyway. Okay," he said. "I'm hungry. How about you, Amos?"

"Yeah."

To Tracy he said, "You're going to make all of us dinner."

Lee said, "No, she's not."

"What?" Richard said, his voice sharp.

"You want dinner," Lee said, "I'll make it for you."

"So you can poison us? Forget it, pop."

"I've got nothing like that in mind. I'll eat whatever you eat."

"I just told you, I want her to do it."

"She's worked a long day. Besides, I'm a better cook than her."

Tracy turned to look at Lee, but Lee was keeping his focus on Richard Billie. Richard said, "You don't want her to serve us, is that it?"

"No, I don't," Lee said. "You want to argue about this too? Or do you want to eat?"

"Don't push me, old man," Richard said. "I'm warning you. Don't push me."

SEVENTEEN

Lee made them bacon and eggs. The Mexican stood near him while he did it, making sure he didn't put little green pellets of mouse killer in the pan or throw bacon grease into someone's eyes. More than once, Lee looked to the back door, wondering how he could push Tracy and the boy out of it. But it seemed like it couldn't work with all three of their captors back here at the time and in any event, the second time he looked at the door Richard Billie caught him doing it, smiled and shook his head. Richard Billie didn't say anything then and somehow that made it worse.

He's a loser, Lee thought. *But he's not stupid. He's convict smart.*

When he was finished preparing the meal, Richard made them all sit at the table together. At some point John looked over at him, scared, and Lee made a funny face back at him, to keep his chin up. It seemed to cheer the boy a little, and then Lee saw Tracy looking at him in a way that was unfamiliar to him.

The big man ate like an animal. Loud, slurping, sloshing noises. Tracy turned her head away quietly, but the Mexican noticed this and smiled over it. The Mexican had excellent table manners.

Richard Billie ate his food with one hand, using a fork. In the other hand, he kept his gun. He seemed to be enjoying this, all of them in close quarters.

Lee said, "I've been thinking."

He made eye contact with Billie.

"I've been thinking, I could pay you to leave."

Richard Billie said, "Haven't we already gone over this?"

"Maybe," Lee said. "But we haven't discussed figures."

"Figures."

"I have a few hundred dollars in the house."

"Oh? How nice."

"But I have more in the bank. If you take me to the bank, all three of you, I'll withdraw money. I'll go with you wherever you want."

"For what?"

"You leave them here."

"In the basement?"

"Yes. They won't be able to alert anybody. And you'll get money and you'll still have me as a hostage."

Richard said, "Who would want you as a hostage?"

Lee didn't answer that one. "You'd have money," he said. "All of you."

"I got money coming to me," Richard said. "A lot. I go with you to the bank, get a couple of miles down the road and a dye pack blows up in my face, covers me with ink. Or I've got marked bills. Or I get my face on videotape. This'll happen whether or not you're dead."

"That won't happen."

"Because you say it won't? Your word of honor?" Richard smiled. "No, pop, there's just too many ways it can go wrong."

"You'd have money," Lee said.

"You're trying to mind-fuck me again. Big shot wheeler dealer. When are you going to learn that you're not running this?"

"I told you, I'm not trying to. You're the one in charge."

"Now you're blowing smoke."

"If you'd just listen to me—"

"Shut up. Clear the table." Richard turned to Tracy. "You. Help him."

Lee said, "Don't give her orders."

Richard said, "I'll do what I want."

"We're doing what you ask us," Lee said, raising his voice. "There's no need to humiliate anyone."

Richard Billie picked up his plate and hurled it against the wall. It shattered there and left a greasy egg stain. Shoulders at the table hunched and then Billie was on his feet staring across at Lee, Billie's hand on his gun. He was daring Lee to keep it up.

Lee kept his hands on the table. He maintained eye contact with Billie, but didn't say anything.

Richard Billie said, "You can clean that up too."

Later, Lee and Tracy stood next to each other at the sink, him washing, her cleaning. John was standing nearby.

Amos was sitting at the table, holding the .38. His attention was focused on the small television set on the counter. He was watching a Jim Carrey movie.

Keeping her voice low, Tracy said, "What are you doing?"

"What?" Lee said, aware of the scolding in her tone.

"You're pushing him," she said. "Do you want to get killed?"

"I wasn't pushing him."

"The man is a psychopath. He'll kill you. Stop messing with him."

"I'm not—"

"You are, Lee. This isn't a schoolyard. It's not one of your excavation sites."

Lee didn't respond to that.

Tracy said, "It's like you're trying to compete with him."

"Is that what you think?"

"I want to survive," Tracy said. "I want all of us to survive. You antagonize him, you endanger all of us."

"I'm not trying to antagonize him. And if you think I'd willingly endanger you and John, then you don't understand me at all."

For a moment she didn't say anything. Then she said, "Now you're mad at me?"

"I have no control over this," Lee said. "Don't you see? I have no control over what happens here. And it—"

And it terrified him. It frightened him down to his socks. A fear he not known since he was in Vietnam. But worse now because they had his family hostage. His grandson's life in the hands of these animals. The mother of his grandson, his son's wife, at the mercy of savage men. He was trying to hold on to something in the face of this. The girl couldn't understand that. She thought he was taking this as another dick-swinging episode.

Tracy said, "And what?"

Lee said, "Listen to me, you're going to survive this. You and John. I swear it. I promise to protect you. Do you believe me?"

Tracy was looking at her father-in-law. She was confused by his expression, his emotion. It was something she had never seen before. Not even when Drew died. Lee had not cried then. Now the man was looking at her and asking her—*asking* her—to trust him. Asking her to just believe him. It threw her. She was trying to form an answer when the big man at the table called out to the others to come into the kitchen.

"Hey!" Amos said. "Come in here. We're on television."

Richard came first, followed by Javier. Richard looked over at Lee and Tracy and ordered them away from the sink.

"Stand over there," Richard said. "*There.* Now stay there."

Then Richard turned to Amos and said, "What the fuck's the matter with you? He might be reaching for a kitchen knife or something."

Brandishing the .38, Amos said, "What's he going to do?"

"Shut up," Javier said to both of them.

And there they were on the screen. Their black-and-white mug shots. Three convicts escaped from the Elk County prison in Kansas the night before. Their names were given. They were at large, believed to be armed, and highly dangerous. Police believed they had killed two men already. A prison guard and a local farmer. The newscaster told the viewers to be on the lookout for a late-model Ford truck with four doors and a Kansas license plate, although police believed the plates could have since been switched.

Tracy turned John's head toward her body. She didn't want him to see this.

The broadcast cut to a law enforcement official in Kansas for comment. A ten-second shot of that and then it was back to the local anchor.

"Okay," Richard said. "Turn it off."

Amos said, "They don't know where we are." He was keyed up over being on television. Scared, but trying to cheer himself.

Richard said, "They know about the farmer, though. And the truck." Richard looked at Lee and Tracy. He said, "What the fuck are you looking at?"

"Nothing," Lee said.

Richard stared at them for a moment. Then he said, "You got something you want to ask me?"

"No," Lee said.

"Good. It's time for you to go to bed. All of you."

Tracy said, "Where are we going to sleep?"

"You're all sleeping in the same room."

"The basement?" Lee said.

"No, not the fucking basement. Quit suggesting things. You're going to sleep in the guest bedroom upstairs. All of you. We'll be guarding it. Anyone tries anything stupid, anyone tries to drop out of the window and break a leg, the kid gets smoked. And if that's not getting through to you, remember there's worse things we can do to him. Now let's go."

There was only one bed in the guest room. It was a queen size. At the door, the fat guy looked at it, then gave Lee a gross, knowing smile. Lee didn't smile back and then the door was closed.

Tracy promptly locked it. Then she held John again.

Lee said, "That's not going to keep them out, if it comes to that. They can kick it open pretty easily." He picked up a wooden chair and propped it under the handle.

Lee said, "I'll sleep on the floor. You and John take the bed."

Tracy said, "We can all fit."

Lee said, "I've slept on floors before."

EIGHTEEN

Richard Billie sat in a brown leather chair with his feet upon the ottoman and sipped from a bottle of Budweiser. The gun was on the table beside him. He kept a lizard's eye on Javier though, to make sure the spic didn't get any ideas about trying to take it. Richard had the remote control to the television and he flipped through channels, sometimes stopping on the ones broadcasting news about the escaped killers.

He liked seeing himself on television. He remembered television cameras focusing on him and Amos when they were first caught by the police and led into the county lockup. Amos put his head down in shame, afraid of his momma or daddy seeing him there. Richard held his head up. People were shouting questions and comments at him and he stared straight ahead, unashamed.

It wasn't an act. He felt no shame over the death of Chrissy Anne Poteet. She had been hanging out with them, drinking their beer, taking their methamphetamine. She was a tweaker and she'd do anything to get meth. Her skank friends were no better. One night, she begged for it and Richard and Amos told her she knew what she'd have to do. She undressed and got on her back, looking skinny and pale and patchier than she used to. It had been nothing to write home about and when they were finished, she asked for the crank and Richard said he'd think about it.

That was when she went all apeshit, screaming and shouting.

Motherthis and motherthat and Richard popped her. She was bleeding then and making strange sounds with her mouth, and Amos said, "Fuck, Richard. I think you might've broke her jaw."

Turned out he'd only knocked a couple of her teeth out, but then she was really screaming, so Richard went to his bedroom and got one of his pistols and came back and shot her in the head. And that put a stop to it.

He looked at Amos then and Amos looked back at him. Then Richard said, "Well, let's get her out of here."

That was when they took her out to the field to bury her. But when they got out there the rain was coming down like a bitch, so they just left her on the ground.

The police came by his place the next day. Stopped him before he could get to his bedroom. Put him facedown on the floor and read him his rights. One of the pigs came out of his bedroom holding the pistol he had used and said, "Lookie here." Being funny.

Later, Richard asked Amos, "Didn't I tell you to get rid of that?"

Amos said he didn't remember that.

The public defender told Richard the prosecutors had 'em by the nuts. The gun with his prints on it, the girl's blood in his car and in his house, witnesses who had seen him and Amos with her, and so forth. The public defender told him that Kansas no longer had the death penalty, but they should plead to life sentences anyway because there was no way they were going to win a trial.

Or, the PD said, they could go to the judge on a blind plea. Tell the judge their story about how everybody was using drugs and the sex was consensual and then things just sort of got out of hand and maybe he could ask the judge for a sentence on a lesser plea of reckless manslaughter.

Richard Billie said, "With a bullet in her head?"

The PD said that Richard sounded like the prosecutor now.

Richard Billie said it was the state's case to prove, so they could fucking prove it in court. The worst that could happen was that he and Amos would get life sentences, which was more or less what this asshole PD was recommending they take anyway.

The state of Kansas took three days to put on its evidence. The PD cross-examined the state's witnesses and called none of his own. The assistant district attorney got emotional during his closing argument, at times looking directly at Richard and Amos and saying things like, "What were you doing there?" Knowing they wouldn't be able to answer him. The PD seemed to look at his notes a lot, and during his rebuttal said that certainly a tragedy had occurred, but who could say what actually caused it? The jury was out for about thirty minutes and came back with life sentences for both of the assailants. The judge thanked the members of the jury for their service and dismissed them from the court.

Richard maintained a strong face when they paraded him before the cameras again. But inside he was thinking about what he would look like and feel like at the age of sixty or seventy behind bars. A lifetime of that shit. For perhaps the first time in his life, he thought about his long-term future. And from that moment on, he watched and he planned and he waited.

Now that he was out, he still had to watch and plan and wait. Amos, he wasn't worried about. But Javier was another proposition.

Now Javier was sitting in another chair in the living room with Richard. Javier sipping coffee from a cup with a saucer to go with it. *Christ,* Richard thought. *Look at him with his cup, saucer, and spoon. Like he's some sort of South American high hat. A Mexican, for Christ's sake.*

Javier stirred the coffee and milk with the spoon. Then he set the spoon on the saucer. He looked at Richard and said, "I've been thinking."

"Yeah?"

"I've been thinking," Javier said, "that there's no reason for us to stay here."

Richard said, "All this stuff on the television, you getting scared?"

Javier smiled. He said, "We have another vehicle here. The girl's. We can take it out of here. Be on our way. The police won't know about it."

"They won't know it's stolen, you mean."

"Right."

"And what about the people upstairs?"

Javier shrugged. "We take care of them first. Leave no witnesses."

"And then what?"

"We drive to Dallas."

"You know," Richard said, "for a while there, I thought you were going to suggest that *you* take the girl's car and Amos and I take the old man's. I thought you were going to suggest we split up."

"But then you wouldn't get your money."

"That's right."

Javier said, "Obviously, I wasn't thinking that."

"Right," Richard said. "You were thinking we'd all ride to Dallas together."

"Sure."

"Meet up with your friends and collect our fifty thousand there. Huh."

Javier shrugged. Like it was simple.

Richard Billie regarded the Mexican again. The Mexican maintained his calm expression. Richard's face broke into a grin. Shit, he had to give it to the spic. He was a cool one.

Richard said, "I suppose you'd want me to take care of the family."

Javier shrugged again. "You or Amos. You're the ones holding the guns."

"Take a murder rap."

"You've already been convicted of that. What more can they do to you?"

"In this state, they can give me lethal injection. I know that much."

"You're going to do it anyway."

Richard nodded. "When I decide," he said. "In the meantime, we might need them."

"Why?"

Richard didn't respond. He said, "Have you called your people yet?"

"You know I haven't," Javier said. "You've been watching me since we busted out. Me and the old man. You want to stay here?"

"I want to rest. We can go to Dallas, take the woman's car. But what's waiting for me in Dallas?"

"Money."

"Yeah, maybe. Or maybe it's a pack of homeboys holding guns."

"Come on, man. Don't you trust anybody? You got me out. You think I'm not grateful?"

"I think I remember you trying to cut out on us in Sedan."

Javier made a gesture. "A misunderstanding," he said.

"Right," Richard said, thinking the spic had ass to spare, calling it a misunderstanding. Richard said, "Maybe you do have the money to pay me what you owe me. And maybe you don't and you don't want to admit it. Or maybe you got it and you don't want to pay it to me."

"I got it. Don't worry about that."

"If you got it, you can have it brought here. Then you can go. Take whatever vehicle you want."

"But not till then, huh? Are those your conditions?"

"Those are some of them. Something else: I don't want your friends knowing where you are."

"You ask a lot."

"I'm not asking," Richard said. "You call who you need to call. Tell them to bring the money to Tulsa. We'll have someone meet them away from the house and bring it back here."

"Someone meet them? If you think I'm okay with Amos—"

"No, not Amos. We'll send someone else."

The Mexican looked at him for a moment. Then it was he who smiled.

Javier said, "Man, you've been giving this some thought, haven't you?"

"I'm always thinking," Richard Billie said.

NINETEEN

Donna Wolfe was in her Pilates class, toning up her abs, when she heard her cell phone ring. It was in her bag leaning against the wall. Donna let it ring. The instructor was one of these hard-ass types who yelled at you if you weren't paying attention or doing the exercises right. It rang again and Donna still didn't answer it.

She went to check it when the class ended and as she reached for it, it rang again. She answered it.

"Hello?"

"Jesus Christ, where you been?"

She said, "Hey." She was careful not to say his name. She said, "I was in class. I couldn't answer the phone."

"Get to Rico's. I'll call you in ten minutes."

The phone clicked off before she could say anything else. She looked at the caller ID. A 918 area code. Where was that?

It wasn't in Kansas.

Shit. He had done it. He'd actually done it. He had busted out. He had told her about a fight coming up that he wanted to bet on. Saying it was sometime in the next ten days . . . she didn't think he'd be able to do it.

She drove to Rico's, a bar and grill that was near the North Park shopping mall. She didn't get there in ten minutes, though. There was no way she'd be able to do that.

He was out. He had gotten out. Telling her to move to a landline that the police wouldn't have bugged. Telling her to

107

avoid using her cell phone so that the scanners wouldn't pick it up. It meant he had done it.

In the gym parking lot, she got into a Mercedes convertible that Javier had given to her. A birthday present. Brand new, red glossy paint and all the options. Back during the good times. Clubs, champagne, the best restaurants. Her best girlfriends envied her. This rich boyfriend with his Oscar De La Hoya looks. *Where did he get it?* they'd ask with knowing smirks.

Fuck 'em. At least she wasn't hooking. She'd never done that. And she'd never danced naked on stages either. When she met him, she'd been a sales assistant with an oil-leasing company. She'd had a recent tryout for the Dallas Cowboys cheerleaders. She survived the first cut, but not the second and they told her she could try out again next year, but at age twenty-five, she knew she'd be too old.

She met Javier after that and had sort of fallen in love with him. His looks, his clothes, his charm. She liked the whole package. He called her "my lady." And he usually treated her like one. He told her he was in the people-pleasing business. He introduced her to a couple of his friends, big men with names like Hector and Miguel who didn't say very much, and after a while she wondered if they were more associates or bodyguards than they were friends.

He took her on trips to Mexico City and Acapulco. Exotic places with white beaches and clear blue water. He told her a lady like her shouldn't have to work and worry about money. He gave her a shoebox with twenty thousand dollars in it and told her to hold on to it for him. A few weeks later, she asked him what she should do with it and he told her, whatever she liked.

Eight months after she met him, she got a call from his lawyer, Eddie Marks. The lawyer told her that Javier had been arrested outside of Wichita, Kansas, for transporting cocaine. One of the state police officers jabbed Javier in the back with his nightstick, so, strictly in self-defense, Javier gave the state cop a pop on the nose, breaking it. Eddie said it looked like a total setup, but he was going up to Wichita the next day to straighten it out. He told Donna that if she needed anything, anything at all, she should give him a call.

While Donna thought, *shit*. Fucking lawyer wasn't wasting any time, was he? Short, tubby Eddie Marks actually thought he could get in her pants while Javier was in prison. It insulted her on more than one level.

Then the fears kicked in about what would happen if Eddie couldn't spring Javier out. Would she have to go back to work? Give up the condo? Sell the fucking Mercedes? Go back to her old, shitty life? How do you go back?

She said to Eddie Marks, "Just get him out, will you? I need him."

Eddie Marks said, "Don't worry, darling. I'm going to take care of everything."

And Donna thought, *Darling? Christ help me.*

Eddie Marks came back from Kansas alone. Reported to whoever ran the Dallas arm of the Tijeras Cartel that the DEA and the Kansas State Police had a pretty good case on Javier.

Eddie Marks checked in with Donna a couple more times after that, just to see how she was or if she needed anything and after the third time he called, Donna told him she really didn't think it was a good idea for him to be calling her all the time because Javier might hear about it and tell his friends to straighten Eddie out. Eddie Marks laughed nervously and told her he wasn't afraid of Javier or his *hombres*. But he didn't bother her anymore.

It took fifteen minutes to get to the phone booth outside of Rico's. She waited next to it for another four and then it rang and she picked it up.

"Hello?"

Javier said, "Where were you?"

"You said ten minutes and then hung up. I couldn't make it here in ten minutes."

"You could have tried."

Donna sighed. She said, "Where are you?"

"Anyone follow you?"

"*No*. Where are you?"

There was a pause. Then he said, "I'm in Tulsa."

"My God. You got out, then?"

"Yeah."

"Oh . . . shit. I mean, that's great. When are you coming here?"

"I can't do that right now. I need you to do something for me. I need you to call Miguel and have him call me at this number."

"What for?"

"Shut up for a minute. I'm going to tell him to give you some money and bring it here to me. Then I'll be coming back."

After a moment, Donna said, "For how long?"

"We'll talk about that later. Now get a hold of Miguel. Donna?"

"Yeah."

"Be careful, baby. People may be watching you."

Richard said, "Give me the phone back."

Javier looked at him. "Why?"

"Because I don't want you to have it."

Richard had made him use Tracy Coughlin's cell phone because he didn't want any of the Mexican's friends to know the home number of Lee's house. If they knew the number, they would be able to locate the address. And then there would be nothing to stop Javier's friends from coming directly here.

Javier said, "What's wrong with me having her cell phone?"

Richard said, "I don't want any unauthorized calls."

"Oh, so now you're authorizing? You going to shoot me if I don't give it back?" Javier said, "How you going to get your money then?"

"Put it on the table, Javier."

Javier smiled. *Have it your way.* He put the cell phone on the kitchen table and stepped back.

TWENTY

They were working at a cafeteria table that had been brought in for the extra law enforcement officers. Cullen had his laptop computer open on the table. He was more adept with technical gadgets than Prather.

Prather was in paper, going through the department of corrections' files. Cullen got a call on his cell phone from Ernie Bridges, the KBI agent working with the techs out in the field. Cullen took some notes and then got off the phone.

"That was Special Agent Bridges," Cullen said. "They found a .40 caliber shell in the field near the victim. Matches the Glock .40 caliber they took off the prison guard."

Prather said, "Glock .40. More and more cops using it these days."

That or a Glock 9mm. Cullen carried a Glock himself. Prather preferred his own cut-down version of the 1911 Colt .45.

Cullen said, "Likely it's got a law enforcement modification. One chambered and another fourteen in the clip."

Killed with an officer's gun, Prather thought.

Prather said, "They took the victim's vehicle."

Cullen looked at his computer screen. He said, "But nothing yet. They could have switched vehicles. It could be in a barn within a hundred miles of here." Cullen leaned back. "You're out of prison, you've got a gun. What would you want?"

Prather said, "Food, shelter, a change of clothes. Money."

"They've got officers at the homes of the relatives of Billie and Denton. They're natives. Sandoval is from Texas. Sort of."

"What does that mean?"

"Well," Cullen said, "he's got people in Mexico City too. And Belize. He wasn't in for murder, unlike the other two. He might have gone away for ten or twenty years, presuming he didn't get his sentence flipped on appeal."

"But he busted out."

Cullen said, "Maybe he saw a chance and he decided to take it. Maybe he liked the odds. If he makes it, he can hide in Mexico."

"You think that's where he's headed?"

"It's what I'd do," Cullen said.

"It's what I'd do too," Prather said. "I've been looking at his visitors' list. He got two visits from a woman named Donna Wolfe. I called someone at the prison, and he told me she was quite an attractive young lady."

"She from Dallas?"

"Yeah. See what you can find out about her on your little whiz box there."

TWENTY-ONE

Eddie Marks was holding court at a large circular table at The Health Club, Dallas's newest fashionable steakhouse. There were four other people at the table, trading gossip and tales of their latest travels and glad tidings of oil being over ninety dollars a barrel. They were laughing and drinking and enjoying themselves. Then the table grew quieter as two serious-looking men in suits walked up to stand over them.

Eddie looked up, but continued cutting his steak. He said, "Something I can do for you?"

"Mr. Marks?"

"Yeah." Eddie still held his utensils.

"I'm Special Agent David Carr of the FBI. This is Special Agent Ray Courtland."

Eddie Marks said, "I'm eating my dinner now. Are you here to arrest me?"

"No, but—"

"Then I suggest you call my office in the morning and make an appointment."

Agent Carr said, "We need to discuss this with you now. We can do it here, or privately."

"I told you, I'm eating."

"It involves one of your clients," Agent Carr said. "Do you want to discuss a confidential matter in front of these people?"

Eddie Marks continued chewing his food, showing them contempt. Then he set down his utensils and wiped his mouth with his napkin, performing for his people at the table, and the agents were willing to let him do it.

"Over here," Eddie said, showing them he was in control.

But they stopped him about ten feet from there.

Agent Carr said, "Javier Sandoval escaped from prison sometime last night. A prison guard and a Kansas farmer have been killed. Were you aware of that?"

For a moment, Eddie Marks did not say anything. People at his table were looking over at him.

Eddie said, "What?"

Agent Carr said, "Your client has broken out of prison and possibly murdered two people. Were you aware of that?"

"If you're asking if I've heard from him, the answer is no. But if I had, any discussion between him and me is attorney–client privileged."

"Not if you're helping him commit a crime," the other agent said. "We're not asking what you discussed with him. We're asking if you've been in contact with him in the last twenty-four hours."

"This is the first I've heard of it. But you have no business—"

"He calls you, you let us know. Do you understand? He's a fugitive now."

"You have no authority to tell me what to do. I am an officer of the court."

"Counselor, you assist him now and you're aiding and abetting a fugitive. As well as a murderer."

"An *alleged* murderer. All I've got is your word he did these things. And the word of people like you doesn't mean squat to me." Eddie Marks looked from one agent to the other. "I bet you guys have tapped my phones already."

The agents said nothing.

Eddie said, "And now you're threatening me with criminal charges if he does make contact with me."

Agent Carr said, "Did we threaten you?"

"I think so."

"I have a law degree too," Agent Carr said. "You have no legal cover if you assist this man in the commission of a crime. That's what you'll be doing if you do anything but encourage him to surrender."

"Stop threatening me. I told you, I haven't heard from him."

Agent Carr took a business card out of his jacket pocket. He held it aloft for a moment then stuffed it in the front shirt pocket of the lawyer.

"If you do," the fed said, "you call us right away."

Twenty-Two

In the car, Courtland said, "Do you think he's heard from him?"

"I can't tell," Carr said. "He seemed surprised. But he's a lawyer."

"You said you were too."

"I never practiced." Agent Carr had gone straight from the University of Michigan Law School into the FBI. Courtland had an MBA from Ohio State. They were both sturdy, tall men with athletic builds. Courtland black, Carr white. Carr was the senior agent.

Carr said, "Well, what do you think?"

"He's a jerk," Courtland said, "like most of them."

"He used to work for George Menefee," Carr said. "He was the counselor to most of the big-league Mexican drug cartels. That's where he learned his trade. But I don't think he holds the same esteem with the Tijeras Cartel that Menefee did."

"You mean, you don't think he's management."

"That's my sense."

Courtland said, "I wonder if that was a good idea, though."

"What?"

"Confronting him like that. Now he knows we're looking for his guy."

"He'd have known that anyway. Just as he knows his phones are tapped."

"Well, that's what I mean. If we hadn't have spooked him, he might have said something on the phone that could have helped us."

"I doubt it. Sandoval wouldn't be dumb enough to call him at his office or home. Besides, I want Marks to be scared of us."

"You think he is?"

"Few people are more scared of criminal charges than lawyers. And maybe he's scared of his client too. Did you see his face when I told him Sandoval was out?"

"What?"

"I don't think he was all that happy to hear it."

"Well . . . maybe."

Agent Carr said, "The thing about these cartel lawyers is, they don't just represent one of the guys in it. They want all the business they can get. They want *all* the cartel on their side. So if they got a situation where they have to decide whether they're going to protect the individual or the cartel, they're going to go with the cartel."

"You're surmising."

"Yeah, I am. But I'm pretty sure I'm right. The question is, what will the Tijeras want to do? Will they want to get Sandoval out of the States and into Mexico? Or will they want him cut loose?"

Courtland said, "You want answers to those questions, you need to speak to DEA. All I want to do is catch him and put him back in the box."

Twenty-Three

In time, John went to sleep. He still had his clothes on, curled up next to Tracy. Tracy sat up in bed. From time to time she looked out the window. There were trees and a huge lot out there. She wondered if she opened the window, would the man on the other side of the door hear it? If she could lower John down, holding him by his hands, extend her waist and let him hang, would John be able to be quiet as she lowered him and then dropped him? Would he land on his feet? Would he break a leg? Or would he land on his head instead or break an arm? The boy screaming out in pain?

The one with the ponytail kept threatening John. He said that if they did anything wrong, the kid would be the one that got it. John would be killed. And that there were worse things they could do to him.

Worse things.

John gets hurt in the midst of an escape and then they would do God knows what to him; kill him, at a minimum, and then kill her and Lee.

Richard Billie frightened her. Horrified her. Even before she had seen confirmation on the news that he was a killer, she had sensed it. She had sensed distinct menace and violence. In medical terms, they called such people sociopaths. Someone without conscience. Someone who derives pleasure from manipulating people. From tricking and deceiving them.

Is that why he had kept them alive? Was he getting off on seeing them frightened out of their wits? Seeing them suffer? He could have killed them all before. Why hadn't he?

She remembered the man smashing his plate against the wall. In that moment, she thought he was going to kill Lee. Kill John's grandpa right in front of them. She had never been more scared in her life than she had been at that moment. Even more so than when she saw the military sedan pull up in her driveway and she said aloud, "No. Oh God, no."

Her worst fears confirmed when the marine colonel regretfully informed her that Drew had been killed.

Had it been "better" because she had feared it would happen? Was it worse to be in the same room with the threat of death? Not with a bomb or an Iraqi insurgent, but an armed escaped convict in your kitchen, smashing dishes and itching to kill your son's grandfather.

She presumed Lee was lying on the floor next to the bed. She could not hear heavy breathing. Was he asleep too? How could he sleep through this?

When she gave thought to lowering John out the window, she came back to Lee. She had made a sort of bargain with herself: If her instincts about Richard Billie and the other two were correct, then they were going to have to try to escape. Because the alternative was death. In that respect, she believed she was willing to sacrifice her life if it meant she could save John. If she could get John away safely, she would accept her death.

But what if it meant sacrificing Lee too? Could she exchange John's life for Lee's? Was it even for her to decide?

What was about it Lee Coughlin? He had never harmed her or mistreated her. Had never been rude to her. Was he really in any way responsible for Drew's death? Had he done anything to earn her unkindness? Was she, like the woman suing the hospital, seeking someone to unload her anger on? Or was Lee like her son, a family member who simply had to bear the brunt of her black moods and fear of living. Tracy thought about her relationship—such as it was—with this man. She had never really known him. He was quiet and not given to discussing his feelings.

Normally, such personality traits didn't bother her. She was generally put off by people who revealed too much of themselves too early. Talking constantly was a way of hiding things too. She had sometimes told herself that Drew was too afraid of Lee. But on giving it more thought, she suspected that wasn't really true. Drew had not feared his father. What he had feared was disappointing his father.

And that realization confused Tracy. For it revealed something about Drew that she knew had to be good but at the same time made her uncomfortable. It demonstrated that Drew loved his father and, more, admired him.

Which Tracy envied. She could admit to herself that she was a little jealous that Drew could love his own parents and she could further admit that such a jealousy was silly and not something that should be fostered. A man can love his wife and his son and still love his father and mother and sister. There was no cap on such a thing.

But that was not the whole of the envy. Unlike Drew, she had never had such a relationship with her own father. Like Lee, Tracy's father had also been quiet and withdrawn. But beneath the still waters was a man that she had learned was not charitable, not warm. A small man that was perhaps angry at the hand he had been dealt in life and never got past it. A man that most people would dismiss as a selfish prick. Or maybe a man who had never grown up. Wanting to always watch his channel on television, grumbling when he was asked to do a domestic, paternal chore like taking her to basketball practice or helping her mother, never offering any help on his own. He had been more like an asshole older brother than a father.

When her father died a few years ago, Tracy had wept for reasons she couldn't fully fathom. There had been no melodrama that she could remember. He had not abused her or her mother. He had not gotten drunk and smashed things up. There was nothing that he did that was overtly destructive. Rather, he just gave nothing of himself. And when he finally passed, Tracy was mostly relieved. She cried not for loss but for what had never been.

She was vaguely aware that the childhood experience had formed her. Had made her hard and impatient with people. But she was glad that she was at least aware of the flaws. And she knew that Drew's presence in her life had softened her.

Now she said, "Lee."

And looked over to the right side of the bed.

But he wasn't there. "Yeah," he said.

And then she looked over toward the closed door. He was sitting on the floor between the bed and the door. Sitting with his back to the wall. Why was he sitting there?

In a lower voice, she said, "What are you doing there?"

Lee said, "I thought you were asleep."

"No. You should be sleeping."

He didn't answer her. She got off the bed and gestured to him. Then she remembered that it was dark and maybe he couldn't see her. And she called out to him again.

"Come here."

They went to the side of the room away from the door, both of them conscious of a man that would be out in the hall keeping guard.

In a whisper, Tracy said, "I've been thinking: is there a way we could get John out this window?"

Lee said, "I've thought of that. I don't think it would work. I think it's too dangerous."

"It's dangerous if he stays here."

"I know that too."

Tracy said, "You want to take your chances with these guys?"

"No. I'm not hoping to get anything from them."

Tracy thought, he's not counting on them to be merciful. Which meant they agreed about something.

"Then what?" Tracy said. "We just wait for them to do what they want?"

"They're expecting us to try to escape. Or, to try to get John out of here. Probably they're posting someone at the window below," Lee said. "When you were coming here, I had a plan. I was going to push John out the front door, then shut it and try to delay them. So you could both get away. But he separated John from me before I could do it. Now I don't think that was a coincidence. I think he knew what I had in mind."

"We could try."

"We could try. Drop John out the window. His leg gets broken and then they'll kill him. And then they'll kill you. Tracy, they will. Please believe me."

"Why are they doing this to us? *Why?*"

"Because they're criminals."

"No," she said. "I meant, why are they keeping us alive?"

Lee sighed. "I don't know. Maybe they want us alive for some reason. Maybe to use as hostages." He stopped and said, "Tracy."

"What?"

"I want you to promise me something. I want you to promise me you won't try anything without asking me first."

She looked at his face in the darkness, and perhaps for the first time, saw him as a man. Not as her son's grandfather or as her husband's father. As family, but not family. A man who loved and hated and feared like any other. She remembered the scene in the kitchen, Lee challenging the leader.

She said, "You want to be in charge. Is that it?"

She saw his face contort a little then. And part of her regretted saying it.

He said, "You're misreading me. I want to keep you and John alive. If we don't all act together, I can't guarantee that."

Tracy said, "You can't guarantee anything."

"*For God's sake, don't you think I know that?* Why are you arguing with me? Can't you at least trust me until we're out of this?"

On the bed, John was stirring. Lee and Tracy looked over at him, and Lee was aware that he had let his voice rise. They kept silent until the boy stopped twitching and then went back to sleep.

Lee did not make eye contact with his daughter-in-law. He said, "Try to get some sleep." Then he walked away from the bed.

Twenty-Four

Russell Duprey was tall and bull shouldered, but he had smooth skin and looked like he was about eighteen. He reminded people of Baby Huey. He was in the Coldwater County Detention Center, serving out a sixty-day sentence for violating the rules and conditions of his probation. He had been to Coldwater County before. It was crowded and the black guys were always asking him where he could get them some good dope, but it was better than being in the state penitentiary.

The county guard came to his cell and told him to come along and Russell wondered if his lawyer had succeeded in getting him out. He knew it wasn't likely—his lawyer hated coming to this fucking place. But he wanted to believe in something.

The guards handcuffed him and attached the cuffs to a belly chain and then they led him into the interview room and right away he knew his lawyer hadn't done shit.

Two cops in plain clothes. One of them an older guy wearing one of those cowboy mustaches, the other a young cop wearing a military haircut.

"Hello, Russell," the older one said. "I'm Special Agent Prather. This is Special Agent Cullen."

The guard left the room, closing the door behind him.

"Yeah? What do you want with me?"

"Perhaps you've heard," Prather said, "Richard Billie and Amos escaped from prison late last night."

Russell Duprey looked from the mustache to the crew cut.

Then back to the mustache.

"Yeah. So what?"

Prather said, "Is this the first you've heard of it?"

"Yeah. I've been here for the last thirty days. It's not my problem."

Cullen said, "They killed two people. A guard and a farmer."

Russell shrugged. "That's too bad, but I didn't . . ."

"We know," Cullen said. "You were here. But last month, before you flunked your UA, Richard called you from the penitentiary."

For a moment no one said anything, the agents letting the silence work on the inmate.

Russell said, "I don't remember that."

"Yeah?" Cullen said. "The phone records show it. He didn't call your cell phone either. He called you at home. I mean, we got it."

Prather said, "You see the problem, Russell?"

"No, sir, I don't. Man's got a right to call me."

"But *why* did he call you?" Prather said. "What did he want?"

"I don't know."

"Ah," Prather said, "come on, Russell. You can do better than that."

"I don't remember."

Cullen said, "I understand you get out of here in about thirty days. Another month or so and you'll flunk another UA and go right back in. But that's nothing compared to a twenty-year stretch for aiding and abetting a fugitive. And we haven't even gotten to being an accessory to murder."

"Now, hold on—"

Cullen said, "We're not talking about two-, three-month stretches. We're talking about a fucking lifetime behind bars. Coming out an old man, if you come out at all."

"Hold on, hold on. I didn't—he didn't tell me nothing about

breaking out."

Prather said, "You sure?"

Cullen said, "Then why would he call you?"

Russell looked at the table.

Prather said, "There's got to be a reason, son. Richard Billie was sentenced for life. He wasn't in a position to make plans outside. Unless he made other plans."

Russell looked from one agent to another, trying to figure out which one would want to harm him less. He said, "You know why he called me? To give me shit. Just like you are."

Cullen said, "For what?"

Russell Duprey sighed and said, "You think I want anything to do with him? He's crazy. The man is crazy. After he and Amos bumped off that girl, he called me and asked if I'd testify for him. I said, 'How the fuck am I going to testify for you? I wasn't even there.' He said, 'Yeah, but I can tell people you were.' That's the kind of guy he is. I was scared of him. He was in county at the time but I was still scared of him."

Prather said, "He wanted you to testify for him? What could you have done for him?"

"I couldn't have done a goddamn thing. Even if I wanted to. I tried to tell him that. He said I could say that the girl shot herself. Then he changed his mind and said I could testify that he killed her in self-defense. Self-defense. I mean, how could that be? But it didn't matter to him. He didn't want to go down for it so he was looking for anything. Thank God he was in jail at the time."

Prather said, "Did you know the girl?"

Russell sighed. Then he said, "Yeah, I knew her. She was a crank whore. They shouldn't a killed her though."

"Is that why he asked you to testify? Because you knew her?"

"I knew her a *little*. But it didn't matter to him. That's what I'm trying to tell you. Richard doesn't care if it doesn't make sense. Even if I wanted to help him—and I didn't—no one would have believed it. I think I was working that night. The prosecutor would have found out about it and then prosecuted me for perjury. It didn't matter to Richard. That's how he is."

Cullen said, "You said he called you to give you shit. Elaborate."

Russell said, "He called me at home and I answered it not knowing it was him. He said, 'Russell, I just wanted to let you know I'm getting out of here.'"

Cullen said, "That's it?"

"Yeah, that's it. He didn't say he was going to kill me. He didn't threaten me. Well, not directly. He just said he was getting out, trying to fuck with me. I didn't know if he meant appeal or breakout or if he was just fucking high. I said, 'All right, Richard' like it didn't bother me and hung up the phone. I didn't want him to think he'd rattled me. I tell you, I never dreamed he'd be able to do it."

Prather said, "He did, though. You think he'll come looking for you?"

"I don't know," Russell Duprey said. "Guess I'm safe here, huh?"

TWENTY-FIVE

In the car, Cullen asked him if he had taken the profiling course at the FBI Behavioral Science school at Quantico, Virginia. Prather said he had not, though he had read some materials another officer had brought back.

Cullen said, "I've put in for the school. But there's a line of officers that want to go."

Prather said, "There always is."

Cullen said, "You ever apply?"

"No," Prather said, and was willing to leave it at that.

Cullen said, "What do you think of it? The profiling business, I mean."

"Oh," Prather said, "I guess I have mixed feelings about it. I'm all for training and education. But the profiling thing may be more fashionable than it is useful. Let's say I'm skeptical about it."

The younger cop said, "It doesn't hurt to go, though."

"No, it doesn't. You want to be in law enforcement long term, it doesn't hurt to have the training on your resume. And you can make good contacts at Quantico."

A moment passed and Cullen said, "I'm not looking for another job."

"I didn't say you were," Prather said, not caring if he was or not. Prather said, "If you're wondering if Quantico training would help you with what we're doing now, I'd say it might, but probably not. The prison file says Billie's got an average I.Q.

Amos Denton's is lower than average. Richard Billie's been diagnosed by the correctional counselor as having an 'antisocial personality disorder.' Which means, like a lot of the guys in the pen, he's been stealing and fighting and bullying and getting in trouble since he was a teenager and making most people he ever came in contact with scared or miserable or dead. He's a stone-cold killer but they want to assign a medical term for it. For some reason."

"Russell said he's crazy."

Prather said, "It's possible he's crazy, but I doubt it. What he was asking Russell to do—testify for him at his trial—that may have sounded crazy to Russell, yes. But Billie had a reason for it. He wanted to stay out of prison. That's self-interest and desperation, not insanity, and you'll find it any convict. You'll want to go right up here."

Cullen slowed the car and made a right turn. They were in the town of Sedan now, approaching Russell Duprey's residence.

Prather wanted to catch Richard Billie and his cohorts and put them back in prison. The agent was not lusting for blood. Billie had done nothing personal to him. And to Prather, law enforcement was not a personal business. Prather had been raised in a religious home and the concepts of good and evil had never quite left him and he did not believe this to be a bad thing. Prather believed Billie was another loser like most of his kind. Billie was not a mad genius and he did not deserve such consideration. He was a violent and highly dangerous menace who needed to be separated from society. Prather was skeptical of profiling the way a hunter would be skeptical of profiling a man-eating Bengal tiger. Prather was skeptical of relying on pseudo-science to track prey. It was important to know the tiger's habits and where and how he could be caught, but sometimes there would not be the luxury of giving much more thought to it than that. Particularly if he was loose. The primary thing was to catch him before he took more lives.

Now they were approaching the house. A Mustang and an old Ford Escort sat in the front yard.

Prather said, "Cut the headlights."

Cullen did so and they rolled to a stop.

Cullen had been thinking about using the car's spotlight to view the front of the house. Now he put the idea aside, taking the older agent's cue.

"Okay," Prather said quietly. "Let's go."

They approached the front of the house, Prather holding his pistol at his side, Cullen then doing the same. They stepped up on the porch and took opposite sides of the door.

On the porch, they could see light toward the back of the house. Probably from the kitchen.

Prather knocked on the door with the butt of his steel-cased flashlight, the raps not too loud or too soft.

"Police officers," he said in a firm voice.

He repeated this twice and then switched on the flashlight and pointed it through the front window. Panning right to left and then back again.

He didn't see anyone.

Well, Prather thought. They had gotten Russell Duprey's permission to search his premises. In a way they had. So Prather put his hand on the knob of the front door and turned.

It was unlocked.

They stepped in, still flashing the light again, both of them still holding their weapons. Cullen found a light switch and turned it on.

They called out hellos and got no answer. They turned on more lights and searched the house. They stayed together as they went from room to room, and it was in the main bedroom that Cullen saw the orange fabric on the floor, resting in the doorway of the closet.

"Mike," he said and pointed.

The orange prison fatigues.

"Man," Prather said. "Call state police."

Twenty minutes later the front yard was covered with police cars from the state and county, including a K-9 unit. They began an organized search and they soon found the bodies in the garage behind the house, both of them shot in the head.

Sheriff Don Edwards was soon there and he looked even worse than before. He looked at Special Agent Prather and said, "This is what I was afraid of. They're not going to surrender."

Twenty-Six

Agents Carr and Courtland returned to the Dallas FBI field office after they left attorney Eddie Marks. That was where they got the faxed letter from KBI Agent Mike Prather informing them that he had reviewed the visitors' list at the Elk County prison and learned that Javier Sandoval had met with a white female, twenty-five years of age, named Donna Wolfe who resided in the University Park section of Dallas. Agent Prather said witnesses had said that the woman was very attractive, appeared to be the girlfriend of Sandoval, and that there was a distinct possibility that Sandoval would attempt to contact her. He advised that agents interview Ms. Wolfe ASAP.

Courtland said, "It's late."

"We're not waiting till morning," Carr said. "You want to drive?"

It was past ten when they reached Donna Wolfe's condominium. They rang the doorbell several times and peered in through the window. She wasn't home.

TWENTY-SEVEN

Hector and Miguel were standing in front of the club, Hector smoking a cigar, Miguel sipping orange soda from a Dairy Queen cup. Hector was leaning up against Miguel's 1989 Mercedes Benz 560SEC, black and shiny. The club owner told them Hector couldn't smoke in there, and Miguel pulled him out before he started breaking things.

It was a nice warm night. Pretty ladies walking by, high-dollar vehicles cruising in the street. It was part of what Miguel liked about America.

A pretty Hispanic girl walked by with a little boy that could have been her brother or her son. She was about two-thirds through her lime popsicle and she tossed it on the ground.

"Hey," Hector said, "that's littering." Looking at her ass now.

He watched it swing back and forth and about two seconds later heard the girl say, "Why don't chew eat it?"

They laughed at that, looking almost soft at that moment. Two men in their late twenties. Well dressed and holding positions of some respect in the Tijeras Cartel.

Miguel looked down the street and said, "Here she comes."

And Donna Wolfe's Mercedes came into view. She slowed as she went past them and found a parking spot down the street.

Miguel said, "Wait here."

He walked down the street and met Donna as she was coming out of her car. He gave her a hand and she seemed to accept it with reluctance.

Miguel said, "Anyone follow you?"

"Not that I know of."

"That you *know of?*" Miguel shook his head. Beautiful blond driving a bright red Mercedes that a drug dealer bought for her. Conspicuous.

"Come on," he said.

He led her into a bistro near the club. It was dark inside and they went to a private booth toward the back.

A waiter came and took their orders. Miguel ordered an espresso. Donna ordered a Tom Collins.

The waiter left and Donna said, "Javier called me. He's out."

A moment passed and Miguel said, "Are you sure?"

"Yeah, I'm sure. He called me from Tulsa, Oklahoma."

"Why there?"

"I don't know."

Miguel studied her.

"Really, I don't. He said he needs money and he needs you to call him."

"Then what?"

"You're supposed to give me the money and then I'll bring it to him."

"What?"

"That's what he said."

Miguel said, "You got the number?"

Donna gave it to him.

Miguel studied it for a second. It was a lot to process. Not the number, but what it meant. Javier had busted out.

But why was he in Oklahoma?

Miguel said, "Stay here."

Like many people involved in the drug trade, Miguel switched cell phones often. It was easier to operate than it used to be. Now the radio frequencies were higher and the police scanners couldn't pick up conversations so easily. But it was still a good idea to change phones. If you used the same one for more than a week, you were asking for trouble.

It helped, too, when you spoke a different language.

Miguel spoke Spanish and English. Though he knew there were plenty of cops who could understand Spanish. Hell, they were teaching the Texas Rangers to speak Spanish these days. In another time, they had just taught them to speak to Hispanics with their boots. Miguel envied the Chinese heroin dealers. They didn't just speak Chinese, but a Chinese that could only come from some tiny part of China that maybe only a handful of people knew how to speak and pretty much no Americans. The Chinese were slick competition, man.

Miguel went down the hall to the bathroom. In the bathroom there was a man washing his hands. Miguel stared at the man's reflection in the mirror. The man turned off the taps, made a brief show of drying his hands, and hurried out.

Then Miguel dialed the number.

Four rings and then a voice on the other end.

"Hello."

A white man's voice.

Miguel said, "Who is this?" He was thinking it might be a cop.

The voice said, "Who's this?"

"Man, I'm trying to reach a friend of mine. Said he was at this number."

"A friend from Kansas?"

Miguel said, "Who are you?"

"Another friend."

Then the man was gone.

A few moments later, he heard Javier's voice, saying hello.

Miguel said, "Is that you?"

"Hey," Javier said, his voice brightening. "She find you, huh?"

"Yeah, she found me. Hey, who was that answered the phone?"

"Don't worry, he's with me."

"You sure?"

"Yeah."

"Was he in with you?"

"Yeah."

Miguel was starting to believe they'd done it. He said, "How many got out?"

"Three of us. Listen, I made an agreement with these guys."

"What kind?"

"I said I'd pay them fifty thousand to get me out. They did. And now I got to pay them."

"Bring them down here. We'll take care of them."

"They don't trust me. They want someone to come up here and pay them."

Miguel sighed. "How much?"

"Fifty. Like I said. You got that."

"I'll talk with the man. You want your lady to bring it, huh?"

"I don't know, man. I think she may be hot. Has she had any visitors lately?"

"She says she hasn't. But I don't know."

Javier said, "If she says she hasn't, she hasn't."

"All right, then. You want me to bring it?"

"Yeah."

Javier was quiet then. And Miguel knew he wanted to bring Hector too. Miguel was remembering the white guy's voice, cocky and tough, and Javier was talking like someone was listening to him. Or watching him. Probably both.

Miguel said, "Where?"

"Tulsa," Javier said. "But they don't want you to know where we are. My new friends don't trust me."

"So what am I supposed to do?"

"It's nothing to worry about, man. It's going to be a peaceful transaction. Come up here and they're going to send someone to meet you."

"Who?"

"I don't know yet."

"You going to tell me where?"

There was a pause. Then Javier said, "They want you to call again when you're in town."

"All right," Miguel said. "I need a little time. But I think about eight hours."

"Good."

Twenty-Eight

Javier was smiling as he handed the cell phone back to Richard. Javier said, "Now what's the matter?"

Richard Billie said, "You're pulling something."

"Man, what do you want? You want money, someone's going to have to bring it."

"You said something about a girl. Why can't she bring it?"

"She visited me in Elk County. You think they don't know that?"

"Who?"

"The fucking police. Man, don't you know anything?"

"Why don't you explain it to me."

"They know about my woman. She comes here to bring us the money, they're going to be following her. You want that?"

"They might follow your friends, too."

"No, man. They know what they're doing. Look, Richie. You standing there watching while I'm on the phone, you hear everything I'm saying. You hear me give the man an address?"

Richard Billie was still giving him the eyeball.

"Did you?" Javier said. "You need to sleep, boy. You're too uptight, seeing things that aren't there."

"I'll sleep later. Why don't you go to sleep?"

"I will." Javier walked off. He stopped at the door, turned and said, "You'll still be here when I wake up, huh?" Waited and then smiled again before he left.

Javier went upstairs. Amos was sitting in a chair near the

guest bedroom. Amos swiveled his head over to him.

Javier said, "You look tired."

"Not so much," Amos said. "I slept in the truck."

"That makes one of us," Javier said. "What happens if you fall asleep? That old dude may get the jump on you."

"I ain't worried about *him*."

Javier thought, *I am*. The old man had fire in his eyes. *Cojones*. Richie and Amos weren't holding the guy in the right perspective. In a lower voice, Javier said, "Maybe you should be. I've seen guys like that before. Wouldn't surprise me if he made a move."

"He's an old man."

"We got his family here. And he may not be as old as you think."

But Javier wasn't thinking the man wasn't *old*. He was thinking the man wasn't *soft*. Certainly not as soft as they thought. He seemed hard and maybe pretty mean too. The old man was pushing Richie here and there, maybe looking for weak points. Maybe trying to wear him down. Javier enjoyed watching it, enjoyed seeing the old man get Richie's blood up. Maybe the old man would go too far and Richie would shoot him. Or maybe the old man would take Amos out first and then Richie would kill him. That wouldn't be such a bad thing; having Amos out of the way, having Amos's gun.

Javier's eyes flicked to the .38 in Amos's hand.

But Amos was looking at him now. Amos said, "If you're going to ask me if you can take over, the answer's no." Challenge now in Amos's expression.

Javier said, "I'm not going to ask you for anything."

Javier walked down the hall to the master bedroom. He closed the door behind him. Inside the room was a king-size bed with a blue down cover, a television on top of a bureau and a remote control on the nightstand. Shit, no gun there. But the room had its own private bathroom.

Javier went in the bathroom and flicked on the light. He looked at himself in the mirror and saw a tired man. Tired, but free. Out of that goddamn cell and that goddamn state.

But man, he had fucked it up. Transporting narcotics on the I-35 corridor. Courier duty was beneath him. But they had been a man short and the demand in Kansas City was pressing. Pulled over by state police that had to have been tipped off. They had the coke wrapped in sandwiches that were wrapped in about three inches of cellophane, but the police dogs sniffed through that shit in no time. Then one of the patrolmen talked smack to him, calling him "taco bender" or some shit, then poking him in the back with a baton, and Javier had to hit him.

Shit. Like that, he was busted.

Then he met Richard and Amos. Two hard-core rednecks with absolutely nothing to lose. They would be his ticket out.

And they had got him out. And now they were thinking about killing him. Do to him what they had done to those crackers in Sedan.

If he paid them the fifty he had promised, would they still do it? Would they still want to kill him?

Maybe. But even if they didn't, would the Tijeras understand having to pay two Kansas assholes fifty thousand dollars for Javier's freedom? What would Caesar do?

They had the money to pay it. They had made much more money through Javier than that. In essence, it was Javier's money. He had made it for them. Though Caesar might not see it that way. But to give it to Richard and Amos would cost him some respect within the cartel.

And what would happen to the shit kickers once they got the money? Within a week, they'd be caught. There was no El Paso or Mexico City for Richard and Amos. They were men born for the institution. And if they survived capture, they would finger

Javier for killing the guard and maybe this Tulsa family too. For killing a white family. And that wouldn't play well with the cartel either.

It bothered him, being under the supervision of these crackers. But Javier was a patient man and a cool one. The thing to do was wait. Wait for Miguel and Hector to get here with their own guns. Wait for Richard to lose more energy. Wait for Richard to kill the old man. Wait for Amos to go after the woman. There were all sorts of distractions. Time was on his side.

Twenty-Nine

Richard came up the stairs later. He said to Amos, "Where's Javier?"

Amos made a gesture. "He's sleeping."

Richard said, "Why don't you go to sleep too?"

"I'd like that," Amos said. "But—" Amos was looking at the door to the guest bedroom.

Richard gestured with his head and together they walked downstairs.

In the living room, Richard said, "You thinking about the woman?"

"Aren't you?" Amos said. "I mean, it's been a long time."

Richard shook his head. "Not now," he said. "You do that, we'll have to kill the old man first."

"So?"

"Not yet."

Amos said, "Why not?"

"We may need them."

Amos looked about the house. Nice and well furnished. And he did want to sleep. Still . . .

Amos said, "Man, I'd like to get out of here."

"Why?"

"I don't like being cooped up."

"You prefer the joint?"

"Fuck, no. But how long can we stay here?"

"No one knows we're here. Besides, we can't leave until we

get our money."

"Yeah? When's that going to be?"

"It should be here in the morning. Get some sleep, Amos." Richard looked up to the ceiling. "They ain't going anywhere."

"All right." Amos started walking to the couch.

"Hey," Richard said.

Amos stopped. "What?"

"The Mexican. Did he say anything to you?"

"When?"

"A few minutes ago. When he came upstairs?"

Amos shrugged. "Not much. Why?"

"No reason," Richard said. "Just watch him, that's all. He may be of a mind to fuck us over."

"I don't see how he could," Amos said.

And Richard thought, *No, Amos probably couldn't.*

THIRTY

The FBI Special Agent in Charge (SAC) called KBI Agent Prather around eleven o'clock that night and told them his agents had not yet located Donna Wolfe.

Agent Prather said, "Why not?"

The SAC said, "They've tried her home. But she's not there."

"And what else?"

"What do you mean?"

"I mean, have they checked with her relatives? Have they got officers looking for her car?"

"She's not wanted."

Agent Prather listened to the man in the FBI giving him opposition. FBI. The top law enforcement agency in the country and who was a state agent to question them?

Agent Prather said, "Sandoval may have been in contact with her. Maybe she's meeting him somewhere. Do you have agents waiting at her home in case she comes back?"

"What would be the point of that, if she's going to pick him up somewhere?"

Lord Almighty, Prather thought. He said, "It's important that someone speak to her as soon as possible."

"Okay," the SAC said, "but he's not the only escaped convict. What about the other two? Don't they have family in Kansas?"

"Yes. We've checked them out and we're continuing. They didn't go to a family's house, they went to a friend's—an associate's—and they killed two more people."

"In Kansas," the fed said. Like it needed to be pointed out.

"Yes," Prather said, "in Kansas. But they're on the move."

"Okay. So you're working Kansas and I'm working Texas," the federal agent said. Meaning, let's stay off each other's turf.

Prather put that aside and said, "My records show that Sandoval's a pretty high-level officer in the Tijeras Cartel. And he's associating with a couple of lowlifes from Kansas."

"So?"

"So maybe it's Sandoval that's calling the shots. Billie and Denton don't really have a place to go. Where would Sandoval go?"

"He'll want to go back to Mexico. Probably by way of El Paso. But that's speculation."

Prather said, "All law enforcement's been alerted, including law enforcement in Oklahoma. All media outlets too. They're in a stolen truck, but I'm thinking they've probably switched vehicles by now."

"Yeah," the SAC said. "And maybe they've split up too."

"I've thought of that," Prather said.

The SAC said, "What do you know about the other two guys?"

"They're bad guys. Both of them have murder convictions. But you probably know that already."

"I know they're bad, but are they smart enough to get far?"

"They don't need to be smart to go on a killing spree, which they've already started. Like I said before, they have nothing to lose."

The SAC said, "Well my people at DEA have a little higher interest in Sandoval. They say he's a bad dude, too, but they don't underestimate him. They think he had something to do with the murder of an undercover agent in Laredo, but they can't prove it. More than a couple would like to see him dead."

"Well . . ." Prather said, uncomfortable. He was not a supporter of law enforcement vigilance. He thought it was not only unprofessional, but that it also got in the way of effective police work.

"But," the SAC said, "what I'm trying to say is, he is smart. He's a killer too, but he's not looking to go out in a suicidal blaze of glory. He's connected to some powerful people in Mexico and he can live pretty sweet if he can get there."

"And you think he wants to get there."

"Absolutely."

Prather said, "I wonder what sort of promises he's made to Billie and Denton?"

"What?"

"Oh, nothing. Just thinking out loud. Listen," Prather said, being diplomatic now. "I appreciate everything you're doing. I know you're down there and I'm up here. But I think it would be helpful to all of us if we could question Donna Wolfe."

After a moment, the SAC said, "I'm going to check on that."

The SAC, whose name was Roger Howe, intended to check on it. He believed his assistant SAC would know who had been sent to question Sandoval's girlfriend. And it was on his mind to call the assistant right away. But then another agent told him that Tina Shimoda from Channel Six was on line two, wanting just a few minutes of his time, and Howe remembered seeing the newscaster's pretty face on television and on a big billboard by the LBJ interchange and Howe said, okay, he would take the call. The interview took almost forty-five minutes and by the time it was finished, agents Carr and Courtland had left Donna Wolfe's condominium and gone home.

Thirty-One

Drew was picking John up and lifting him above his head and John was laughing. Thanksgiving, maybe, with a football game on the television in the background. Drew and John and Tracy sitting on the couch, laughing and smiling. It was good to have Drew back, looking happy and at home. Drew turning now and saying something to him . . .

Lee opened his eyes.

Darkness.

Lee was on his back on the floor, cold and stiff.

Christ. Back in reality.

It was not the first dream he had had about Drew since he had buried him. They were getting less frequent. About one every couple of weeks now. Though he had never been a religious person, Lee wondered if the dreams were meant to tell him that Drew was okay now, perhaps in a better place. . . . it would be nice. But why was it that he always dreamed of Drew in a family setting? Drew with him, his son, his wife. Did Tracy have similar dreams?

He had never asked himself if there had to be a reason. Did Drew have to die for his country? Did he have to go out there in the first place? Why had he gone? And why was he, Lee, alive when his son and his wife were dead? His wife had been better than him. And his son had been better than him too. A better father, anyway. Engaged with John in a way that Lee had probably never been engaged with Drew. Maybe there hadn't been time. Men of Lee's generation did not spend much time struggling over whether they were good fathers. They provided and that was what they thought was most important.

There hadn't been time, Lee thought. When Drew and Katy were young, he and Susan had always seemed to be working. Struggling to keep their heads above water, worrying about this month's bills and then the month's after that. Telling themselves not to think too far in the future because it could bring too much despair.

And if there had been time, what would he have done different? Now that Drew was gone, Lee did not think of the things he "should have told" Drew. He doubted he would have told him anything. He just would have been around. He would have been here. And for a man like Lee Coughlin, that meant far more than words.

After the funeral, Jessica—Lee's secretary of ten years—said to him, "Aren't you mad?"

He didn't answer. But he caught the drift of what she was talking about. A man shouldn't have to bury his own children. It wasn't natural. If someone had to be taken, couldn't it have been him rather than his son? An old man with most of his life behind him?

Now, sitting in the darkness, Lee wondered if he should have to be buried with his grandson and his daughter-in-law.

No, he thought. *Stop that.* They were his, but they were not his. They were not his to give up on. Not his to surrender to despair. They were Drew's. Drew's family and he had a sacred duty to protect them.

I'm sixty-three years old, he thought. Again thinking of his age and his mortality. But no longer thinking of time spent with his grandson, but of how little his life meant in the face of theirs. And in that moment, he asked for some higher power to take him instead. He asked for a bargain. His life for theirs. He would accept those terms without hesitation.

But how to do it? What could he offer these men that would persuade them to release Tracy and John? That he hadn't already offered? Was it money they wanted, or was it just bodies? The sick pleasure derived from torturing the helpless and the innocent?

He could tell himself that they would be merciful. Hope for it. But he had been in combat himself, been in business too, and his life experiences told him that men like Richard Billie were not given to compassion. It just wasn't in them. Lee could hope for it, but hoping for such things could be dangerous too.

Lee got to his feet. He stood by the door and waited, still and quiet. He put his hand on the knob, turned it slowly. Turned it so that it was free from the doorjamb. Waited. Then cracked it open.

A sliver of light in the darkness.

He waited for a voice, some stirring on the other side. The click of a revolver's hammer.

Nothing.

Lee opened the door further. He looked out.

An empty chair.

He drew breath. His heart pounded.

There was no one in the hallway. Just an empty chair. Lee checked his watch again. Almost three o'clock in the morning. Quiet, still time. Could it be they were all asleep? If he could get to one of them, one of them that was armed? If he could get a gun, he could get them out of here. Kill one of them or all of them if necessary. Get Tracy and John out. Get them into a vehicle and tell them to drive to the nearest police station or well-lighted convenience store.

Lee looked back at the bed. Tracy and John were sleeping there. Tracy curled over John, holding him in her arms, her back to the door.

The sight of it stirred him. Tracy. Had she had her own conversation with higher powers, telling God that she would be okay with dying so long as John lived? Lee did not doubt she'd sacrifice herself.

Lee stepped out into the hall, closing the door behind him. Did that and then thought, now what?

He was upstairs in the hallway alone. He didn't know who else was up here. The door to the master bedroom was closed. Probably someone was in there, sleeping in his bed. There was another bedroom on his right, but the door to that one was open. Maybe they were all up here.

Lee took a breath. Exhaled quietly. And listened.

Downstairs, a sound. Low murmurs.

Lee looked over at the staircase on his left. The stairs went down in front of him, stopped at a landing, then turned right. It led into the living room. It was out of sight now, but Lee had figured out the muffled noise he was hearing now was from the television. He had not been able to hear it in the bedroom. But now he could hear it.

It meant that someone was down there watching television. Watching it, unless they'd fallen asleep in front of the television. Watching it or . . . *shit*. How could he know?

Richard found whiskey in a cabinet in the kitchen. He poured himself a glass, had a couple of sips, then poured it down the sink. He never had formed a taste for whiskey. He put the whiskey away and took another beer from the man's refrigerator. That was more like it.

How long had it been since he'd had a beer? Sat in front of the television with a cold one. It was one of the many things he missed being inside. Cable television, comfortable furniture, beer and decent food. This was a good place to be.

The girl wasn't bad either. Nothing you'd see on a stage in

Ark City. Not a show girl with a shiny face, but still a cute thing with a good-looking rack. A widow. Was she getting laid? Was the old man wanting a piece of her? Richard snorted at the thought of it. He'd done the old man a favor, locking him in a bedroom with her. *No, Daddy; wait for little Johnny to go to sleep* . . . Yeah. Not fucking likely. She was the sort that looked down on you, would make you work for it and never smile while it was going on. Like it was a lottery win just to be there.

He was aware that she would hate him even if he didn't have her hostage. That's how bitches like her were. But, hell, he'd never raped a girl. He may have knocked a few around here or there, but they'd always been the sort that got off on it. It pissed him off that they had hung the rape charge on him with Chrissy Anne. Chrissy Anne was a crank whore; she'd given it to them as she would have given it to anyone with good dope. Would have done it with a barnyard animal if she'd done it with Amos. But the fucking prosecutors weren't satisfied with a simple murder charge; they had to throw a rape charge in there too. Turn Chrissy Anne into a good girl for the jury. Richard's lawyer even believed it, though he'd never admit it. Didn't any of these people realize the bitch was bound to die sooner or later?

They were doing the second run of Leno now on television. They showed it at ten-thirty and then again at two-thirty. He was watching it now because there really wasn't anything else on. The old man didn't have Cinemax or Showtime. No porn. Leno was interviewing some blond puss with an English accent who was skinnier than a bird.

Richard heard a door close upstairs. He pulled his attention off the television and the blond and looked up to the ceiling.

Javier?

Maybe it was him, walking out of his room. Walk down the hall to take a leak. Or come downstairs to get something to eat. Maybe . . .

But then, wasn't there a bathroom attached to the bedroom that Javier was in?

Richard picked the Glock off the coffee table and walked to the foot of the stairs. He looked up the steps to the place where they turned left. Dark, but nothing there.

He started up the stairs, holding the gun in front of him. He got to the landing, turned left and then the door to the guest bedroom was in view. It was closed.

Was that the one that had been opened?

Shit, he shouldn't have had those two beers. They were making him tired. Good to be out of prison and good to have a cold beer, but he should have been sleeping. He had been too keyed up to sleep earlier, too keyed up and not really trusting anyone. He should have stayed up here and sat in that chair and kept watch on the door. But he couldn't do that and watch television. Shit. It was like having a job, having to keep an eye on things and people.

Richard walked up the rest of the stairs. Then he stood in front of the bedroom door with the captives on the other side. He put his head against it and listened to hear what was going on on the other side. He put his hand on the doorknob.

The door to the next room opened and Richard looked up just as the old man rushed him. Richard cried out—"Hey!"— and then the old man hit him in the dark, his arms outstretched, and they both went down the stairs, rolling and tumbling, and when they reached the landing, the old man's back hit the wall and then they were moving down the next set of steps, Richard shouting Amos's name now and he lost the gun somewhere, but the old man was still with him and then somehow they were at the foot of the stairs and the old man was on top of him, holding down his chest with one hand and punching him in the face with the other. And Richard was almost screaming now for the fat fucking ape to do something and then Richard saw the old man lift his face just as Amos's boot came into it.

The old man cried out now as he was kicked back, and Amos stepped in low and smacked the old man across the face with the gun. And then the old man slumped over.

Richard was finally free and he scrambled over to the Glock and picked it up and he was leveling it at Lee and then he heard the girl above him screaming, *"No."* And Richard stood up and said to her, "Just stay there. Stay there or I swear to God I'll kill him."

Amos was standing over the old man now too, holding the .38, its hammer clicked back.

The boy was standing behind the woman now, clinging to her back. He tried to get past her to grandpa, but Tracy held him in place.

Richard said, "I swear to God, I'll kill all of you. Just stay there."

Richard walked over to the couch and picked up a cushion. He came back holding the cushion in one hand and the gun in the other. Lee, still conscious, comprehended it, but it came quicker than he thought it would.

Richard said, "I see I'm going to have to teach you something."

Then he placed the cushion in front of the gun's muzzle and fired a shot into Lee's thigh.

THIRTY-TWO

Javier watched it happen from the staircase. He hit the light switch and walked down to stand behind the woman. He reached out to take her by the shoulders, but it was too late, she was running down the stairs, *Christ*, putting herself between Richard and the old man.

Then she was next to the old man, saying things to him and looking at the dark wet patch that was spreading on his leg.

And there was Richard with blood coming out of his nose, shaking with fear and rage. And Javier smiled to himself. Look at homeboy. Got his nose bloodied by an old man.

Javier stood next to the boy. Javier put a hand on the boy's shoulder.

"Why don't you go back to your room?"

The boy shrugged the hand off. "Get off me."

Then he too went down the stairs, joining his mother and grandfather.

"You bastard," Tracy said.

Richard Billie said, "You're lucky I didn't kill him. It was his fault." Richard noticed the Mexican on the stairs, now coming down to join them. Richard said, "He tried to jump me."

Javier said, "Tried?"

"Fucking snuck up on me, man. Where the fuck were you guys?"

Amos didn't say anything. He was still pointing the .38 at the old man, who looked like he wouldn't be able to get up.

155

Javier said, "I was in bed. What happened?"

"I went upstairs," Richard said, "because I heard something."

"And he was waiting for you," Javier said.

"Well . . ."

Javier shook his head. Like only a very simple person could have fallen for it.

"Fuck you, Sandoval," Richard said. "You're fucking sleeping. Someone's got to watch them. Anyway, he won't be trying anything now."

Lee was shaking. With effort, he concentrated on Richard. He said, "That was stupid. Someone will have heard that gunshot."

"Shut up, old man. There's a lot of distance between you and the closest house. You want, I can put the pillow against your face for the next shot."

"Don't," Tracy said. She kept her voice steady as she made direct eye contact with Richard. "Don't," she said. "We get your point. You could have killed him and you didn't. We understand you."

Tracy looked to Javier and then Amos, appealing now for mercy, and then back to Richard Billie. She said, "Let me treat him. He'll bleed out otherwise."

"Let him, then," Richard said. "He asked for it."

"What's it to you?" she said. "The life of an old man. You've already won. Don't let him bleed to death. In my car, I have a first aid kit. Please, let me treat him."

Richard said, "Why should I?"

"Because . . ." She couldn't think of a way to persuade him. A way to see how it would benefit him. There would have to be something in it for him.

They were all looking at her now. Waiting for her to come up with something. She looked to Lee, his face pale and clammy. Christ, he would be going into shock soon.

"Because," Tracy said, "if you kill him now, you'll have to kill all of us. And that may bring the police here. If not, I'll have my hands full keeping him alive."

Her heart was pounding loud enough that she could feel it in her hands and in her temples. She thought she could say, *Why haven't you done it already?* They must have had a reason for not doing it already. A reason for letting them live this long. She could ask him. But somehow she knew that wouldn't be a good idea.

Finally, Richard said, "All right. You can take him upstairs. Amos will get your kit out of your car and bring it to you. But you listen to me. The next time any one of you tries something, I'm going to kill the boy. Not hurt him, not wound him. Kill him. No more kindness. You hear me, lady?"

"I hear you."

Richard nodded. He looked at Javier and said, "Help her get him upstairs."

She ordered John to sit in the corner and turn his head away. She put towels on the wound. It was a big one; a hole going through his thigh and coming out in a large chunk in the back. What they call a "flesh wound" on old television shows, but she was afraid that an artery might have been nicked. The bright red spurts signified the most serious type of bleeding. It would have to be controlled quickly. A loss of two quarts of blood would produce a severe state of shock. A loss of three quarts would be fatal.

Tracy prepared a sterile dressing and held it over the bleeding point. She did this for half an hour. Then she put a pillow under his leg and elevated it.

She called out to her son.

"John," she said. "It's okay. You can come over here now. See. He's okay."

She said this even though he had passed out. But she wanted the boy to see that Lee was still alive. His pulse was less rapid now. But his skin was still pale.

"Grandpa?"

"He's sleeping now, sweetheart. He'll be okay."

Now she was lying to the boy. She didn't know if Lee would be all right. If the shock became severe, his pulse would become more rapid or dissipate altogether and his pupils would dilate. Complications of shock could kill him, even if he didn't have any physical injuries.

She could not let John know. Not now. She wasn't sure herself if Lee would survive. There was no need to terrify John.

"Come here," she said.

She led him to the side of the bed. They sat on the floor together, their backs against the bed. She pulled him in toward her, cuddling him. With her free hand she reached up and took her father-in-law's hand and held it. It was still cold and clammy. She prayed for it to warm.

"Okay," she said. "Okay." She was wanting to lull John to sleep. Get him to sleep through this nightmare. But she was also faintly aware that she was saying it to herself. *Okay.*

Lee would have to rest at least twenty-four hours. That is, if he were to survive it. A gunshot in the leg and maybe they didn't mean to kill him with it. But it was a bleeder and Lee was showing signs of early shock. It wasn't something he could just sleep off.

"Mama," John said.

"What honey?"

"Is Grandpa going to die?"

"I don't think so, honey. Try to sleep now."

"I don't want to sleep."

"Try anyway."

"But—"

"We're all going to be okay," Tracy said. "We're with you now. Both of us."

She waited for the boy to say something else. But he didn't.

She waited for him to ask what happened down there. What would she have said if John asked her that?

What had happened? Had Lee tried to escape? Richard Billie seemed to be saying that Lee had set some sort of trap for him. Billie with blood running from his nose. Lee must have done that. It would not have surprised Tracy. She had never doubted that Lee Coughlin was a very tough man. In a way, Drew had always feared him.

She had never believed and had never seen any evidence that Lee had abused Drew as a child. Certainly, Lee had always been a gentle giant with John. But once in a great while when Lee spoke in a certain tone, Drew could not help but reply with a "yes, sir." A serious one, too, Drew regressing to boyhood. Maybe it was a Southern thing, calling your dad sir. Or maybe there had been a few occasions during Drew's teenage years when he had tested his father's resolve and regretted it. Christ, Drew admiring him and fearing him to the end.

She had thought these things before. But now when she thought of it, she could not summon the usual anger at Lee. Or even at Drew, for that matter. Maybe it was because she was holding Lee's hand now and praying for him to live. Maybe it was because John was here and she could not bear the thought of John losing his grandpa, with or without Drew.

Or maybe it was because she had seen Lee herself. Seen him fierce and strong, smashing his fist into Richard Billie's face. It had frightened her, but she had seen that it had frightened Richard Billie too. If not for the fat one, Lee would have beaten Richard to a pulp. Maybe even to death. And Richard Billie knew it.

For at the end of the day, he was a punk. Take away his gun

and there was very little to him. A vicious killer, but a coward. Lee knew it and maybe Richard knew it too.

And so she vacillated. She was angry at Lee for having tried to take out Richard, for trying to take his gun from him. It had gotten him shot and might still kill him. *Stupid,* she thought.

Or maybe not. Maybe it could have worked. If he had gotten the gun, he could have killed or disarmed the big one, Amos. And then kept the Hispanic guy at bay. And then she and John would have been saved. He had risked his life to try. Whatever else she could say about him, she would have to remember that.

THIRTY-THREE

Downstairs, Richard washed his face in the bathroom sink. He got most of the blood off his face. He touched his nose and winced in pain. Fuck, it could be broken. He dried his hands and came out to the kitchen where Amos and the Mexican were sitting.

Javier was smiling.

"Something funny?" Richard said.

"No, man. I'm not laughing."

"You better not. It could've happened to you too."

"I doubt it," Javier said.

Amos said, "He's a tough guy. We should have known he'd try something."

"Fuck him," Richard said.

Javier and Amos were sitting at a table with cans of beer and a bag of pretzels. Amos held a cold beer can to his head. The fight had stressed him.

Javier said, "He hits you, you shoot him."

Richard said, "What would you have done? Huh, Mister Machismo? Cut him open with your switchblade?"

"Man, get out of the sixties. What I'm asking is, why didn't you kill him?"

"I have my reasons."

"Why don't you tell me your reasons."

"I told you, we're going to need them. And if you don't stop giving me shit, I'm going to use this thing on you too."

"Yeah, man. Whatever."

"I told you, we're going to use the girl to pick up the money. She wouldn't do it if he were dead. I need her thinking that she'll be saving him."

Javier said, "Did you see that hole you put in him? He's not going to live through the night. She's a nurse. You think she's not going to figure that out?"

Richard Billie was thinking he would kill the woman and the child, in time. And when he did, he wanted the old man alive to see it happen. See it before he was finished too. But he didn't want to explain it to this fool.

Richard said, "This is really eating you up, isn't it? You can't be in charge, so you want to nitpick."

"I'm just saying . . ."

"You ain't saying shit that's worth listening to. So why don't you keep your fucking mouth shut until your muchachos get here with the money."

Richard's hand was on the Glock now, lying flat on the table. Richard's finger rested close to the trigger.

Javier took it in and made eye contact with Richard. Javier smiled again, thinking, Big man with a gun.

But he kept that comment to himself. Stood and walked out of the room.

After he was gone, Amos said, "Richard, I don't know . . ."

Richard Billie sighed. "What?"

"He's Latin, man. You insult their manhood, they'll kill you for it."

Richard almost did a double take. Fat boy questioning him now. In a tone that was both fierce and tired, Richard said, "You getting smart now too?"

"Hey, I'm the one that bailed your ass out," Amos said. "Don't go forgetting that."

Richard saw an insolence in Amos that was new to him. In

that moment, he remembered Amos choking the prison guard to death. A big, dangerous bear when aroused.

Richard held up a conciliatory hand. He said, "I'm not forgetting anything, Amos."

Amos Denton looked at him with something of a prison stare. Then he, too, walked out of the kitchen.

Thirty-Four

The girl's name was Tia, and she said she was Chinese, not Vietnamese, and for eight hundred bucks she would come to your house and give you a massage and then spend the night in your bed and do whatever you asked her. The girlfriend-for-a-night rate. Eddie Marks didn't think it unreasonable. He had dated his share of Dallas women who required diamonds and designer handbags and European vacations and, after a while, he didn't see much difference. Besides, Tia had a certain amount of style for a pro. She would undress and climb in bed and crook a finger at him, motioning him to take off his pants. And sometimes she would feign jealousy when he referred to other women, knowing that Eddie's ego needed to be stroked too.

Tonight, she was still in her kimono, massaging Eddie's shoulders, when there was a rap on the front door. Eddie was lying on his stomach on a massage table—which Tia had brought—a towel covering his backside, and he asked Tia baby if she could please get the door, giving himself a little something extra there. He wondered what it would be like to have Tia live with him as a sort of full-time servant. Maybe her and a blonde and a redhead and maybe a Japanese girl to give the whole thing symmetry. Like James Coburn had in that *Flint* movie.

He changed his mind when Tia returned from the front door with Hector and Miguel—*Christ*—not even warning him that they were here. Flint's women wouldn't have done this to him.

Eddie Marks would have liked to have remained cool, staying on his stomach while he greeted these guests. *What can I do for you, gentlemen?* But he couldn't stop himself from jumping off the table, wrapping the towel around himself so they wouldn't be able to see his vanishing erection.

"Hey, guys," Eddie said. "Kind of in the middle of something here."

He thought they might smile back at him, maybe make a joke and say they were sorry.

But they didn't.

Miguel said, "Caesar wants to see you. Now."

Eddie looked to Tia to see if she would give him any support. She was rolling her eyes. And Eddie regretted that he'd paid her upfront.

He rode in the back of Miguel's Mercedes. Hector sat in the front seat next to Miguel. They conversed in Spanish, which Eddie didn't understand beyond a few words.

They had given Eddie time to get dressed, and he had put on slacks and a white dress shirt and a suit jacket but no tie. Dressing almost like he was going for an interview. Pretending not to be scared.

He remembered when he had first started practicing law, when he had first gotten into criminal defense. Back then, it had been nickel-and-dime cases. Breaking and entering, possession with intent to distribute. He had won a few trials and made something of a name for himself and then his old boss Menefee had started referring some of the big-time cartel members to him. And then it changed. Instead of Eddie interviewing the clients, the clients started interviewing him. As if he was seeking a place in a large corporation. Which, in a way, he was. He sensed a change then, a loss of his independence. But there had been so much money on the table. Much more than the five- or even twenty-thousand-dollar retainers he had demanded from his previous clients. More than he had been able to turn down. In his earlier life, he had told clients they were to never call him after hours unless it was an emergency. He had made that very clear. He had remained in control. Now, he had men showing up at his house at midnight, sending quasi-girlfriends home before he could get laid. Men not asking but telling him to get dressed and to come along. He did not ask himself if Tia had more freedom than he did.

Miguel got off the downtown exit. Minutes later he pulled into a parking garage. They ascended the levels of the garage, the wheels screeching as it made the turns. When they reached the eighteenth floor, Miguel parked the car.

They got out and Hector pulled the seat forward for Eddie. Eddie looked at the two men and Miguel gestured to a black Jaguar XJR with a big black guy standing next to it.

"Go on," Miguel said.

Eddie walked over to the Jaguar. It was quiet up here. There weren't even any other vehicles. Eddie saw the downtown buildings over the garage walls that now seemed frightfully low. Eighteen floors up . . .

The black guy opened the back door to the Jaguar and Eddie got in.

The door shut and Eddie was looking at Caesar Cavazos.

The U.S. Department of Justice had issued an intelligence bulletin saying that Caesar Cavazos was the leader of the Tijeras Cartel. That he had been a member of the elite special forces of the Mexican Army and had been trained in the United States at the School of the Americas at Fort Benning, Georgia. In the late 90's, Cavazos had defected to one of the very drug cartels that he was supposed to be fighting. Soon after the defection, Cavazos had taken over the cartel himself. The Department of Justice referred to these former members of the Mexican military as "Los Zetas."

Under the leadership of Caesar Cavazos, the Tijeras Cartel had killed rival members of competing cartels, journalists and even some policemen. Some of these murders had taken place in Mexico. Others had been committed in Dallas, Laredo, Houston and McAllen.

Caesar Cavazos was a slim, handsome man in his midfifties. He wore tailored suits and Italian shirts and he looked far more like a businessman than a gangster.

Now he said, "Hello, Edward." His voice like soft leather.

"Hello, Caesar." Eddie had only met him a few times, but he believed he could get away with the familiarity.

"Have you heard about Javier?"

"Yeah," Eddie said. "A couple of feds came and told me he broke out. Naturally, I told 'em to go fuck themselves."

A beat. And then Cavazos said, "You spoke with federal agents?"

Christ. "No," Eddie said. "I mean, they tried to discuss it with me. But I didn't tell 'em anything."

"Would you have been able to anyway?"

"No, I would not have. Caesar, Javier hasn't called me. I swear to you, he hasn't."

"You didn't know he was going to do this?"

"No. He didn't tell me."

"You've advised people before to disappear. To run. When you thought they were going to lose."

Eddie waited a moment, debated whether or not to admit he'd done that. Then he said, "Yes, I have."

"What about his appeal?"

"Javier's?"

"Yes."

"We had a chance, but not much of one."

"Stop talking bullshit. Would you have won the appeal?"

"Probably not."

"Did you tell him that?"

"Yes. I told him."

"Are you sure?"

"Yes, I'm sure. Look, he's my client. I don't screw my clients."

Cavazos smiled. "I'm your client too, Edward. And so is Donna."

Another moment passed, Edward wondering if the rumor about Cavazos carrying a knife was true. Eddie said, "Yes, that's true. I don't see a conflict of interest."

"No. If you behave."

"There's nothing between her and I. I swear."

"You don't have to convince me. Javier's the one to worry about."

"Nothing. I swear to you."

"Okay. I believe you." Cavazos put a hand on the lawyer's knee. "I believe you, okay?"

". . . okay."

"Here's the thing. I haven't heard directly from Javier. Donna has. He escaped but it seems like he has to pay these men some money before they'll let him go. I'm going to get the money to him. But the police are going to try to get to Donna to find out where he is. Javier . . . he has a weakness for this woman. So . . . we have to keep her."

Eddie could see that Caesar was stepping around it, explaining why they would not kill Donna.

Cavazos said, "So I am counting on you to protect her from the police. To ensure she doesn't tell them anything. To protect her and Javier and us. We're all family, huh?"

"Yes, sir."

Cavazos gave the lawyer a long look that he didn't like one bit.

Cavazos said, "Is very important, understand?"

"I understand."

THIRTY-FIVE

Hector drove Eddie Marks home and Miguel rode with Caesar in the back of the Jaguar. The big black guy was driving the Jag.

Miguel said, in Spanish, "How is he doing?" Referring to Caesar's new driver.

Caesar said, "It's an adjustment. He hasn't acquired a taste for tamales and *atole*. He thinks Mexican food is all nachos and cheese."

Miguel said, "I was in Arlington last week, they got a *licuado* stand on the street. Right there downtown. They blend it to order."

"Real *licaudos*?"

"Yeah. Just like in San Juan de los Lagos. Just as good."

"I'll have to see."

The Jaguar left the parking garage, turned south.

Miguel waited for Caesar to come to it. Caesar didn't like to be rushed into talking business. It was his way and Miguel respected it.

Caesar let some silence drift between them. Then he looked out the window and said, "When Javier asked for the money, did you promise it to him?"

Miguel said, "I said I'd check with you."

Caesar nodded. This was the correct answer. He put out a little more silence and in time he said, "Fifty thousand."

"Yes."

Miguel hoped that Caesar would not ask him what he—Miguel—thought. Javier was Caesar's lieutenant. But Caesar had never said if Miguel was his second in command. Miguel knew that Caesar might think that Miguel was threatened by Javier. Competing with him. Miguel did not think he was. But he didn't want to be put in the position of having to persuade Caesar of this. Caesar had a fondness for Javier that almost seemed familial.

Caesar said, "What's going on?"

Miguel said, "He got out with a couple of guys who are probably holding him."

"Like a hostage?"

"I think, yeah. I think he promised them money if they helped him break out."

"Who are these guys?"

"I didn't get their names. If they broke out, it's probably on the news. We can find out."

"Gringos?"

"Yeah. I talked with one of them. He was a fucking *cono*. Talked shit to me."

"Yeah," Caesar said, "but they got Javier. You don't know where they are?"

"They're in Tulsa. Hiding somewhere. We don't know specifically where they are."

"Okay," Caesar said, "come to my house in the morning, I'll give you the money. I want you to bring him back. That is the main thing."

"And what about these two fucking guys? You want me to just give them the money?"

"I just told you, I want Javier back here. Alive and unharmed. If Javier wants to take care of them, it's up to him."

Miguel nodded, aware now of his place.

★ ★ ★ ★ ★

Miguel's suspicions about Javier being related to Caesar were correct. Javier was Caesar's son. Javier, however, was not aware of this. Caesar was.

Unbeknownst to either of his wives, Caesar had kept a mistress in Belize for about six years. Her name was Adrianna and, at seventeen, she had soft, pale skin and small, firm breasts. In the fourth year of their relationship, she became pregnant. Caesar was not willing to marry her. Yet he was also aware that Adrianna was from a devout Catholic family. With Caesar's encouragement and permission, she married the owner of a restaurant, whom she had been courting. The restaurant owner—whose name was Sandoval—allowed himself to believe that the baby was his.

Caesar's attraction to Adrianna waned after that. She grew heavy and maternal. But he supported her and the boy. And as Caesar made the transition from *federale* to narcotics trafficker, his support payments increased as well.

Meanwhile, his marriages produced only daughters. Javier was his only son. And when Javier reached his twenties, Caesar offered him a job.

A couple of years ago, Caesar took Javier aside and told him that there was a DEA informant in their operation. The name the man used was Luis Nolla. But Caesar had information that the man's real name was Andy Septien. Andy Septien was from San Diego, California, not Tijuana, and he was a motherfucking rat who needed to be killed. Javier said he would take care of it.

Javier knew Luis/Andy. Knew where he lived, where he ate, where he shit. Javier thought it was important that the man not only be killed but humiliated. A message needed to be sent.

That was why Javier shot Andy Septien when he was taking a dump in a run-down Mexican restaurant in east Dallas. Shot him with his pants down.

Publicly, they would blame a rival cartel for the murder. But they would know better. And more importantly, the DEA would know better. They would know what happened to agents who tried to infiltrate the Tijeras Cartel.

Javier used a pistol with a silencer and slipped out the back door after it was done. Within hours, he was in Mexico City, his alibis firmly established. He did not return to Dallas for six months.

Caesar had been pleased with the job. He didn't think he could have done it better himself. He liked Javier and he planned to have Javier take over the cartel when he retired. Or died. For now, the thing was to get Javier out of the country. Maybe for a few years. In that time, they could get the legal mess straightened out. Time always helped.

THIRTY-SIX

In the morning, Tracy checked Lee's pulse. He was still unconscious, his breathing labored. She checked his mouth to make sure he wasn't constricted by vomit or, worse, blood. He was still cold and clammy, still sweating.

His eyes fluttered open.

Lee said, "Hey."

Tracy said, "Hey. How are you feeling?"

"Not good. How do I look?"

"You've looked better. Do you know where you are?" Tracy wanted to see if he was mentally confused, a common sign of progressive shock.

"I'm in bed in my house. Where did you think?"

Tracy relaxed a little. "It was a medical question," she said.

"Yeah," he said, "I know. You want to see if I'm hallucinating."

With a towel, she wiped the sweat from his brow. She said, "How would you know that?"

"In Vietnam, the medics used to ask us things like that."

Tracy said, "Were you wounded there?"

"No. But I saw men who were."

Tracy turned to look at John. He was still sleeping, her coat over him. She turned back to Lee.

"You never speak about it," she said.

"What? Vietnam?" He said, "Why would I?"

"I don't know."

Lee Coughlin looked up at the ceiling. "We came back and we didn't know we were supposed to talk about it. I went away and people, people my parents knew, they were proud of us. Came back a couple of years later and it was like a different place. People hating us. Throwing their medals on the steps of the Capitol. Or throwing somebody else's medals. I never really wanted to talk about it, one way or another."

"Were you sorry you went?"

"Sorry?" Lee said. "I don't know. I never really thought about it."

"You must have thought about it."

"Maybe I did. We came back through Germany, me and some buddies. Then from there to New York. We had some unused leave so we stayed there for a few days. Saw some girls . . . went to a couple of parties in the Village. God." He was smiling at the memory. "Frenchy, he was the one who took us there. He wasn't afraid of anything."

"Frenchy?"

"Jim French. Another jarhead. He was a charmer. He met these girls at a bar and the next thing we knew we were at one of their parties. All these hippies. I thought we'd get shit thrown on us, called baby killers, that sort of thing. Frenchy, he just wanted to get—he just wanted to chase girls. Anyway, I sat quietly in a corner, smoking. And this young couple eventually sat down next to me and we started talking. Politics. All night, they kept trying to get me to say it was all Nixon's fault. For them, it seemed to be all about him."

"They were trying to bait you?"

"Oh, maybe. I don't know. They wanted some sort of explanation for it. An easy explanation. But it wasn't easy. It started with Kennedy and then escalated with Johnson and the Gulf of Tonkin Resolution which was passed in the Senate, eighty-eight to two. And the French before them. I don't mean my friend French."

"I know what you meant."

"But I guess they were right."

"Who?"

"The people at the party. They seemed to think I was simple minded, not thinking about the bigger picture. And they were right. I probably wasn't interested. I wanted to get home and forget about it."

"Forget about what you did?"

"What I *did*?" Lee turned to look at the girl, perhaps understanding the drift of her question, but not feeling any anger over it. "Yeah, I guess," he said. "More, though, what I saw. No one who sees something like that wants to remember it."

"So . . . you didn't talk about it with your wife?"

"No. Why burden her with something like that?"

"Maybe she would have liked to have been burdened."

Lee's smile almost became a laugh. He acknowledged the look on Tracy's face and said, "Sorry. You young people, you think all married couples should tell each other everything they're thinking. I don't think it works like that."

"It's called communication."

"You can communicate without talking. Sometimes better, in fact."

"Not always," Tracy said. She put aside her sudden feelings of anger. Then she said, "You loved her, though. Didn't you?"

"My wife? Of course I loved her."

Tracy said, "I never met her."

"That's too bad. She would have liked you."

Tracy's lower lip trembled. *He's sick,* she thought. *He's not himself.* She said softly, "Did you miss her?"

"Miss her? Of course I did. Do. She was my wife. My

companion. It's a continuing pain. A hunger that never goes away."

A few moments passed. Then Tracy said, "Does it ever? Does it ever go away?"

He was looking at the ceiling again. Weak still, but suddenly uncomfortable with the drift of the conversation. He said, "It gets better. You don't forget, but it gets better. It's unbearable, but you tell yourself that she'd want you to carry on. That's how I managed it."

"But you didn't remarry."

"No. She told me I should. But . . . I don't think I'm that easy to live with."

"You mean you didn't want to."

He didn't have the strength to shrug his shoulders. He said, "What difference does it make?"

She didn't know what he meant by that. She was thinking about asking him. Maybe asking him if he was angry at the things life had done to him.

But then he said, "Listen." His voice lower now.

Tracy drew closer to him. "What?" she said.

"I screwed up. I thought I could get the gun from Richard and get us out of here. But it didn't work out. I'm sorry."

"Don't say you're sorry."

"Let me finish. I'm not saying this to you because I've given up. I want you to know that you and John are going to survive. But it's going to be up to you now."

Tracy looked at him.

And Lee said, "You're going to survive, you hear me? You and John. But you've got to use your head. Richard's a psycho, but he's weak. He's wily, but he's not that smart. He's falling apart. He's paranoid. He doesn't trust me or you, but he doesn't trust his friends either. Remember when I suggested to him that he put us in the basement?"

"Yes."

"When I said that, I was trying something out. Because I suggested it, he thought I had a gun hidden down there."

"Do you?"

"No. But that's not the point. He knows he can never be trusted, so he figures no one else can either. Use it."

"How?"

"You'll figure out how. I know you will."

"How—"

"*Listen to me:* you're smarter than he is. You're smarter and you're stronger. I know it. You're just going to have to figure out how."

"I don't see how," she said.

"You will," Lee said. He lay back then, his energy expended.

Someone knocked on the door. Three raps and then the door opened.

It was Amos, the big one. He held the .38 in front of him. He pointed it at Tracy and said, "Richard wants you downstairs."

THIRTY-SEVEN

She sat at the kitchen table with Richard and Amos. Richard sat across from her, his hand on the gun he had used to shoot Lee. Amos slurped cereal from a bowl, never quite closing his mouth while he chewed. Tracy was repulsed.

A cold March sun crept through the cracks surrounding the closed blinds. The small television on the counter gave them the morning's news.

Richard said, "We can't let you go yet."

After a moment, Tracy said, "Okay." She no longer believed they would ever let them go. They had seen him shoot Lee. She said, "Are you still waiting for your money?"

Richard gave her a little smile. "Been listening in, huh? Maybe you're smarter than you look."

"You said you had money coming to you." Tracy said, "The sooner you get it, the sooner you can leave us."

Richard said, "Javier's friends called a while ago. They got started a little later than we would have liked. But they're coming."

"Good."

"No, not good. I don't want them coming here."

Tracy frowned. "Why not? They're your friends."

"Don't get smart with me, lady."

Tracy took a breath. "Okay," she said. "What do you want me to do?"

"First of all, I need you to call your hospital and tell them you won't be coming into work today. Then you need to call the boy's school, tell them he's sick. You're going to make those calls in front of me. What about the old man?"

"What about him?"

"What about his job?"

"He owns his own business." Tracy shrugged.

"People are expecting him, though. Someplace."

Tracy said, "I can have him call whoever he needs to call."

"Will he be able to do that?"

"Yes. With my help."

"Good. What's he doing now, anyway?"

"He's struggling to stay alive."

Richard Billie was smiling again. "Honey, don't look at me. That was his fault."

"You didn't have to shoot him."

"You're a nurse. He's your problem now."

Still smiling at her, and Tracy thought, *How?* How could he enjoy this?

Richard said, "We're here for a little while longer. We can get along or we can have more people getting hurt. Now you know I'll do it."

"Yes. I know."

"And we're not going to have any more problems, are we?"

Tracy looked at Amos Denton. He was looking back at her now, food in his mouth. Leering at her. She resisted shuddering, which wasn't easy.

"I don't think so," she said.

The animal look on Amos's face did not go unnoticed by Richard. He chortled. "No," he said. "No more problems. Right, Amos?"

Amos nodded. He was still eyeing Tracy.

"Don't mind him," Richard said.

"Why don't *you* mind him?" Tracy said, her tone sharp and angry.

It took the grin off Richard Billie's face. He quickly got to his feet. Grabbing her roughly by the arm, he pulled her up. "Let's make those calls," he said.

"Jan? This is Tracy. . . . Listen, I can't come in today. I think I'm coming down with a flu."

Richard Billie was standing next to her, still holding her arm. He put his head close to hers.

"I know," Tracy said, "and I'm sorry. But I think I'll be better tomorrow. . . . Okay. Goodbye."

She clicked off the phone.

"Now call the school," Richard said.

She made the next call. And as she dialed, she thought about what would happen if she called Katy and said that John wasn't coming into school that day. Signaling Katy that something was wrong. Hadn't it been done in a movie she'd seen? But Richard Billie was still close enough to her that he could hear what the other party was saying on the phone. Katy would say, *What? What are you doing, Tracy; this is Katy you're talking to.* And that would be the end of that. She didn't like this creature holding on to her arm, putting his ugly, dirty face close to hers. She could smell him now. Could sense that he was smelling her.

She reached the principal's assistant and told her that John was coming down with a cold and that he wouldn't be at school today. The assistant said that was too bad and then asked if Tracy was going to be taking him to the doctor. Tracy said, no, she didn't think it was anything too serious. The assistant didn't know that Tracy was a nurse. The assistant said something about an upcoming book sale and was Tracy planning to come? Tracy was getting upset now, strain showing in her voice, and she said, "I'm sorry; I don't have time to talk about it right now."

The principal's assistant said, "Oh. Well, all right." Wounded. Tracy said goodbye and hung up the phone.

Richard said, "What was that about?"

"It wasn't about anything. She wanted to chat and I didn't want to."

He was eyeing her now, a mean look on his face. Lee was right: he didn't trust anybody. He *was* paranoid.

"Were you trying to tell her something?"

"No," Tracy said. "Goddammit, do you think I'd endanger my own son?"

He tightened his grip around her arm and she winced involuntarily.

"You better not," he said. Then he shoved her away. "Amos," he said, "take her upstairs." Richard handed Amos the old man's cell phone. "Tell the old man to call whoever he needs to call. Watch him while he does it."

"You coming?" Amos said.

"No," Richard said, irritated. "Handle it, will you?"

"Okay," Amos said. He took Tracy by the arm, not grabbing her as roughly as Richard had. "Come on," he said.

She walked in front of him when they went up the stairs. She could feel his eyes on her, remember his meaty hand on her arm. He could not see the look of revulsion on her face. *It's not for him to see,* she thought.

On the landing, she turned to face him. "Your friend doesn't have very nice manners," she said.

"What?" Amos said. He was confused.

"Richard," Tracy said. "He's not very nice."

It wasn't so much what she was saying. It was the little-girl facial expression and her body language. She was confiding in him. Telling him in her way that she preferred him to Richard. A little-girl thing that could work on this boy.

Amos said, "Oh, he don't mean anything."

"I mean, I'm nice, aren't I? Why can't he be nice?"

"I don't know," Amos said, uncertain.

Tracy decided to leave it at that. She continued up the stairs and knocked on the guest bedroom door.

John asked who it was.

"It's Mommy," Tracy said. And John opened the door.

John started to move to her for a hug, but Tracy put her hands on his shoulders and held him steady. In that moment, she looked straight into his eyes and screwed her face up. She was trying to tell him that Mommy might be telling some lies. Maybe he would understand.

"Honey, go sit over there in the corner."

John said, "I'm hungry."

"We'll get you food. Mr. Amos here needs to help Grandpa make some calls."

Amos took in the crumpled figure lying on the bed. The old man looked worse now. Amos could smell the man's wound. Amos said, "Huh." A grunt of acknowledgment, if that. He wondered if the old man would live through the day.

Amos said, "Can he make the call?"

Tracy walked over and held Lee's wrist. The pulse was the same as when she left him minutes earlier. His eyes were closed though. She decided that he was pretending to be asleep.

Tracy said, "He's passed out. Hopefully, he's not in a coma."

"Coma?"

"He's lost a lot of blood."

Amos said, "You make the call for him, then."

"I don't know who to call."

"He's got an office, doesn't he?"

"Sure."

"Well call his office. Tell them he won't be in today."

She decided to push him a little further. She gave him another little-girl face. "I don't know the number of his office."

"Look," Amos said, "Richard told me I was to have you call his office or someone and I'm not leaving until you do it."

"Do you have to do everything he tells you?"

Amos looked at the little lady again. "No," he said. "But you need to make that call."

"After I do, will you let me make some breakfast for John? Or do you need to check with Richard on that too?"

Now his expression was becoming fierce. She wondered if he would hit her. "Make the fucking call," he said.

Lee found the number marked "office" on Lee's cell phone and pressed it. She waited for Amos to come stand close to her as Richard had done. But he remained where he was. A woman's voice picked up the call and Tracy said, "Hi, this is Tracy Coughlin, Lee's daughter-in-law. He asked me to call you and let you know he won't be able to come in today."

"Oh," the woman on the other end said. "I wasn't expecting him this morning anyway."

Tracy said, "Why not?"

"He was going to check a couple of sites this morning, and then maybe check in with us this afternoon. He spends more time on the sites supervising than he does here."

"Oh," Tracy said. "Well, can you let those people know that he won't be there this morning?"

"I can," the woman said, "but he usually gets in touch with the crew chiefs himself."

"He can't today," Tracy said.

There was an uncomfortable silence. And Tracy knew that the assistant was thrown a little bit. Tracy made eye contact with Amos. She gave him a little nod to show that everything was okay.

The woman said, "Why? Is something wrong?"

"He's just not feeling well."

"And you're his daughter?"

"Daughter-in-law."

Tracy kept quiet. The woman maintained her own silence and then Tracy broke it by saying, "Okay? Good. He'll be in touch."

Tracy clicked the phone off. She handed it to Amos like it was something he had been kind enough to loan her.

"Okay," he said. "You and the boy come down to the kitchen, eat something."

It was something, she thought. At least she had him taking a stand against Richard. She called to John.

THIRTY-EIGHT

Miguel was putting the gas cap back on the tank of the Mercedes when Hector came out of the convenience store. Hector was holding a Big Gulp of Mountain Dew. In his other hand, he had lottery tickets.

Miguel took it in and shook his head. Fifty thousand dollars in the trunk of the car and Hector was buying lottery tickets.

An eighteen-wheel truck ran by, drowning out the sound of the music coming from the car stereo. The truck dieseled off and they could hear Eminem again. Hector's CD.

Miguel said, "What'd you buy that for?"

"Can't get 'em in Oklahoma. We'll be across the state line in twenty minutes."

"You can get them in Oklahoma now. And what'd you get that big drink for? I'm going to have to stop every half hour so you can take a piss."

Hector got in the passenger's side and closed the door. Miguel got in the other side and started the car.

Hector said, "If we stop again, I can buy another ticket. Double my chances."

"We're not stopping again," Miguel said.

THIRTY-NINE

Amos sat in the kitchen in a chair that he had scooted close to the television. About four to five feet from it, but he held the remote control in his sausage fingers and switched channels like a teenager.

John Coughlin sat at the table eating cereal. Tracy made some toast for him and asked him to eat that too even if he didn't feel hungry. She didn't know when they would let him eat again. Richard Billie sat at the table with them. He had ordered Tracy to make him bacon and eggs and coffee. She looked at Richard and his gun and his proximity to her son and she had become very, very still and Richard said, "Don't worry about him. Just get to work." That awful cold smile on his face again.

As she stood at the stove only a few feet away, she saw the fear in her son's eyes and wondered if she had ever experienced anything so horrifying. Her son—her and Drew's little boy—sitting at the same table with a monster. All the monster would have to do is raise the pistol and shoot and, like that, her son would be dead. And she would be standing right here to watch it.

And he knows, Tracy thought. The son of a bitch knew that he was frightening her nearly to death. Frightening an eight-year-old boy. He knew and he was enjoying it. Tracy cooked and prepared food and coffee, all the time looking over at their captors enjoying their power, and being more scared than she had ever been in her life, her insides quivering so that she thought she might lose control of her water. But she didn't and she almost had to put herself in a sort of trance to hold herself together.

A little boy, she thought. *How can you enjoy frightening a little boy?*

Maybe he's paying you back, she thought. Paying her back for getting tough with him this morning. Maybe he was reminding her that she could sass him all she liked, but he still had the gun and he still had her boy. And now how fucking tough was she? Where was that hard-ass bitch tone now?

God help her, it was working. Richard Billie was simply sitting at a kitchen table with her little boy and if he pointed the gun at the boy and asked her to dance naked around the kitchen, she'd probably do it.

She finished preparing Richard's meal and coffee. She started to bring the plate and coffee cup over to the table. A thought flashed through her mind to throw the hot coffee in his face.

Richard Billie looked up at her and smiled.

"Set the coffee down there, hon."

God, he knew she'd been thinking about it.

Richard reached across the table and pulled the coffee over to his place. Then he reached for his plate. He ate with one hand, leaving the other one on the gun.

Then he gestured to Tracy and told her to sit down.

Tracy said, "John. Go upstairs with your grandpa."

"No," Richard said, "let him stay for a while. A family should eat together."

"I haven't any food," she said.

"Fix yourself something then." It was another order.

Tracy made toast and poured herself a cup of coffee. She cautiously took a seat next to her son.

Richard Billie said, "Well, isn't this nice?" Scorning her and her son now.

Tracy said nothing.

And Richard said, "Huh, Amos?"

"What?"

"I said, isn't this nice."

"Yeah, sure," Amos said. He wasn't getting Richard's drift. On the television, Matt Lauer was asking Heather Mills if she was an inspiration to other handicapped people.

Richard said, "My mama didn't make me breakfast when I was a kid. Had to make it myself."

Tracy realized he was directing it at John. Calling him a mama's boy. She hoped John wouldn't catch it.

But now Richard was looking directly at the boy. Richard said, "She pour the milk for you too? Tuck you in at night?"

John looked back at him, frightened now.

"Huh?" Richard said, pressing him.

Tracy said, "Why don't you knock it off?" She kept her voice casual, as if she were talking to a teenager.

Richard turned to her and said, "Excuse me?"

Tracy said, "You've already shot a sixty-three-year-old man. Do you need to follow it up by picking on a child?"

"Lady, I'll do any damn—"

The door opened and Javier walked in. Richard grabbed his gun and turned in his chair, moving very quickly when he did it. Alarmed and jumpy.

Javier smiled at him. "Good morning," Javier said.

Richard didn't respond. He remained mentally coiled, tensed. Javier walked past him and went to the counter for a cup of coffee. He came back to the table and took a seat. Tracy noticed he had changed clothes. A pair of nice slacks and a knit shirt. Lee's clothes.

Javier looked about the table. Woman, little boy, Richard. Javier smiled at it all. He said, "Where's the morning paper?"

"I don't know," Richard said. He said to Tracy, "Does he get it?"

"I have no idea. Why don't you look outside?"

"I'm not going out that front door."

John said, "I can get it."

"What," Richard said, "and take off running. You do that and I'll—"

"*Never mind,*" Tracy said. And now she looked directly at Richard and said, "Stop it. Stop talking to him."

Richard gave her a look that suggested that this time she was going to be punished for her insolence.

But Tracy went on, "There's no need to torture him. He knows what you'll do. Just stop talking to him."

"Say please."

"Please."

"Ooh," Javier said, "maybe we been cooped up here a little too long." He was amused by it.

This time Tracy addressed Javier. She said, "I'm taking him upstairs. You can come with me and make sure that we're not trying to escape."

Richard said, "You don't talk to him, lady. You talk to me. I'm the one in charge."

Tracy said, "I'll cook for you. I'll serve you. I'll get your goddamn paper. But don't bully my son. *Don't.*"

"Okay," Javier said, getting to his feet. "Let's take him upstairs."

"Hold it," Richard said.

"Richie," Javier said, his voice and gestures conciliatory, "you're in charge, okay? But I want to eat breakfast in peace. I'll be right back."

Richard looked at Javier and thought, *Shoot him now.* Put a bullet in his spic face. Then kill the rest and be on their way.

But Javier said, "Come on, man. We're getting the money

today. And then we're home free."

And then Tracy was on her feet too, taking John by the arm and following the Mexican to the kitchen door.

Then Richard put his arm on the boy and stopped them. Richard's hand gripping little John's wrist.

Tracy tensed and felt a fear and hatred she'd never felt before. She stood motionless as the monster addressed her son.

Richard Billie said, "Okay, boy. You're going upstairs with your granddad. Your mama's going to come back down here with us. Now you try anything stupid like climbing out the window, we're going to kill her."

Tracy gasped, and Richard kept his focus on John and said, "You understand me, boy?"

John was shaking, unable to form words.

Richard said, his voice a little fiercer, "I said, do you understand me?"

"Yes, sir."

"Good," Richard said. He released his grip. "Now get out of here."

She was shaking as she climbed the stairs and she couldn't stop it. She kept her hands on John as he walked in front of her, kept saying to him that it was okay, that everything would be okay, that he was a brave boy, but she couldn't stop shaking inside. She hoped that John was not aware of it.

Then they got to the guest bedroom. She turned to Javier and said, "Let me have just a second with him."

"In there?"

"Please."

Javier gestured an okay and she went inside and closed the door. She looked over at Lee. He seemed to still be asleep. Then she crouched down and said to John quietly, "He's a dangerous man, honey. Unless I tell you otherwise, you do what he says.

Don't try to escape. It's going to be okay. Do you understand me?"

"Yes, ma'am."

"Now, try not to cry. Mommy's going to be downstairs, but Grandpa will be with you up here."

"But—"

"He's going to be okay too. I promise. Believe me. Okay?"

"Okay."

"I love you, pumpkin."

John said he loved her too. She hugged him fiercely and kissed him on the face. "Be good," she said.

She went out the door and closed it behind her.

Javier smiled at her. She recoiled inside. He was not a bad-looking man. Handsome, actually. But he was one of her captors.

"Come on," he said, gesturing to the stairs.

And then it occurred to her why she had appealed to him at the breakfast table. It might have been because he was there and perhaps the least wicked of the three. But that probably wasn't it, she thought. He's vain, she thought. He's a good-looking man and he knows it. He's probably always done well with women. By siding with her over Richard, he had won a point. Shown Richard and Amos the advantage he would always have when it came to the ladies. Never mind that the lady in question was trying to protect her son. That she was fearing for the lives of her family. In the mind of this stud, she *preferred* him.

With this in mind, Tracy turned to him on the stairs and said, "Thanks."

"For what?" Javier said.

"For helping me out down there," she said. "I don't mind helping you guys, but your friend can be a little rude."

"He's not my friend."

Tracy put a little smile on her face. "Well, that's good to know," she said.

Javier smiled back at her. And Tracy thought, *Good.* And then hoped that Javier wouldn't take this as some sort of sign that he could molest her.

Then she thought, *What if I did get him alone?* Entice him with her body, maybe get him down into the basement for some good country loving. Wait until he was distracted, then smash a barbell over his head.

Okay, that would take one out. But it would be the one without a gun.

They reached the bottom of the stairs and Tracy saw Amos and Richard standing by the front door. They were both peering through cracks between the curtains and the window. They were both holding their guns at their sides.

Richard turned and saw them.

In a low voice, he said, "There's someone out there." He motioned to Tracy and said, "Come here."

FORTY

Richard grabbed her by the arm and pulled her hard enough to jerk her toward him.

Again, he said, "There's someone out there. Look through here."

Tracy pulled back the curtain. She saw nothing in the front yard. Panned right and took in the driveway. Behind her Jeep and Lee's Dodge Ram truck was a Chevy pickup. In the bed of the pickup was a large water container. A black man got out of the truck and seemed to examine Lee's Dodge.

"Who is that?" Richard said.

"I don't know."

He squeezed her arm tighter. Tracy winced and said, "I don't know. This isn't my house."

Amos said, "That's a water tank in his truck."

"Fuck," Richard said, "I can *see* that. What's he doing here?"

Tracy said, "Maybe he's here to clean Dad's truck."

"Shit," Richard said. "What, by appointment?"

"I don't know. I don't live here."

A few moments passed. Javier stayed by the foot of the stairs. Richard held Tracy close to him, his pistol just touching her stomach. Amos continued to peer out the window.

Then Amos said, "Shit. He's still here."

Now the man was coming to the front door.

Richard Billie cursed again.

Amos said, "We got to get rid of him."

Tracy wasn't sure what he meant by that. She didn't want to give it too much thought.

Javier said, "Get him in here."

"No," Tracy said. "Just stay quiet."

"He's not leaving," Richard said. "He's seen two vehicles. He's coming up here."

"Then let me get rid of him," Tracy said.

"No," Javier said, "get him in here."

Tracy turned to Richard and said, "Please. Let me answer the door. I'll get him out of here. There'll be no trouble."

Amos said, "Richard—"

"Shut up," Richard said. "All right," he said to Tracy. "Get him out of here."

"Richard," Amos said.

Now the man was coming up the front steps.

The captors stepped back, out of sight.

The doorbell rang.

Richard whispered to her, "Remember. One screwup and the boy dies." He released her arm.

Tracy opened the door.

"Hi," she said.

And now she saw that he was a pleasant-looking man of about thirty. Tall and solid, wearing a baseball cap.

"Hello," he said. "I'm Ruben. Is Mr. Coughlin home?"

"No. I'm afraid he isn't. I'm Tracy, his daughter-in-law. What can I do for you?"

"Well, I usually wash his vehicle every ten days or so. I see that it's in the driveway and it's pretty dirty." Ruben smiled. "He's taken it out to one of his sites, I suppose."

"Yes. Probably."

"Well, he usually gives me the keys and I move it further down the drive and wash it there. But he's not home?"

He seemed perplexed by that. He wasn't home, but his

vehicle was in the driveway.

"No," Tracy said. "His daughter picked him up this morning. They left in her car."

"Oh. Well, I can wash it and get the money from him next time. I've done it before."

"Uh, maybe not. I don't want to . . ."

"Or not," the man said. He raised his hands to show he wasn't pushy. He said, "How about you? Is that your Jeep?"

"Yes."

"I can wash that, if you like. Eight dollars for the external wash and dry. Fifteen for the inside and outside. I've got a vacuum cleaner in the truck too."

"No, thank you."

"Okay." He smiled again. And then he was looking out at the driveway again. Seeing two vehicles there, curious, and Tracy was thinking, *please don't. Please don't ask any more . . .*

But Ruben Matthews was a decent, thoughtful man. He had worked with Lee Coughlin for almost two years now and he had always liked that Coughlin spoke to him like a man. Never patronizing or putting on airs. Ruben Matthews could see that Coughlin was a man who had worked with his hands and hadn't forgotten it.

Now Ruben was thinking that if Coughlin had left his vehicle here and gone with his daughter, the man must have some sort of health problem. He was older . . .

Ruben said to the young woman at the door, "Is everything okay, miss?"

He saw her mouth working, tightening. She said, "Everything's fine. Tomorrow, okay?" Her voice firmer now. She was stepping back, narrowing the space in the door.

"Okay," Ruben said. He began to walk back to his truck.

Inside, Amos said, "*Shit.* Did you hear that?"

Richard Billie said, "Yeah, I heard. Go around the side door, catch him. Do it away from here."

"No," Tracy said.

But Amos was already leaving. Hurrying.

"No," Tracy said. She started after him.

Richard pointed his gun, staying her. Tracy heard the kitchen door open and close and she trembled at the thought of it. And she prayed that the poor man outside was already in his truck and had already backed out of the driveway.

Ruben Matthews was in his truck and had the gear in reverse when he saw the heavy white man hurrying down the driveway, waving at him with one arm. The other one behind his back. A small alarm then in Ruben's head, but not ringing loudly enough as he brought the truck to a stop and put it in park.

The big man came around to the passenger side of the truck. Opened the door, climbed in the cab, and took a seat next to Ruben. That's when Ruben first saw the gun.

Amos pointed it at him and said, "Let's go."

Ruben drove to the end of the road. Then made a right turn as the fat man told him to. Ruben took the man in and thought, *convict*. He'd seen the type before. Trashy man, with nothing to lose and no respect for life.

Amos said, "Keep both hands on the wheel."

Ruben did so. He nodded his head slowly, showing the man he was going to cooperate, fighting his panic.

Ruben said, "Where's Mr. Coughlin?"

"A friend of yours?" Amos said.

"Yes."

"He's fine. You'll be fine too, you do as I tell you."

"I intend to do that. I don't want any trouble."

Ruben Matthews wanted to believe that. He wanted to believe this turd wouldn't kill him. But the boy had already admitted that he was holding Coughlin in his home. And not just Coughlin, but the man's daughter-in-law too. He thought of her now, pretty young lady scared for her life and probably Coughlin's too. She had tried to get him out of there. But he had hung about, asking if everything was all right. *Damn.* Yes, he had asked that and now he was probably going to die for it. He thought of his wife, Sheila, his little girl . . .

Ruben said, "I've got an idea."

The man with the gun was smiling at him. A cold, steely smile. "What?" the man said.

Ruben said, "I can drive you out north of town. Drive out in the middle of nowhere, you leave me and you can have the truck. Do what you like."

"Yeah?" he said. The man was still smiling. Like Ruben was being funny now.

Ruben felt a stone inside of him. His mouth dry.

Amos said, "We'll see." He was still smiling.

For the next few minutes neither of them said anything. Ruben tried to keep his terror in check by taking some comfort in the spare town traffic around them. He told himself that the man was going to wait until they were out in the country and then he would do something. But not out here with all these other cars and businesses nearby. Soon traffic thinned out and they crossed the Arkansas River on the Twenty-First Street Bridge. Downtown fell behind them.

Then they were in a rougher area. Public housing and littered parks. They came to an intersection near the highway and Amos told the driver to keep going west, over another bridge crossing the highway and a railway yard that cut through a refinery.

"Turn here," Amos said, directing the truck into the parking lot of an abandoned, blackened warehouse. Ruben did as he was told and then Amos told him to continue behind the building where tall grass and weeds had crept over the back lot.

"Okay," Amos said, "stop."

The truck was rolling now, the transmission still in drive, but

Ruben Matthews's foot was not on the gas and he looked over to his left to the scrub that would come up over a man's waist, a field of it and the river beyond and then, with the truck still rolling, Ruben opened his door and jumped out.

"Shit," Amos said, as he looked over and saw the black guy running away at good speed. Amos scooted over to the driver's side and took control of the wheel.

He turned the vehicle to his left and went after Matthews. Not flooring it, but accelerating, and he saw the man turn around, despair and panic on his face, then turning back and running full out now.

Amos gave it more gas and in a couple of seconds he was right up on the guy. Firing one shot and missing, but the next two connecting and putting the guy down. Amos stopped the truck and put it in park. He got out, walked over and used another round on the guy's head just to be sure.

FORTY-ONE

Donna Wolfe drove the Mercedes only two blocks before she pulled over and hit the electric switch to put up the convertible top. It was goddamn cold this morning. She had lost her jacket sometime during the previous night. It was something of a blur now. Lost her jacket and left the top down on the car. Good thing it hadn't rained. Try explaining that to Javier.

If he got here. Oh, God. Javier. What if he'd been in town last night? What if he knew what she had been up to? He would kill her if he knew.

It had happened so quickly. Like the old days. She had just said goodbye to Miguel and Hector and she was feeling excited and scared. Keyed up. Javier had broken out of prison and he was coming back. She didn't know if she should be scared or if she should look forward to it. She didn't know what she thought. And then her phone rang and it was Earlene and she said she was with Jamie and they had just left Scarlett's and were heading out to the Stripe and she should come. And Donna thought, *I shouldn't*. And then said it too, but Earlene shouted come on and then Donna could hear Jamie giggling in the background and saying, "Tell that skanky bitch to get her ass down here." And it all sounded like too much fun then and Donna said, "Okay. I'll have one cocktail with you."

An hour or so later they were drinking martinis laced with Vicodin and Donna was feeling very loose and wonderfully drowsy. Free and easy. *Euphoric.* She was feeling *good.* And midnight came and went and before they knew it, it was two A.M. and they had piled in her Mercedes with a couple of other people, shrieking with delight, and Donna thought later one of the guys may have tumbled out the back when she turned a little too quickly at an intersection, though she wasn't too sure about it. They ended up at a party at some guy's house in North Dallas and there was a heated pool in the back and there were a lot more girls there, a good many of them taking their clothes off and jumping in the pool. And Donna vaguely remembered saying no and maybe it was Jamie who said, "Come *on*," and then she too was naked and splashing about in the water. She remembered that.

After that, it was a little indistinct. She woke up in a bed in one of the bungalows with a towel for a blanket. Looked over and saw a naked boy next to her. The boy looked about seventeen and after a few moments she remembered who he was. She checked herself then and more or less confirmed for herself that she had been with him. Then she found her clothes somewhere on the floor and crept out of there. The walk of shame, as Earlene would say. Dress loosely fit and wrinkled, undergarments missing . . .

God, she thought. A seventeen-year-old. Was he the same one going around with a bowl of heart-shaped pink pills, offering them to the guests? A crystallized form of methamphetamine called strawberry quick that the kids were into these days. He had seemed older last night. He had seemed charming and sexy and cool. God, if this got back to Javier . . . he would be back in Dallas soon. Maybe later today.

Back in Dallas, and then what? How long would he stay? A day or two and then he would be on his way back to Mexico. Right? That could be good and bad. Good because it wouldn't give him enough time to find out if she had misbehaved. That was the thing with these Latins. They could be real firecrackers in bed and great romancers, but they lived and died over their women. Their code of machismo. If Javier found out she'd fucked some kid in North Dallas, he'd kill her and the boy. If he could ever find out who the boy was. She certainly wouldn't be able to tell him.

Still, even as she thought of it now, it brought a slight smile to her face. A hard-chested, smooth-skinned boy asking her what school she went to. A kid ten years her junior. It gave her some pride.

She parked the car in the garage behind her condominium. She undressed in her bedroom and put a bathrobe on. She turned on the taps for the shower and waited for the water to get hot. She would feel better when she was clean. Get some sleep and then have some coffee and then maybe call Earlene and see how much she knew. She hoped it wouldn't be much, but realized that such a hope was probably vain.

That was when her doorbell rang.

Her heart pounded. *Javier!* He had followed her. Or he had been waiting outside. He *knew. Where have you been, you filthy whore?* He would kill her. It would be on the television that night. *Escaped Convict Kills Slutty Girlfriend.*

Stop it, she thought. He called last night from Tulsa. He wouldn't be back this soon. Of course he wouldn't be.

The doorbell rang again.

Donna looked at the bathroom, heard the shower running. And the doorbell rang again. Whoever it was probably knew she was at home. She turned off the shower and went to the door. She was still in her bathrobe.

Her heart was still pounding when she looked through the peephole. Reason told her it wouldn't be Javier, but she didn't want to trust reason then.

Shit. It wasn't Javier. What a relief.

It was two guys in suits. Cops. One of them leaned forward

to the peephole. It was the white one. The other was black. Donna's experience with law enforcement told her these guys probably weren't with the Dallas PD. Too thin and clean-cut. They were feds.

And they seemed to know that she was home.

Because now the white one was saying, "She's here." Then he said to the door in a louder voice. "Ms. Wolfe, open up. FBI. We need to talk to you."

She unlocked the door and opened it and then she said, "I'm not talking to you without my lawyer present."

Agent Carr said, "We're not arresting you. We just want to ask you a few questions."

"Right," she said. "You can read me Miranda or not read it to me. It doesn't matter. I'm not talking to you without my lawyer present."

The white agent looked at the black agent. They both seemed to mentally shrug and then the black one said, "You better call him right away then."

FORTY-TWO

Amos got the black guy's truck away from the abandoned warehouse and then crossed the bridge back over the railway yard. It was good to get out of the house. The girl there was good-looking but it was not easy being there with all the fighting going on. Javier wanting to kill Richard, Richard wanting to kill him, both of them wanting to kill the old man and the girl and the kid. It was like being in his parents' house again. Everybody wanting to kill everyone else. They were bored and tired and wanting to get out of there.

Amos saw the highway come into view again. Highway 75. Take it south and it would bring him to Texas. He had a vehicle now and he would be alone. About half a tank of gas. He had lifted the black guy's wallet and searched through it when he got back in the truck. About eighteen dollars. So he had the vehicle now and a highway in front of him, but how far could he get with eighteen bucks?

He would have to go back to the old man's house and sit and wait, keep waiting until Javier's people brought them their fifty thousand dollars. Then they'd be set. They'd have real money. Fifty thousand dollars and they could get out of this dump. Go down to Florida where it was warm. Further down to the Florida Keys. Live in a shack and hear the waves at night. Amos didn't think much beyond that.

The bridge ended and the truck descended an incline to a stop sign. Amos checked the gun. It was the old man's .38

Chief's Special. A snubnose with five shots. Amos had just used four of them. One shot left. Shit. Had he used that many? He'd have to ask the old man where the extra ammo was when he got back. If the old man was alive to tell him.

He could have used the .38 on the old man last night. But it was dark and he wanted to avoid unnecessary noise if he could. He was surprised to see the old man had gotten the better of Richard. The old man on top of Richard, just pounding the shit out of him. Who would have thought he had it in him? Amos thought the kick in the guy's face would have broken his nose or jaw but it didn't seem to. Maybe that's why Richard had shot him afterwards. To give him some sort of damage. But that probably wasn't it. Probably it was because the old man had gotten the better of Richard, maybe even scared him, and Richard wanted to make him pay for that.

Or make him die slowly. Amos remembered his mom's uncle getting shot in the leg during a hunting trip. Hunting in the woods and drinking beer and someone accidentally shot the man in the thigh, pretty much the same place Richard had shot the old man. They put Amos's great-uncle in the pickup and drove him back to town, forty miles away. Must have hit an artery or something because by the time they reached town, the man had bled out and died.

Maybe it would be the same way with Coughlin. Maybe he was dead already and the woman was trying to keep it from the boy so the boy wouldn't start crying.

The stoplight turned green and Amos pressed the accelerator. He went about two blocks when up ahead he saw the car moving toward the edge of the parking lot of a hamburger stand. It was a Pontiac Firebird, old and shabby looking, with a couple of black kids in it, and they were slowing as they got to the street, but then they decided to go at the last second, the driver punching the accelerator, and Amos stood on the truck's brakes and locked it up, the tires screeching out and the kids in the Firebird trying to squeeze it out in time, but it was no use and all three occupants of the two vehicles knew it was coming and then the truck slammed into the Firebird and both vehicles came to a halt.

Amos had not been wearing the seat belt. Consequently, his head slammed forward on impact and hit the steering wheel. It was not enough to knock him out, but it stunned him and left him momentarily disoriented. Noises came to him, indistinct at first, then taking form. Voices, moans, traffic stopping, steam. Amos lifted his head, shook it, and looked through the windshield.

The Firebird was totaled. Its side was smashed in, the guy on the driver's side lolled over onto the passenger's seat like a rag doll. The passenger was sitting back in his seat, blood streaming from his nose. There were a couple of fishing poles that had been thrown forward from the back seat. People from the hamburger stand were starting to come over.

The steam was coming from the truck's radiator. Amos looked around the cab of the truck. The .38 was lying on the passenger floorboard. One round in the chamber. He looked out the passenger window again. More people coming from the parking lot of the hamburger stand, most of them black. One of them dialing a number on a cell phone now.

Amos turned the key in the ignition. The engine turned and then turned and then caught. Amos put the gear in reverse and started to back the truck up. There was a large scrape as it disengaged from the wreckage of the Firebird.

Voices murmured and raised. Alarmed. The fellow was leaving and it was clearly the guys in the Firebird who were at fault.

Amos backed the truck fifteen feet. Then he put the gear in drive and stepped on the accelerator and drove away, a couple of people running after him. The truck's engine made a strained noise as it kept going.

In the cab of the truck, Amos thought, dumb fucking spooks. Pulled out right in front of him. Dumbshit niggers were going to get his ass arrested. The second bridge that would take him back over the Arkansas River was up ahead, but he could hear sirens coming from that direction. He made a left turn before the bridge and hammered the accelerator again, the truck's engine making sort of a whistling sound now. He looked at the temperature gauge and saw that it was pegged to the right. There wouldn't be much time before the engine blew.

Now he was driving north, parallel to the river, and he sensed that he was boxing himself in. Keep moving, he thought. Keep moving and don't panic. He made another left turn down another residential street. He kept going until he saw an alley bordered by overhanging trees. He figured that would be the best place to leave the truck.

He got out and took the .38 with him. He could hear sirens as he ran down the alley.

Forty-Three

A fire engine went by, its sirens screaming. Amos turned his back from the street as other emergency vehicles followed. He was standing at the pay phone at a run-down gasoline stop. He found the number in the telephone book, deposited the change and made the call.

The phone rang. And rang. Five rings and then an answering machine picked up.

Amos didn't hesitate. He raised his voice and said, "Rich! Pick up, it's me. Goddammit, I need help. Pick up!"

A moment and then he had Richard on the phone.

Richard Billie said, "What happened?"

"There was an accident," Amos said.

"What do you mean, accident? Where's the spook?"

"He's dead. I was driving back and these fucking guys smashed into the truck. A bad wreck. I had to get away before the police got there. The truck's totaled."

Richard Billie squeezed his eyes shut. Then opened them. He said, "Are you still with the truck?"

"No. I dumped it. Listen, you gotta come get me. They're gonna be looking for me."

Richard looked over his shoulder. The girl and Javier were sitting in the living room. They weren't looking at him, but he knew they were both listening in.

Richard said, "I can't come get you." If he left Javier alone, Javier would just leave and then he'd be out fifty grand. Also, he couldn't trust Javier to watch the hostages.

Amos said, "*You have to.* They're looking for me. Goddammit, Richard, I get caught, they're going to find you too."

Richard acknowledged the threat. He could hang up the phone or tell the fat piece of shit to get fucked. But that wouldn't get him anywhere. The reality was he needed to bring Amos back here.

"All right," Richard said. "Where are you?"

"I'm at a Git-N-Go on Southwest Boulevard. Across the street from a lot by the railroad. That's where I'm going to be."

"Where?"

"I'm going to hide behind the railroad cars. They're under the highway overpasses. They might use a helicopter to find me."

"Okay," Richard said, "I'm going to send the girl to come get you."

"She'll do it?"

"She'll have to," Richard said.

"Tell her to hurry," Amos said.

Richard hung up the phone and went into the living room. Javier sat in a chair, his legs folded. He was still drinking his coffee. The girl sat on the edge of the couch.

Richard looked at her and said, "That was Amos. He needs your help."

Tracy said, "What happened?"

"A car wreck. He had to hide. You're going to go pick him up."

Tracy said, "What about the man who came here? The man who owned the truck?"

"Don't worry about him."

Tracy looked from the Mexican and then back to Richard. She had not forgotten that Javier had urged her to get the black man into the house. Javier had wanted the same thing as the other two. He was no better.

Tracy said, "He killed him, didn't he?"

Richard said, "I told you not to worry about it."

Tracy squeezed her eyes shut. A good man who may have had a wife and children. Comes to the door to wash a customer's vehicle and twenty minutes later he's murdered.

Javier said, "Miss, you didn't even know him."

"Shut up," Tracy said, her voice fierce. "He didn't do anything to you."

"Be that as it may," Richard said, "we've got a situation here. And you are going to help us whether you like it or not. That car washer is dead but your boy is still alive."

Tracy stared at Richard, comprehending his meaning.

And Richard said, "Yeah. That's why you're going to go get Amos and bring him back here safely."

"Why can't you do it?" Tracy said. Then turning to Javier, she said, "Or you?"

Richard said, "I'm deciding who does what. You're going and he's staying here. Now get up."

Tracy got to her feet and then Richard said, "You'll take your car. But you're leaving your phone here. Neither one of us is going with you. So until you pick up Amos, you'll be on your own. You stop and call the police or pick up a gun at a pawnshop, you'll be killing your boy. It's that simple. I look out the window and see a police car or a telephone repairman or a flower truck I don't like, I go upstairs and put one in his head. Then I'll finish off the old man. And that'll be your doing, not mine. I told you before, I got nothing to lose. You do. Do we understand each other?"

Tracy nodded. Mechanically, as if she had been forced to stand outside herself to function.

"Good," Richard said.

★ ★ ★ ★ ★

They watched her back the Jeep out of the driveway from the living room window. The Jeep motored off down the road and Richard let the curtain fall back to cover the window.

Javier said, "You sure that was a good idea?" He was still pushing him.

Richard said, "Well, I wasn't going to let you go. If that's what you're thinking."

Javier smiled and said, "I wasn't thinking that."

"I'm not worried about her," Richard said.

She kept both hands on the steering wheel to keep them from shaking. But she was still shaking inside. Quivering with fear and helplessness. She thought of John and Lee and told herself that she had to keep it together. For them and for Drew. But she was holding onto something else too. Anger. A growing rage.

A psychiatrist had once told her about something called the Principle of the Least Interest. She, the shrink, had told her that in a relationship between two people, the person with the least interest in maintaining the relationship held the most power. He or she had the ultimate bargaining power of saying, "Okay, I'll just leave." Then the other would give in to their demands. A harsh and simple tenet of negotiation used between husband and wife, boyfriend and girlfriend.

Tracy thought that the principle was a little too mercenary for her tastes. If two people married, they should trust each other and work with each other toward a common goal. Or goals. Family, companionship, support. Her marriage with Drew had never been reduced to power plays or unspoken threats. But maybe they had just been lucky. Maybe the marriage would have soured in time.

But she didn't really believe that. She never had believed

that. You could try and reason your way out of grief by thinking such things. The marriage wasn't really that great anyway, and so forth. But they had been very happy and there was no getting away from it.

But a version of the principle was at work here. In this situation, Richard Billie had the advantage over her. He had said it himself: *he had nothing to lose.* And she did. If she called the police, it was possible that they could capture Amos and then return to the house with her along with about fifty or so police officers. Surround the house and work to bring out John and Lee alive. But Richard Billie had said that if he even so much as sensed a cop he would run upstairs and put a bullet in little John's head. He said it and he knew Tracy knew that he meant it. It might cost him his own life, but he didn't care. It was hard to beat someone who didn't care.

She thought about another person playing the devil's advocate, saying, "But he's going to shoot John anyway. Maybe this way you'd have a chance."

Yeah, maybe. But the odds were too slim. She had seen the cold, empty look on Richard's face when he shot her father-in-law in the leg. Cold-blooded and vengeful. She had seen that and she had no doubt now that he would kill a child for no other reason than to make her sorry she'd fucked with him. Anything could trigger it. Even if all she did was to return to the house without Amos.

And that's as much thought as she cared to give it. At least for now. She would have to obey the monster's vile instructions to the letter. So it was that she drove west and pulled off the exit ramp to Southwest Boulevard and hoped with all her might that she would find Amos in the railway lot across the street from the convenience store.

She found the store and made a right turn into the graveled lot across the street. In the lot were a couple of abandoned cars with flat tires and cracked windshields. The day was darkening, clouds coming in low, threatening rain. Soon the Jeep was under the shadow of the highway overpass. Tracy let the Jeep roll along to the back of the lot. She stopped the vehicle and put it in park.

In front of her was a fence and beyond that, stationary railway cars, mostly yellow or a dark red. She turned around to look at the convenience store on the other side of the street. She knew what she feared then.

She turned back and looked out into the rail yard. God, she thought. Please don't let him be caught.

Then she saw him. Coming out from behind one of the cars. Big, white, and menacing. Now he was familiar to her. Now she needed him to be alive and free. This was the person she needed to see.

He crossed a series of tracks then went through a hole in the fence. He ran to the Jeep and got in.

"Hey," he said. Familiar with her too.

Tracy did not respond to his greeting. Instead, she looked in the rearview mirror.

And saw a police car in the parking lot of the convenience store.

"Jesus," she said. "Get down. There's a police car across the street."

He turned around to look for himself. And she said, "Please. Hurry."

"All right," he said, slumping as much of his mass as he could to the floor. "But remember," he said, "I've still got this." He pointed the .38 at her.

"I remember," she said, without even thinking about it. She was on autopilot now. She backed the Jeep up and turned it around.

She got it to the street then, without using her indicator,

made a left turn. She drove carefully, not using too much acceleration. The police car faded in her mirror. Then she looked out the windshield and saw another coming toward her.

She made a slight gasp.

"What?" Amos said.

"It's just another cop," she said. "It's okay. He's past us now."

Amos said, "Don't fuck with me now."

"I have no intention of fucking with you," Tracy said. "Your friends have my son at gunpoint."

Amos didn't reply to that. He wasn't sure he'd heard the girl use the word *fuck* before. He was looking at her face, tight and determined. A little different than she was yesterday. He said, "Can you still see them?"

"No. I think we're okay."

Amos rose from the floor and took his seat. He turned around and looked out the window, the gun still in his hand, pointed loosely at her.

"Well," Amos said, smiling. "You did all right."

Christ, she thought. He was smiling at her. He had killed a man, murdered a perfectly nice man who had probably never harmed anybody, and now he was smiling at her. It made her feel unclean.

She said, "You killed him, didn't you?"

"What?" he said. "Oh, well he tried to run away."

Tears came to Tracy's eyes. So casual. And dishonest about it as well. She said, "You didn't have to do it. You could have just let him go." She was trying not to say these things out loud, but she couldn't seem to stop herself.

Amos said, "You knew what would happen when he came to the door. He just got unlucky. What's he to you, anyway? You didn't know him, did you?"

She was stifling sobs now. She said, more or less to herself, "That's what Javier said."

"What?" Amos said.

"Nothing."

They drove in silence for a while.

Then Amos said, "Looks like it's going to rain."

Tracy looked over at him. It's unreal, she thought. It's just unreal. He killed a man and now he says it looks like it's going to rain. What do you say to that? Was he going to try to rape her before they got back? Would he look at her while he did? Or would she be, like the man who came to the door, simply an object?

Tracy said, "You've got a cut on your head."

"Yeah?" Amos touched it and winced. "Yeah. I hit it on the steering wheel in that wreck. Fucking assholes pulled right out in front of me."

"Yeah," Tracy said. "Some people." She didn't have the energy to keep it in.

Amos didn't respond to that. He just continued to look out the window. They would be home soon.

FORTY-FOUR

When Eddie Marks was a law student, he clerked for a criminal defense firm of marginal reputation. The office was an old brownstone with fire escapes climbing up the sides and it overlooked a parking lot. One afternoon he stood at the receptionist's desk, pointlessly flirting with a woman eight years his senior, and he looked out the window and saw a red Acura NSX pull into the parking lot. A top view of it and the car was new at that time. The Nipponese Ferrari, they were calling it. It excited young Eddie Marks and he said so. The receptionist was a knowing type with frizzy hair and a tight top, and she drifted over to the window to see what all the fuss was about. Looking at the red sports car down below, she said, "Geez. The guy that's driving the car is going to be fifty years old and bald." A few seconds later the driver got out and proved her right. She had predicted this without knowing anything beforehand.

About fifteen years or so later, Eddie Marks bought his own red car, though not an Acura. His was a candy-apple-red Corvette convertible. His own little Barbie car.

Agents Carr and Courtland were standing on the front step of Donna Wolfe's condominium when the red Corvette pulled up to the front curb. Eddie Marks was behind the wheel, visible through the windshield and open top. Agent Carr noticed that Marks had a big head. A moussed-up head with big wraparound sunglasses to help keep it in place. Would he open the door to get out or just vault out of the car like he was Dan Tanna?

216

He opened the door and brought his briefcase with him. Like it was going to do him some good.

Agent Carr said, "Hello, Eddie."

The lawyer didn't appreciate the glibness. He went to Donna Wolfe and put his arm on her shoulder. She winced, just, but let him stay there. Eddie Marks put on his professional tough lawyer face and said, "You are not to question her."

"We haven't," Agent Carr said. "She said she wanted to call you and we've been pretty much waiting since."

Eddie Marks said, "Then why are you still here?"

This didn't faze the agents. It was Courtland who said, "We wanted you to be aware of something."

"What?"

Carr said, "We wanted you to be aware that we've put in an exigent circumstance request with Judge Henry Iacovetta at the Western District for telephonic records for your client and you to check incoming and outgoing telephone calls."

The lawyer said, "He won't give it to you."

"Yes, he will," Carr said, "and you know it."

"Probably within the hour," Courtland said. "Then we can check the records with the telephone company and there won't be anything you or her can do to stop it."

Eddie Marks shrugged. "Go ahead, then."

Carr said, "We will. But your client should know that if we find any evidence that she's been in touch with Mr. Sandoval, she'll be arrested for accessory to escape and aiding and abetting a fugitive. That's to start."

Courtland said, "If we're feeling angry, we can add accessory to murder."

Eddie Marks laughed. "Well," he said, "now you're just talking shit."

"Are we?" Carr said. "We have an escaped fugitive and four murders already. If people were killed after she helped him, a case can be made. But even if one can't, she'll do seven to ten just for helping him escape."

The lawyer said, "Donna, go inside. You don't have to listen to this."

Carr started to say something, but Courtland said, "You're right. She doesn't. But she should. Maybe she should ask herself if you're more interested in protecting Sandoval than her."

"Fuck you."

Courtland said, "She can go inside, maybe throw her cell phone in the incinerator. But we're still going to get the records from the phone company. And if we find evidence that she's been in touch with him in the last twenty-four hours, she'll be arrested. And by then she might figure out she'd be better off with another lawyer. But it won't matter then because deal-making time will be over."

"Donna, go inside."

Donna Wolfe said, "What sort of deal?"

"Donna," the lawyer said.

But now she was looking at the agents. Thinking about her behavior the previous night, about what Javier would do to her if he found out about it. Wondering now if Eddie Marks was as interested in her welfare as he was getting in her pants.

Eddie Marks said, "Donna, don't listen to these guys. They're trying to scare you."

Carr said, "He's right. We are trying to scare you. But we're not lying."

Eddie Marks said, "I got one question for you: have you got an arrest warrant? Got one with you right now?"

The agents hesitated.

And Eddie Marks said, "That's what I thought. This conversation is over."

FORTY-FIVE

They put the driver of the Pontiac Firebird in the ambulance and hauled him off to Tulsa Regional Medical Center. Traffic investigators were on the scene, making measurements and taking photos. The big fire engine was still there along with several city and county police cars.

The patrol sergeant in charge of the scene was named Kurt Sinders. He was talking to one of the first officers on the scene, a young earnest sort named Cale.

Sergeant Sinders said, "Anything?"

"No, sir."

"Don't call me sir." Sergeant Sinders said, "Well, let's go over what we do know. We found a wallet on the floor of the truck with a driver's license telling us the owner of the truck is Ruben Matthews. African-American. No cash inside the wallet."

"Correct. We found the truck about twenty minutes ago."

"And all the witnesses say the driver was white."

"Yeah."

"We got a hit and run. And a possible grand theft auto."

"Yes. Sergeant."

"And we can't find him."

The patrol officer kept quiet. He presumed the sergeant was simply confirming it for himself now.

Sergeant Sinders said, "Have we called the Matthews residence yet?"

"Yes. No answer."

Sinders said, "It's a working vehicle, correct?"

"Yeah. Big tank in the back. I presume it's used to wash cars."

The patrol sergeant was thinking that so many witnesses probably hadn't mistaken a black guy for a white guy. Which meant that the truck had been stolen and that's why the driver had fled the scene when the accident wasn't his fault. The owner wasn't home, which could mean he was sitting at a lunch counter somewhere, shaking his fist at an empty parking lot. But that wasn't likely. The truck hadn't been reported stolen.

So the truck had probably been jacked. Which meant there was a possibility that the owner of the truck had been killed and was maybe dumped in an alley somewhere.

But who would want to jack a truck used to wash cars? It wasn't the sort of vehicle that a thief would steal. Maybe it was a junkie. Maybe it was just random . . .

Sergeant Sinders said, "Stay here for a minute." He took out his cell phone and made a call. When the line picked up on the other end, a voice said, "Homicide."

"Yeah, Sergeant Kurt Sinders here. Could you get me Captain Devereaux?"

"Hold, please."

Then a voice came on, saying, "This is Mal."

Mal Devereaux, supervising captain of the detectives. He was an ex-marine and one of the most respected people in the Tulsa Police Department. He was a homicide detective but hadn't forgotten how to talk to the men and women on patrol.

Sinders said, "Hey, Mal. Kurt here."

"Hey Kurt, what's going on?" Mal Devereaux's voice was familiar and friendly.

Sinders said, "I am on Twenty-Third Street in the western division. We got a hit and run with a stolen vehicle. A driver of a vehicle hurt pretty bad. No homicide that I'm aware of. We got a wallet, found in the truck, showing a picture of an African-American named Ruben Matthews. And the tag of the truck shows it's his."

"And?"

"Well, he's a black guy. And all the witnesses said that the driver of the truck is a white male. He's the one that fled."

"So you think there's been a carjacking?"

"Yeah. We've got patrol cars out looking for the runner. He's already abandoned the truck."

"So why are you calling me?"

"Well," Sinders said, "it's just a thought. We were all briefed at the beginning of shift about the three escaped convicts from lower Kansas. Maybe the runner was one of them."

Mal Devereaux didn't say anything.

Sinders said, "Just a thought."

Devereaux said, "You still got witnesses there?"

"Yeah."

"They gave you photos at line-up this morning, didn't they?"

"Yeah. I've got them in the car."

"Well, show the witnesses the photos and see what you get. If something comes of it, call me right back."

"I will."

FORTY-SIX

She parked the Jeep close to the garage and they went into the house through the back door. Richard and Javier were there waiting for them.

Richard said to Amos, "You check her?"

Amos said, "What?"

"Did you check her? See if she's got a weapon on her."

Amos sort of shrugged.

Richard said, "Goddammit, boy. What's the matter with you?"

Before she could say anything, Richard put his hands on Tracy and felt her body from top to bottom. He didn't stop and linger over anything, but he wasn't considerate about it either. He got behind her and pulled her jacket off.

"She's fine," Richard said.

To Amos, Javier said, "What happened?"

"He's dead," Amos said.

"Where?" Javier said.

"In a field behind a—look, don't worry about it. No one's gonna trace it back to us."

Tracy stood and watched this reptilian exchange. Three men talking about the death of another like it meant nothing. Which to them, it did. She was so repelled by it, she had barely noticed Billie running his hands over her body.

Richard said, "Nobody saw you?"

"No."

God, Tracy thought. *They're all such liars.* Even with each other. Of course someone had seen him. The man had been in a fucking car wreck. He had run from it. Abandoned the truck. How could he have not been seen?

She said, "I'd like to go upstairs now."

Richard looked at her and smiled. He said, "What are you so blue about?" He said it when he knew why. This, Tracy knew.

She said, "I'd like to go upstairs now." Still showing no emotion.

"All right, sis." To Javier, Richard said, "Take her upstairs."

They started to go and Richard gave her one more twist. "Hey," he said. And when she turned to acknowledge him, he said, "Cheer up. You did good."

He was still laughing when she walked out of the kitchen.

Javier opened the door to the bedroom upstairs. John rushed into her arms, and she felt a relief she had never experienced before.

John said they hadn't hurt him. He said they hadn't even come up to check. He said, "I could have left. Maybe tried to get away." He looked at her in such a way that she knew it was a question. He was afraid that she would think he was a coward for not trying.

Tracy recognized this and so she said, "Run away and leave Grandpa alone? Leave your mama alone?"

"No," John said. "I wouldn't have done that."

Tracy said, "Sometimes it's hard to know what to do. What the right thing is. Do you understand me?"

"I think so."

"These are bad men. Very bad. But we're going to be okay. All of us. You just have to do exactly what I tell you to do. Do you understand that, John?"

"Yes, Mama."

She kissed him and pulled him toward her again. Taken out

of autopilot then, but not so much. She said, "I want you to go lie down and shut your eyes. Try to nap."

She helped him to a place on the floor and put a blanket over him and adjusted the pillow under his head. She sat cross-legged there and soon he closed his eyes. When they remained shut for a few minutes, she went to Lee.

She checked his pulse and found that it was obtainable and regular, but still faint. Using a cloth, she cleaned the sweat off his brow. He opened his eyes as she did so.

"Hey," he said.

"Hey. How are you feeling?"

"I don't know. Thirsty."

"I'll get you something."

"Later," Lee said. "What's going on?"

She hesitated.

Lee said, "What's the matter?"

She lowered her voice so John wouldn't be able to hear, and her voice broke as she began to tell him what happened. "They killed him," she said.

"What? Who?"

"A black guy. He came here to wash your truck. He said he knew you—"

"Ruben?"

"Yes."

"Oh God. No."

Tracy was crying now, continuing in a hurried voice. She said, "He came to the front door and they made me answer it and I tried—I tried to get him to leave. But he saw your truck in the driveway and then he asked if everything was okay. And that's when they decided to get him. Amos, the big one, went out there and got in his truck. And then they left. And . . . and . . . oh God, I'm so sorry."

Lee Coughlin gathered himself. He reached and clutched her wrist.

"It's okay," he said. "It's okay. It's not your fault."

"I should have—I should have said something to him. But they made me . . ."

"Stop it," Lee said. "I told you, it's not your fault. Tracy."

She lifted her head and acknowledged him. The old man demanding that she look at him. Using her name.

Lee said, "He's dead now."

She nodded her head.

"But they killed him," Lee said. "You didn't."

Tracy said, "They're going to kill us too."

She didn't doubt it anymore. She thought maybe she could get them to fight against each other. Flirt with the Mexican one, be nice to the big one, get them against the mean one. She thought she could play each of them off against the other. And now she realized she had been deluding herself all along. There was no good one. There was no ugly one. They were all three of them bad. They all wanted a man dead simply because he had walked up to the front step of the house.

Lee said, "No, they're not."

"They're—"

"No, they're not."

"Who's going to help us?"

She waited for him to say the police. Or a divine intervention. Or a miracle. Some virtuous force from outside to come in and bail them out. But he didn't.

What he said was, "You are."

FORTY-SEVEN

Amos still had the .38 snubnose on him, but he had used four shots to kill the car washer. He went back and counted them out. Three shots from the window of the truck, missing the first time, maybe connecting the second time, definitely connecting the third time. The fourth one in the head just to make sure. It was a five-shot gun and he had one round left.

He sat in the living room with Javier and Richard. Amos was still holding the gun at his side. And he wondered if Richard knew how many rounds he had used. He wondered if Richard knew he only had one shot left.

Would it make any difference if he knew? Amos wondered.

He could tell Richard, "Hey, I need more bullets." And then maybe Richard would say, go upstairs and ask the old man where he keeps his extra ammo. And that would be that.

Or maybe Richard would look at him and smile and say, "Well, you're okay." And Richard would have something over him then.

Amos was getting anxious about it.

One shot left and what would he do if the police came in here? One shot on a short-barreled gun that wasn't much use when the target was more than twenty feet away. If the girl hadn't come and gotten him by the railway yard, he'd've practically been defenseless against the cops. What would he do if they showed up here? Or if they ran into them later on the road? What if Javier's spic friends somehow found out where they were laying up?

Ask Richard. He'll go to the old man and find out where the ammo is. Just do it.

But Amos didn't like that idea. And even if he did, he certainly wasn't going to ask Richard in front of the Mexican.

Amos stood up. He began to drift toward the stairs.

"Where are you going?"

It was Richard who was asking him, looking over his shoulder while he sat on the couch.

"Upstairs," Amos said. "Use the john."

Richard said, "There's one downstairs."

Amos said, "I thought maybe I'd lie down afterwards. I didn't get much sleep last night."

Richard stared at Amos, paranoid still, and Amos looked back at him like he had nothing to hide. Amos didn't have to act too much. If Richard started giving him heat, he would tell Richard that he had bailed all their asses out by taking care of the car washer while they were watching television.

Amos said, "Okay?" A little tension in his voice.

Richard made a gesture that told him he should suit himself.

Upstairs, Amos thought about actually going to the bathroom first. Just to make some sort of effort to support the lie. But when he got there he couldn't wait. Softly, he knocked on the bedroom door and then he opened it. It was unlocked.

The girl was sitting on the floor next to the bed, administering to the old man. Amos could smell the blood and sickness now. He didn't think the old man would last the day. But his eyes were open.

Amos pointed the gun at the old man and the girl. He said, "I need more ammo for this. Where do you keep it?"

The old man seemed to struggle to look at him. Then he said, "Did you empty the gun?"

"No, goddammit. I didn't say that. I need more, though."

Lee said, "There isn't any more."

"You're lying."

"Do I look like I'm in a position to lie to you?"

"I need more bullets."

"I don't have them."

"Listen," Amos said, raising the gun and pointing it directly at Lee. "I've got one more round in here and I'm going to use it on you if you don't tell me where I can find more bullets."

Lee kept his voice steady. He said, "I told you, I don't have any. Not in the house. I keep extra rounds in my office, but not in my house. You don't believe me, check yourself. Or go to a Walmart and buy some."

As Lee said this, he squeezed Tracy's hand. Because of this, she kept her mouth shut.

Amos continued to stare at the old man, leveling the sight on the old man's forehead. He could squeeze the trigger and put him down for good right now. But a shot would boom out in this room and bring Richard running up the stairs. *What did you do that for?*

Amos let the moment pass. He lowered the gun and walked out.

FORTY-EIGHT

It was late afternoon when Captain Mal Devereaux drove the unmarked Crown Victoria to West Tulsa. Ten minutes earlier, he had received a phone call from the patrol sergeant telling him that one of the witnesses had identified the man driving the stolen truck as Amos Denton, one of the escaped convicts from Kansas. The parking lot of the hamburger stand became a sort of command post and within forty minutes, it was filled up with cars from the FBI, OSBI, and Tulsa County Sheriff's Department. It was Captain Devereaux who requested that the police helicopter be flown in to search the area for a heavyset Caucasian male in his early to midtwenties, presumed to be armed and dangerous.

The helicopter buzzed over them, circling the area and going out over the railway yards a few blocks away. Captain Devereaux briefed the Tulsa County sheriff and the Tulsa Police Department assistant chief and the local FBI ASAC. All of them were here at the site and a few of them wondered if the driver of the truck was their guy or if witnesses had wanted to be interesting.

About thirty minutes of that and then they got a call from the officers in the helicopter, saying they think they found a body lying in a field between the river and the southwest refinery.

Captain Devereaux could still hear the helicopter's blades whirring to the west. He turned and could see it hovering in the distance, maintaining its height over a spot. Not more than a mile away. He turned to Patrol Sergeant Sinders and said, "I'll ride with you."

A convoy of police cars left the hamburger stand, sirens whooping as they moved down the street and crossed over the railway bridge and came to a stop a few blocks later. They drove to the front of the lot of the abandoned warehouse and then behind it, got out of their cars and hurried to a spot underneath the helicopter and saw the body of an African-American, and Mal Devereaux was not surprised when Sergeant Sinders told him that was the same guy who owned the truck.

FORTY-NINE

Prather was on the sidewalk of the Elk County Sheriff's Office talking with his ex-wife. He had not spoken to her in months. But she had picked today to call him to complain about their daughter. Their daughter, Julie, was now a junior at Kansas State, studying art history, of all things, and was he aware that she was now living with a guy?

Prather said, no, he was not. She had not told him. He did not ask his ex-wife if this was another misunderstanding. Betty had a slight history of overreacting to events. Prather wondered if they could discuss this another time. His ex-wife said, "When? After Julie gets pregnant?" And Prather looked up at the sky and wondered why Betty had picked today to discuss such a thing. Julie was twenty years old now and what was he supposed to do when she was at college.

Prather said, "Look, I'll call her. Okay?"

"When?"

"When I get time," Prather said. He had always hated arguing with Betty. He wanted to end the conversation diplomatically. He stood away from the people smoking cigarettes, taking their afternoon breaks.

Cullen came out of the building and called out to him.

"Mike! There's a detective from Tulsa on the phone for you. They might have seen Amos Denton there."

Prather ended his call and ran inside.

★ ★ ★ ★ ★

"Prather."

"Agent Prather?"

"Speaking."

"This is Captain Devereaux, Tulsa PD. We've got a man killed here and we believe there's a possibility the shooter may have been by one of your escapees."

Believe there's a possibility, Prather thought. Well, it was something. He said, "Captain, I've got Special Agent Will Cullen here with me. Do you mind if I put you on speaker?"

"No."

Prather pressed the button on the phone and said, "You got an identification?"

"Here's what we got," Devereaux said. "A white male, heavy-set, in his twenties. He was driving a truck and ran into another vehicle. Witnesses say the other vehicle was at fault. Nonetheless, the white male in the truck took off. Turns out the truck was stolen from Ruben Matthews, a black male. He used the truck to wash cars. Ruben Matthews is dead. Shot three times, last time in the head execution-style. We have one witness at the wreck who says she saw Denton through the windshield of the truck."

"Through the windshield?"

"Yeah," Devereaux said, "I don't know how strong it is. But we have a murder and an identification. Any sign of your guys up there?"

"Not lately. I don't know if you're aware, they stole a truck here and shot the owner in the head too. Later, they killed two more people, who they knew. Shot them in the head too. All of the murders so far have been done with a Glock .40 caliber. Is that what was used on your victim?"

"We don't know yet. We've got techs out here, but we haven't found any shells from a semiautomatic. We believe that a revolver was used."

A pause as Cullen and Prather exchanged looks.

Prather said, "Not the same gun."

"No, it isn't," Devereaux said. "But they could have gotten another gun. Was one taken from the victims?"

"You mean here?"

"Yeah."

"We don't know."

"Well, Mr. Prather, I'm not going to tell you that we definitely have one of your guys down here because I don't really know."

"I understand," Prather said. "But it's something."

"You want to come down, we'll do everything we can to assist you. But, again, I'm not positive it's one of your guys. What I'm saying is, I don't want to mislead you. This could be a lead; it could be nothing. I don't want to take you away from your post for nothing."

"I understand," Prather said. "Tulsa's about a couple hours drive from here. So it's certainly possible they're there."

Devereaux said, "Any of them have family here?"

"No."

"Have you gotten any other tips?"

"FBI has been trying to get information out of Javier Sandoval's girlfriend in Dallas. But she's apparently lawyered up on them."

"Do they believe she knows anything?"

"They're not sure. They tried to bluff her out, but . . . they're still working on it."

"Okay," Devereaux said. "Well, I just thought you'd want to be updated. Can I have your cell number?"

"Yeah. And I'll take yours. Listen, I'm going to check a few things. I'm going to think about coming down. Thanks for the call."

After they exchanged contact information, Devereaux got off

the phone and Prather stood at his desk and pondered.

An ID through a windshield.

But a homicide. Could be related.

Prather thought of the case he had worked on three years earlier when a man in Coffeeville named Ralph Adam Krans answered an advertisement in the newspaper for a used car. The voice answering the telephone number was that of a young female and she agreed to meet Ralph Adam at her home. He showed up there armed with a .357 revolver, raped her and killed her and then took her car across five states before they finally caught up with him in Tennessee and he died in an exchange of gunfire with the police. Before that, he had taken four more victims in his killing spree.

For what? Prather thought. For the little money they had on them or the plates they had on their vehicles. Or maybe just to do it. When it was all over, the only "motive" the police could find was that the man had been in contempt of court for not paying child support. Ralph Adam Krans was a loser, hardcore, and he knew his days were numbered once he killed the first girl in Kansas. Maybe he just wanted to have some fun before he died. Stick it to the man, the system, and five innocent people before getting done in himself.

That was how it usually was with these cases, Prather thought. Losers with nothing left. Wanting to go out in a blaze of glory and take some innocent people with them. Ralph Adam Krans got his fifteen minutes of fame at the end and probably got the satisfaction of knowing that if he hadn't earned their respect, he had at least earned their fear.

Cullen said, "Well?"

"I don't know," Prather said. "It's pretty thin."

Cullen said, "They could be hundreds of miles from here. They could be across the street. We don't even know if they're still together."

234

Prather said, "Billie and Denton are locals. Sandoval lives in Dallas. I don't think Sandoval would want to stick around here."

"Okay," Cullen said, "presuming he'd want to go to Texas, why would he be in Tulsa, Oklahoma? And they didn't see Sandoval there, they saw—they said they saw—Denton."

Prather said, "Let's brief the state police on it."

The Kansas Highway Patrol had a commissioner and a chief, the chief being subordinate to the commissioner. The commissioner is appointed by the governor and the commissioner is the one who selects the chief.

Prather had mixed feelings about the KHP chief. The chief, whose name was Thomas Ludlow, had fired one of his captains because the captain had driven his patrol car off duty. The captain had merely done what pretty much all the state troopers had done. Indeed, what Chief Ludlow himself had done and was still doing. (He was videotaped driving his patrol car to church.) It turned out that the use of the state car had been pure pretext—the termination was related to a personal feud between the commissioner and the captain, a not uncommon occurrence at law enforcement agencies.

Prather didn't think Chief Ludlow was personally corrupt. He had probably gone along with the termination because the commissioner had forced him to. Ludlow was a couple of years short of getting his thirty years in, and he was too old and too tired to be making enemies and endangering his pension.

Chief Ludlow had come down from Topeka after the prisoners escaped.

It surprised Prather, the chief personally involving himself in this. Ludlow had never been much of a hands-on officer. Prather suspected that Ludlow preferred Elk County to the infighting at the state capitol.

Prather personally briefed Chief Ludlow on the Tulsa development.

Ludlow sat behind a desk, blinking here and there. When Prather was finished, the chief said, "Hmmm. I don't think that's much."

"It may not be," Prather said. "But I wanted you to be informed."

Chief Ludlow said, "We think they're in Kansas City."

A moment passed while Prather waited for an elaboration. He didn't get one and he said, "Why?"

"We've received a tip," the chief said.

"From who?"

"CI."

The chief liked to use acronyms. CI rather than confidential informant. Perhaps it made him feel like he was in the game.

Prather said, "Who's the informant?"

"It's confidential."

God. Prather said, "Well, can you tell me what organization forwarded this information to you?"

"KCK police."

Kansas City, Kansas police, which was separate from the Kansas City, Missouri department.

The chief said, "They have a description that matches the stolen truck. Two men in it."

"They get a tag?"

"No."

Prather was having trouble understanding why this would come from a confidential informant. He said, "But three men escaped. And the make of that truck is very common."

The chief said, "We're on standby."

Prather waited for another elaboration. Again in vain. He excused himself and returned to Cullen.

Cullen asked, "How did it go?"

236

"Bad. He should have retired last year."

Prather told Cullen about the chief's Kansas City lead.

"That's it?" Cullen said.

"Oh, he thinks it's gold. He just wants to be able to say something. Look," Prather said, "I want you to hold down things here. I'm going to Tulsa to check it out. I might be back in about eight hours."

"You sure?"

"It's a stronger lead than anything else we got. If I stay here, I'll end up being sent to Kansas City."

Cullen said, "Call me if you need anything."

FIFTY

It was late afternoon when the federal agents got the telephone records from Donna Wolfe's cell phone company. They found that she had received a telephone call the day before from a 918 area code. The number was listed to a Tracy Coughlin, residing in Tulsa, Oklahoma. The other numbers they found were all Dallas based: girlfriends, shops, and relatives.

Agent Carr said to Agent Courtland, "So what do we have?"

"The number of a woman in Tulsa," Courtland said. "We can call and ask Donna Wolfe who she is. But she's already lawyered up. We can ask Marks if he'll agree to an interview and ask her herself with him there—"

"Which he already told us he won't agree to."

Courtland said, "So what then?"

Agent Carr sighed. "We don't have enough to arrest her."

Courtland said, "Maybe she hasn't been in touch with him."

"She has."

But Courtland wasn't so sure. They had no evidence that she had been in touch with him. Carr had a gut feeling and the U.S. attorney wouldn't take that as enough consideration to file charges. They had tried to bluff her into giving something to them and it hadn't worked.

Courtland said, "Well, let's call her ourselves. Ask her what her relationship to Donna Wolfe is."

Agent Carr picked up his desk phone.

★ ★ ★ ★ ★

They were in the living room watching television when the cell phone rang. Richard Billie had two phones in his pockets. The old man's and the girl's. It was the girl's they had used to make the calls to Texas. Richard had been careful about that. He had made sure that the Mexican couldn't get close to the phones. He didn't want the Mexican giving out the address to his friends.

Now they were expecting a call from the Mexican's friends telling them that they were in town and ready to deliver the money. Expecting the call and wanting the call. Richard didn't know how long he would be able to keep an eye on the Mexican and Amos and the hostages as well. He wanted to be out of here, with fifty thousand dollars traveling money.

Amos and Javier watched him as he took the phone out and looked at it. It was still ringing. A 972 area code. A non-local call. Was it the Spics?

Richard answered the call.

"Yeah?"

"Hello," a voice said. "I'm trying to reach Tracy Coughlin."

A white voice.

Richard said, "You've got the wrong number." He clicked off the phone as the man started to say something else.

Richard felt his heart pound.

Javier was looking at him now. Amos too, though not as intently.

Javier said, "Who was it?"

"I don't know. A white guy." Richard did not tell them that it sounded like a cop.

Javier said, "How do you know it wasn't one of my boys?"

"He didn't sound Mexican."

"Yeah?" Javier said. "What does that sound like?"

"You know what I mean," Richard said.

"Could have been Miguel."

Richard looked back at the Mexican. "Really," he said. Like it was stupid to argue about it.

"Okay. Maybe not. Maybe the girl's boyfriend." Javier was quiet for a moment. Then he said, "Maybe you shouldn't have answered it."

"Maybe you should mind your own fucking business. Your guys are supposed to call me on that phone. What do you want me to do?"

Now Amos was looking at him too.

Richard said to both of them, "Look, don't worry about it."

Then the phone rang again. Richard looked at it and saw the same number as before. This time he didn't answer it. He relaxed, a little, when four rings passed and the messaging service picked it up.

But then he played the message back and heard this:

"Hello, Ms. Coughlin. This is Special Agent David Carr of the FBI. Would you please call me at 972-555-5456. I'd just like to ask you a couple of questions. Thank you."

"Who was it?" Javier said.

Richard didn't answer.

And Javier said, "Man, you look spooked. Who was that?"

Richard said, "It was a fed. Goddammit, it was an FBI agent."

Amos and Javier were on their feet, all of them speaking quickly with raised voices, pointing fingers and shouting at the same time.

Javier said, "I didn't tell anybody shit."

Richard said, "Well, your fucking girlfriend must have talked to them."

"She wouldn't do that."

"How do you know she wouldn't?"

"Because if she did she knows I'd fucking grease her."

"All I know is a goddamn federal agent just left a message on this lady's phone."

Javier said, "Well, you're the one's had the fucking phones since we got here. How do we know you didn't contact them?"

"Now why in the fuck would I do that?"

"Well, I sure as hell didn't," Javier said. "I made two calls on that goddamn phone and both times you stood there while I did it."

"You stupid motherfucker," Richard said. "Don't you see? She must have told them."

"They can access records without her permission, fool."

"What?"

"I said they can access phone records without her okay. It doesn't mean she turned us over. Richard, think about it. If she had ratted us out, they'd probably be here already."

"No. No, because I never allowed you to tell her where you were." Richard said, "Even if you're right, why did you have to fucking call her from this phone?"

"*Because you made me, you stupid fucking redneck!* How else are we supposed to get the money?"

Amos said, "Fuck. Does this mean they know we're here?"

"No," Richard said. Though he wasn't sure. If there was a GPS in the girl's phone, they would be able to find them here. But he hoped there wasn't. "No," he said again. "It doesn't mean shit."

Amos said, "What if they call again?"

"We don't answer it," Richard said.

Javier said, "But we need to answer it if my guys call."

"Well then, the next time it rings, you come over here and look at the number to make sure it's them."

Christ, Richard thought. The goddamn phone had become a liability. A thing to be feared. But they needed it. They couldn't use the home phone because if Javier's friends knew that number, they would be able to find out where Javier was. And that would bring them here.

Javier said, "I don't like this, man. I think we should get out of here."

Richard said, "No one's going anywhere until we get that money."

The phone rang again, startling all of them.

"Christ," Richard said. He held the phone up and Javier walked over to look at it. It rang a third time and Javier said, "That's them."

FIFTY-ONE

Javier said, "Where are you?"

Miguel said, "We're south. A place called Glenpool."

Richard gestured with his gun. Javier said to Miguel, "Richie wants to talk to you."

Richard took the phone and said, "Don't talk about where you are."

Miguel said, "Why? You scared?"

Richard said, "You got the money?"

"Yeah. We got it. Why don't you tell us where you are?"

Richard said, "Not going to play that way, amigo. You're going to meet a friend of ours. One hour. You give the money to her. All of it. She brings it back and Javier's given us what he promised. You try to follow her back here, you won't be doing Javier any favors."

"You threatening me?" Miguel said.

"Yeah, I'm threatening you," Richard said, "and him."

Miguel said, "I don't think you know who you're talking to."

"I know," Richard said. "This is business. You want to take it as an insult to your manhood, that's your problem."

For a moment Miguel was quiet. Then he said, "Who's the girl?"

"Her name is Tracy. She's about thirty. Good-looking. Don't hang around and talk to her. Just give her the money and say goodbye. Javier will meet up with you later."

"Where?"

"Fuck, I don't know where. That's up to him. Just give the girl the money and get going."

Javier said, "Tell him I'll call him later."

Richard scowled at the Mexican. But then said to Miguel, "He said he'll call you later."

"Okay," Miguel said. "Now where do I meet the girl?"

"Hold on," Richard said. He put his hand over the phone and said to Amos, "Get me a phone book."

"Where is it?"

"It's in the kitchen. Hurry."

Amos brought the phone book back and Richard spent some time flipping through it. Then he said, "Okay. There's a shopping mall at Seventy-First Street and Memorial. That should be easy for you to find. There'll be a food court there. There's one at every mall. Look for her there."

"That's a big place. How will I know who she is?"

"She'll know who you are."

"How?"

"Because you'll have a red hat on your table. You can buy one there."

"Boy, you thought this out, huh?" Miguel said, fucking with him now.

"I've had time to think it out," Richard said. "Be there in one hour."

Richard clicked the cell phone off.

Javier looked at him and said, "You didn't tell him about the fed."

Richard said, "What would have been the point?"

Richard switched the cell phone off. Now no one could call on it or use it to call out. Richard knew that it also prevented anyone from being able to triangulate the location of the phone using cellular phone towers. He felt better now, taking the submarine beneath the surface.

FIFTY-TWO

It took Agent Courtland about thirty minutes to conduct a check on Tracy Coughlin. He first went to the NCIS base and found that, apart from a speeding citation three years earlier, she had no record of any criminal activity. Through IRS records, he learned that she was a registered nurse at St. Jude's hospital in Tulsa. That she had an eight-old-old son. That she owned a house near the intersection of Thirty-First and Harvard. And that she was a widow who lost her husband in Iraq.

Agent Courtland summarized this to his senior partner. Courtland said, "In short, she doesn't seem like she's mixed up with criminals."

Carr said, "What about Donna Wolfe?"

Courtland shrugged. "I don't know. A girlfriend?"

"In Tulsa?"

After a meeting between representatives of the Tulsa PD, the local FBI branch, OSBI and Tulsa County Sheriff's Office, it was agreed that a statement would be released to the local media that there was a possibility that the Kansas escaped convicts were possibly in the local area. The television stations would be given photos of Amos Denton, Richard Billie, and Javier Sandoval. The stations would also be advised that Amos Denton was suspected in the murder of a Tulsan sometime this afternoon.

Shortly before the statement was released to the media, a

bulletin was circulated to all law enforcement involved in the search for the convicts. And it was in this way that agents Carr and Courtland first learned of a possibility of the suspects being in Tulsa.

It was Agent Carr who telephoned Mike Prather on his cell phone. He had gotten the number from Will Cullen.

Prather said, "Yeah, I know about it. I was going to call you."

Carr said, "What do you think?"

"I'm on my way there. Not so much because I believe that people actually saw Amos Denton at the scene of that accident. The truth is, I didn't have any other solid leads."

Carr said, "Well, let me tell you what we have. Though I'm not sure it's much."

"I'll take anything," Prather said.

"We searched Donna Wolfe's telephone records and found that she'd received a call from a Tulsa number. A cell number. The person's name is Tracy Coughlin. We've checked her out. And she doesn't seem to be anyone associated with any of the fugitives."

"Who is she then?"

"She's a nurse, a mother. A war widow. Her husband was killed in Iraq. An ordinary person, apparently."

"You talk to her?"

"I tried. Listen, a man answered the phone and said I had the wrong number. Then he wouldn't take any more calls."

"Can you triangulate it?"

"We haven't tried that yet," Carr said. "What do you think?"

"I think you should. Maybe it's nothing. But maybe they stole her phone. Or maybe they've abducted her. Somebody should at least talk to her."

"I'll notify the Tulsa branch and tell them to get started on it."

"What about the girlfriend?"

"Donna Wolfe? She's impervious. Lawyer won't let her talk to us."

"Can't you apply some pressure?"

"We don't have anything on her. Just a suspicion. The U.S. attorney won't authorize charges with what we've got."

Prather said, "Well, we've got two tips emanating from the Tulsa area. A possible sighting of Amos Denton and a phone call from the area to Sandoval's girlfriend. Which means they're there. Or were. It's still a haystack."

"We'll find them," Carr said.

"Yeah, maybe," Prather said. "But we've got five people murdered now. Four in Kansas, another in Oklahoma. I wonder how many more before they're caught."

Carr said again, "We'll find them."

FIFTY-THREE

They saw themselves on the six o'clock news. The lead story. The first photograph on the screen was of Amos, black and white, looking like he was born for the penitentiary. The newscaster was saying that Amos was suspected in the killing of local citizen Ruben Matthews. They followed the photo of Amos with ones of Richard and Javier. Then they cut to the street in West Tulsa where there were a lot of police cars and emergency vehicles near the parking lot in front of the hamburger stand.

They sat in the living room, none of them saying anything at first. Amos still held the .38, wishing even more now that he had more than one bullet in the cylinder. Javier looked at Amos, frowning and shaking his head at him like he was stupid, and Amos thought about using the last bullet on him. Then Javier was looking at Richard Billie.

Richard kept his eyes focused on the television screen. Finally, he deigned to acknowledge the Mexican.

Javier said, "Well?"

"Well what?" Richard said.

Javier said, "What do we do now?"

"Same as before. Wait."

"Wait," Javier said. "Now that they know we're here."

"They don't know anything," Richard said. "Even if they did, you think it's a good idea to leave now? You panicking?"

"Fuck you," Javier said.

"I thought you people prided yourself on being cool."

"Fuck you."

Richard brought up the Glock. He didn't point it at the Mexican. Just displayed it. Richard said, "Homeboy, you're about this close."

Javier made a gesture that may or may not have been conciliatory. He smiled and stood and walked out of the room. Richard looked at the Mexican's back and thought about putting one between his shoulder blades. But it passed and he returned his attention to the news.

Then Richard removed the girl's cell phone from his jacket pocket and checked it. It was still turned off. He hoped Amos wouldn't notice this. Richard looked at Amos and said, "Don't worry about it."

Amos said, "Do I look worried?"

Christ, Richard thought. Amos trying to sound tough now. Richard stood and said, "Keep an eye on the Mexican. I'm going to talk to the girl."

Tracy lay on the floor with John under a blanket. She held him to her, in a state of rest that wasn't quite sleep. She heard the doorknob turn and she got off the floor.

Richard Billie came into the room.

On the bed, Lee said, "What do you want?"

Richard grinned at the old man and lifted the Glock, as if to remind him what it could do.

Tracy came around the bed, between Richard and Lee. It made Richard step back without even thinking about it.

Richard said, "You're going to run one more errand for us."

Tracy just said, "What?"

"Javier's associates are in town. They're bringing us money. You're going to meet them, pick up the money, and bring it back here."

"Why can't you do it?"

"Someone needs to stay and mind the store."

"Can't Amos do that?"

"Don't get mouthy with me, honey. You want us out of here or not?"

"Yes. I want you out."

"Good," Richard said. "We both want the same thing. You get the money and bring it back here. And then we'll leave."

"All of you?"

"All of us."

"And let us live?"

"Yeah. What did you think?"

Tracy didn't answer him. She thought, this is a man who can look you right in the eye and lie. It didn't bother him at all. For some reason, she thought this might be his most offensive trait. And now she had to lie back to him.

"I don't know," she said. "Who am I supposed to meet?"

"It'll be two guys. Maybe one. Mexicans. They're going to be at the food court at the shopping mall at Seventy-First and Memorial. You know where that is?"

"Yes."

"They're going to be at one of the tables. I told them to put a red hat on the table. That's how you'll know who they are. Go to them, get the money and bring it back here. And then we'll be finished with you."

"You promise?" Tracy said, knowing he was lying again.

"Yeah."

Richard stepped closer to her, looking over his shoulder at the closed door as he did so. In a lower voice, he said, "Listen to me, these guys are going to try to get you to tell them where we are. They're going to want to know. But you don't tell 'em, you understand? You bring them back here and the boy dies. You and him too."

Tracy felt her stomach heave. Still she heard herself say, "I thought they were your friends."

"They're not my friends. They're Javier's. Do not bring them back here. Do you understand me?"

"Yes."

"And remember what I said about the police. I told you before, I got nothing to lose."

"I remember."

Richard looked at her for a moment, wondering if she was fucking with him again. He wondered if he should smack her then just in case she should forget. But something restrained him. The man on the bed perhaps, the memory of him slugging his fist into his face.

Richard said, "You're going to leave in a few minutes. If you're not back in one hour, the boy dies."

Richard Billie walked out of the room, closing the door behind him. Tracy remained standing, closing her eyes, then opening them.

Behind her, Lee said, "Are you going to go?"

She turned to him. "I have to," she said.

She walked past him and went over to John. She prayed that he hadn't been awake to hear Richard Billie's ugliness. But when he sat up and looked at her, she realized he had heard it.

"Mama," John said.

Tracy embraced him. Held him tightly and fiercely.

"Listen to me," she said. "Grandpa's going to be with you. I'll be back and then this will be over."

"Promise?"

"I promise. Now you promise me you won't do anything without checking with Grandpa first. When I'm gone, he's in charge. Got it?"

"I got it."

"Tracy." It was Lee talking now.

She turned and went to him.

Lee was paler now. With effort, he brought his hand up and placed it on her wrist. She took his hand and held it.

"What is it, Dad?"

She felt him tug on her hand and she knelt down next to the bed, her face closer to his so he could speak in a tone not much above a whisper.

Lee said, "I'm sorry about what happened."

Tracy said, "What are you sorry for?"

"You and John. It's my house they came to. If I didn't have John here . . ."

Tracy said, "You're going to take blame for that?" A bit of scold in her tone now.

"It's my fault."

"No, it's not," she said. "You're talking foolish now. Listen, it's not over yet."

Lee said, "I know that."

She studied his expression for a moment. And he went on.

Lee said, "Earlier, when I told the fat one that there were no bullets in the house for the .38, I was lying. There are some. In my study downstairs."

She said, "Are you sure?"

"It's my house, isn't it?" Lee said, "Downstairs in the desk in the left drawer there's a cigar box with old letters in it. Beneath that, beneath those letters are some extra rounds for that gun. He doesn't know about it."

Tracy said, "You didn't tell him." She was remembering Amos leveling the .38 at Lee's face, threatening to kill him if he didn't say where the bullets were. Lee looking at the barrel of the gun and holding out.

Now Lee said, "He didn't need to know."

"He still has bullets in the gun," Tracy said.

"He has one," Lee said. "Only one. Watch him. If he uses it and then . . ."

"And then what?"

"I don't know," Lee said. "Maybe he'll put it down. And then you can get it."

Tracy thought about saying, Yeah, maybe. And maybe he'll surrender. And maybe the police would show up and save them all from being murdered. And maybe this was all so much piss in the wind. But she didn't voice her despair. She just said, "Okay."

Lee said, "It's something."

"Yes," Tracy said. "It's something."

Lee said, "Remember what I said to you earlier."

"What?"

"I said that you were stronger and smarter than they were."

Tracy said, "Did you say that?"

"I think I did."

Tracy looked at Lee for a moment, trying to comprehend him. She said, "Did you really mean that?"

"Of course I meant it. What's wrong with you?"

"I don't know," Tracy said, her voice breaking. "I'm sorry."

"What are you sorry for?"

"I don't know. Oh. I do know. I'm sorry for the way I've treated you. I've been such a bitch."

"I don't know what you're talking about."

"Yes, you do," Tracy said. "You're just not going to admit it. Because you're too good. That's the problem, really. You've always been so good. I didn't see it before. But he always knew. He knew it and he wanted to measure up to you."

Lee said, "Are you talking about Drew?"

"Yes," Tracy said, almost angry again now. "Who else would I be talking about?" She stopped. Her anger was gone and she looked her father-in-law in the eyes.

Then she said, "We never speak about him, you and I. We never have."

"I know," Lee said. And he looked away from her. "I was afraid it would be too much for me. We can, though. If you want." He added, "Anytime you want."

She smiled through her tears. "What timing, huh?" she said.

"Tracy," he said, "listen to me. Before you came along, I told him not to enlist in the reserves. I did. But he wouldn't listen to me."

"He always listened to you."

"No," Lee said. "Not always. He could be very stubborn."

"You're telling me?" Tracy said.

Lee said, "It was the last thing I wanted him to do. I swear to you."

"You don't have to swear to me," she said. "I believe you. It's no one's fault, Dad. He just . . ." She trailed off, not knowing what else to say.

Lee said, "I said he was stubborn and he was. But not for one moment did I ever think he was dumb. He was always very smart. And he picked himself a champ for a wife. I always knew that."

The door opened. It was Richard Billie again. "Let's go," he said.

Lee kept his eyes on Tracy. "Always," he said.

Tracy squeezed Lee's hand tightly and leaned forward and kissed him.

"I'll see you soon," she said.

FIFTY-FOUR

Mal Devereaux was on the phone with the assistant chief of the
Tulsa Police Department. It was the second time he had to
brief him in the last thirty minutes. Things were happening too
fast. He knew the assistant chief would be relaying everything to
the chief and then on to the mayor. Between the two calls,
Devereaux had telephoned his wife to tell her he wouldn't be
home for dinner.

Because he was captain of the detectives, Devereaux had his
own office. It was a small one in the corner of the detective
squad room. Generally, he left his door open. Unless he had
one of his people in there for a discussion that probably related
to disciplinary issues. On his desk was a mouse pad with a
black-and-white photo of Barney Fife. Devereaux was a friendly,
warm man who liked to joke with people. But everyone who
knew him knew he was very serious about his work.

His door was open now and one of his younger detectives appeared in it. Devereaux excused himself to the assistant chief
and placed his hand over the phone.

"What is it?" he said.

The young detective said, "There's a Special Agent Mike
Prather from the Kansas Bureau of Investigation here. He said
you were expecting him."

"Show him in here."

The detective left then came back with the agent. Devereaux
continued briefing the assistant chief while he gestured Mike

Prather to the chair. Devereaux gave a couple more answers, his tone respectful and deferential. Then he ended the call.

He stood and shook the KBI agent's hand.

Prather said, "I tried to call you. I spoke with a couple of guys from the Dallas FBI. They told me that Sandoval's girlfriend received a call from a number in Tulsa."

Devereaux said, "A woman?"

"Yes. Do you know about it?"

"We got a notice from FBI here. They've sent a couple of agents out to her house to interview her."

Prather said, "How long ago?"

"Maybe a half hour. We're waiting to hear from them." Devereaux said, "I was just telling my assistant chief about it."

Prather said, "The Dallas agents tried to call the number themselves. They said a man answered and told them it was a wrong number."

"Do they think it was Sandoval?"

"No. They said it sounded like a white guy. Take that for what it's worth. They tried to call again and then there was no answer. None since."

"Presuming it's the fugitives holding the phone," Devereaux said, "they've probably turned it off so we won't be able to track it."

"Probably," Prather said. "Or maybe not." Prather sighed. "Are we just blowing smoke here?"

"I don't know," Devereaux said. "I told you before, I'm not all that sure they're here. We got a witness who says he saw Amos Denton drive away in that truck. But the other witnesses said the man never got out of the truck. His face has been on television for the last twenty-four hours. Maybe someone thinks they saw him when they didn't. A heavyset white guy who's got a shaved head. That describes about half the officers in this department."

Prather smiled, in spite of himself. He said, "Are you worried?"

"What do you mean?"

"I mean, are you worried that this is a goose chase and that the fugitives are nowhere near here."

Devereaux said, "Well, it wouldn't be the first time I'd look like a fool. My assistant chief, he's leaning on me because he wants certainties. He's being leaned on too. But I don't really have anything certain."

Prather was beginning to like this guy. He said, "I know how you feel. Well, we got a phone call from Tulsa to Sandoval's girlfriend. We got a white male voice answering the phone and claiming it's a wrong number. We've got a witness who says he saw Amos Denton in a truck stolen from a man who was murdered. I wouldn't call that nothing."

"I wouldn't either," Devereaux said. "But it's pieces. That's all. You're from Kansas. What do you know about these guys?"

"About Sandoval, not so much. The sheriff of Elk County, he's familiar with the other two."

"Anything special about them?"

"Not really. They're hard-core, badasses. They killed a girl, raped her. Killed at least four people in the last forty-eight hours. We don't know what they were doing with Sandoval. He's kind of a big wheel in the Tijeras drug cartel."

"I read that. Which reminds me, something else you should know."

"What's that?"

"It's not official, but DEA believes that Sandoval killed one of their undercover agents. Shot him while he was taking a shit. A very undignified death. DEA couldn't prove it was Sandoval, but they say they know."

"So?"

"So they've got a personal grudge against Sandoval."

"You mean they want to kill him."

"That's what I'm hearing. I don't blame them, exactly. In their place, I'd probably want the same thing. But it might be a problem if these guys have taken hostages."

"Sounds like they have their priorities mixed up."

"Maybe," Devereaux said. "I'm not exactly a fan of DEA myself. Too many guys with crew cuts and Oakley sunglasses thinking law enforcement is combat. But if they think Sandoval's in Tulsa, we're going to have to deal with them too. I wonder if Sandoval's still with the other two."

Prather said, "Well, we know that they escaped together. I can't see them wanting to stick together for long."

"Not chained together, huh?" Devereaux said, "Like that movie with the black guy and, uh—"

"Tony Curtis?"

"Who?"

Prather said, "I forget the name of it. Black guy and white guy chained together and they both hate each other but then become pals. That the one?"

"Yeah."

"Well," Prather said. "I don't see that happening here. They're cons. Billie and Denton, they'll stick together for a while. Too long and one of them will kill the other. But maybe that's wishful thinking on my part."

The young detective was standing in the doorway again. Devereaux acknowledged him.

"Yeah?"

"FBI on line two. It's about the Tulsa girl."

Devereaux picked up the phone.

Prather watched him handle it. Devereaux listened to the voice on the other end, and after a few moments, asked his own questions. Those were answered and then Prather heard the captain say, "Is she at work?"

Devereaux listened for an answer, and then said, "Yeah, I think we should check."

He spoke for a couple more minutes then wrapped up the call.

Then he said to the Kansan, "She's not home. They called the hospital where she works and they said she called in sick."

Prather said, "That *she* called in sick? Or that someone called for her?"

"They said she did," Devereaux said. "But the agents only called the hospital. What I mean is, they didn't send anyone there to interview someone in person."

"You would have?"

"Yeah. But if there's a presumption that they crossed state lines, it's FBI's jurisdiction."

"Not solely," Prather said.

"Yeah, I know." Devereaux sighed. "You think she's been abducted?"

"I think it's possible. If they're in town, it's certainly possible. If she hasn't been, we still need to talk to her."

Devereaux said, "We have to find her first." He regarded the KBI agent and said, "I can call the feds back and ask them to send someone to the hospital and maybe get in an argument about who answers to whom. Or you could drive out to the hospital and check it out. Save us some time."

"While you man the phones," Prather said. There was no hostility in his statement.

Devereaux said, "That's pretty much the size of it."

Prather said, "Dallas feds told me she's got a kid."

"Yeah, that's my understanding."

"So if he's not home, where is he?"

"If he's not with her, then with the father, I suppose."

"There is no father. He was killed in Iraq."

"Oh?" Devereaux said. "I guess I missed that."

Prather got to his feet. "You've got a lot on your mind," Prather said. Then he walked out.

FIFTY-FIVE

Drew had owned a handgun, which he kept stored in a lockbox in their bedroom. The lockbox had been Tracy's idea. She had not minded having the gun in the house before John was born. But she had changed her mind afterward. Drew said that if someone ever broke into the house, he wouldn't have time to get the gun out of the lockbox and protect his family from harm, and Tracy had told him they'd have to worry about that when the time came. It never did. After Drew died, Tracy sold the gun.

She had shot it a few times when Drew took her to the shooting range. That had been it. It had held no allure for her. Nor, she suspected, for Drew. He had not been a gun nut. And he had only owned the one firearm. A revolver, like Lee's, but with a longer barrel.

Driving south on Sheridan, Tracy allowed herself to think about it now. If she hadn't sold it, she could have gone by the house now and gotten it. Had it with her when she got back to Lee's house. But then Richard had checked her for guns the last time she had gone on an errand. If she could get one, maybe she could put it on a windowsill and reach it later from the inside. Maybe she could find some way to sneak it in. Maybe she could throw it up to Lee or John in the second-floor window, like a young boy trying to get his girlfriend's attention in the dark of night. Maybe they wouldn't catch her doing it. Maybe she could sprout wings and fly.

Christ. Where would she get a gun anyway? Could you walk into a pawnshop and just walk out with one? Wasn't there some sort of waiting period? And how would she look now, attempting to do that? A woman on the verge of a breakdown. Maybe they would call the police and then she would lose everything.

Assuming there was time for all that. Which there wasn't.

But you can't just do nothing, she thought. You can't just sit back and wait to become a statistic. An item on the evening news. A reason for people to drive with their lights on in memory of her all-too-early death. Her, John, Lee. They were such good people, they'd say. After all they'd been through, they didn't deserve this.

No, they fucking did not.

"Shit," Tracy said, as she made a left turn into the parking lot of a Quik Trip. She knew what she was going to buy when she got there and she knew she would feel silly buying it. But she had to do something.

She found it on the bottom shelf next to the hand lotions and shampoos. Aquanet, just like her mother used to use.

Tracy parked the Cherokee in the north lot of the mall, behind the Dillard's department store. A light rain was coming down now. She walked through it and went through the rear door of the clothing store. Then she was inside with the sound of voices and shoppers and the faint scent of perfume. She had been here a couple of months ago, the post-Christmas sales. She had bought John a pair of shoes. John. She must think of John and, yet, not think of him. Because if she thought too much, she would collapse, and then she wouldn't be able to help him or help anybody.

Tracy remembered a friend of hers from nursing school. Nancy had been her name. A tough shell on that girl. Nothing seemed to faze her. But then Nancy's husband was stricken with cancer and Tracy found her in the bathroom sobbing like a little girl. Uncontrolled and heaving sobs. And Nancy had been ashamed that Tracy had seen her that way. Tracy had said, "There's nothing to be ashamed of. He's your husband."

A tough nurse, like herself. But breakable like anyone else. She could bring her game face to work amidst the blood and the death and the grief. Work her shift and go home and somehow put it out of her mind. But it wasn't so easy to do when it involved your own.

She had left John and Lee alone in that house. Left them there with those animals while she went out to do the animals' bidding. Went out to run their errand. They had known she would do it and now she was doing it. She didn't want to think about how much she would do for them.

In the clothing store, her heart jumped when she thought she saw someone she knew. Sadie something or other. She had met her and her husband at a party and she hadn't much liked her. *God.* What if the woman recognized her and wanted to stop her and chat? But then she realized it wasn't her, it was just someone who looked like her. And, shit, upon getting closer, she realized the woman didn't look much like the Sadie person after all.

Hold it together, Tracy. You must hold it together.

She walked out of the clothing store and then she was in the heart of the mall. Lit up and well populated. She walked past watch shops and sporting goods stores and small places where they sold high-dollar chocolates. Past the glass elevators and the Starbucks below with its dominant seating area next to the latest model convertible Saab surrounded by velvet ropes. She took the escalator down.

The volume increased when she got to the food court. A lot of people there, more than she had expected. It was the dinner hour now, not the lunch hour. Yet it was crowded. She wondered if it was a lot of families getting in the evening meal before

watching the latest pirate movie. She looked first at the surrounding food stands. Popeyes, Sonic, Charley's Grilled Subs,
Big Easy Cajun, someplace that sold gyros. A lot of meat and
cheese and fried starches. Tracy waded in to the seating area.

She had been here before. But now it was like she never had.
She was searching the place, examining it. Letting herself gaze
from table to table, looking for a Hispanic man with a red hat.
Afraid of finding him, terrified of not finding him.

She stopped and looked at a table. There, next to a discarded
Taco Bell bag was a red hat. A ball cap with *OU* on the front.
She stopped.

"Something wrong?"

She looked to the source of the voice. A white guy, heavyset
and wearing a striped sweater. He was wearing glasses. And
now Tracy saw that he was sitting with two little boys. His sons.

"Sorry," Tracy said. And kept walking.

She looked at her watch. *Christ.* Twenty minutes had already
gone by. Richard had told her she had to be back in one hour.
Forty minutes left. Forty minutes left and what if these fucking
people weren't here? Richard would make no allowances for
things like that. He would hold her accountable for things that
she couldn't control. He would kill John.

She came to the end of the sitting area. She stood still and
did a slow pan, from left to right.

And then she saw him.

A Hispanic man, but not quite what she expected. He was
well dressed, almost European looking. Wearing a black sport
jacket and dark slacks and a white shirt. There was another man
sitting at a table about ten feet away from him. A bigger man,
but Mexican too. They would be together. On the table in front
of the man wearing the black sport jacket was a red hat. A
woman's hat, she thought.

Tracy walked over to them. She got to the table, feeling her heart pounding, and she took the seat across from him. She looked him in the eye.

She said, "Are you waiting for someone?"

The man said, "I don't know. Who are you?"

"I'm Tracy. Richard Billie sent me here."

"Yeah? Who's that?"

Tracy stiffened her lip and said, "You know who it is."

"Do I?" Miguel looked away from her, his eyes seemingly on the pizza stand.

"Yes."

Miguel said, "I see you got a bag with you. Why don't you give it to me?"

"Why should I do that?"

"You don't have to," Miguel said. "Maybe I'll just leave."

"Don't," she said. "*Don't.* Here." She handed him the bag.

Miguel took it and handed it to Hector, who had walked over. Hector took it to another table and went through it. And as he did that, Tracy figured out what they were doing.

"I'm not a cop," she said.

Miguel acknowledged her statement, but then looked over to Hector. Hector finished going through her bag then made an all-clear gesture to Miguel.

"Okay," Miguel said. "Then you're here for the money."

"Yes."

"Are you with him?"

"Who?"

"Richard Billie. Are you with him?"

Tracy grimaced. That anyone could think she was Richard Billie's woman. She said, "No. He's abducted my family. He's holding my son hostage."

"You say," Miguel said.

Tracy made a gesture and said, "At this point, I don't much care whether you believe me or not. He's got Javier and he's not going to let him go unless you pay him the money you said you would."

Miguel said, "I never agreed to pay them anything."

"Javier did," Tracy said.

Miguel shrugged.

And Tracy said, "Why did you come here?"

Miguel leaned forward to intimidate her. "What?" he said.

"Why did you come here?" Tracy said, undeterred. "Was it for nothing? Were you just fucking bored? Either you brought the money or you didn't. If you didn't, tell me now and I'll go."

Miguel said, "Man, you pretty tough."

Tracy shook her head. "No," she said. "I just don't have time to play games with you. They've got my son. I have to bring back money or they'll kill him. Either you have it or you don't."

"We've got the money, okay?" Miguel turned to Hector and gave him a signal. Hector opened a briefcase and took a thick manila envelope out. He looked to Miguel and Miguel made a downward motion with his index finger. Hector put the envelope into Tracy's bag.

"See?" Miguel said.

Tracy said, "How do I know it's in there?"

"It's in there."

"It doesn't seem like much."

"Fifty thousand isn't much," Miguel said. "Not to us." He leaned forward again. "The money's not the point, lady. Javier told these boys he'd pay them. That's his problem. But our people, our organization, we not in the business of paying ransoms. You understand?"

"That's not my problem. That's between you and Richard. Or Javier and Richard."

"Then we discuss it with Richard."

"Can I have my bag now?"

"No, I'm not finished," Miguel said. "We'll give it to you, but we're going with you."

Tracy shook her head. "I can't allow that. Richard told me if you come back with me, he'll kill my son. He knew you'd want to come with me."

Miguel said, "He said that?"

"Yes. Look, he's not stupid. He knows Javier's going to try and get out of paying him."

"So you are with him."

"I already told you I wasn't," Tracy said. "Listen, do you even know the man? Do you know Richard?"

"I spoke with him on the telephone," Miguel said. "That's all."

Tracy regarded the man sitting across from her. Cool and collected, but maybe his determination wasn't so much business as it was personal. Knowing Richard, he had probably insulted this man. Pushed him in some way. And now Miguel wanted to meet Richard in person and tell him something. Maybe something more than that.

Tracy said, "You want to kill him, don't you? You want to kill Richard."

Miguel made another gesture. Maybe.

And she could feel it. Feel it within reach. Yes, he wanted to kill Richard. Maybe even worse than she did. For her, it would be about self-preservation and protection of family. For this man, it would be about settling a score. Responding to an insult. It tempted her. Bring back this one and the other sitting nearby. Let them come in through the front door and pull out their guns and eliminate the beasts keeping them hostage . . . Yes, it would bring an end to it. Maybe.

But it was too risky. They would have to get them all on the ground floor before either Richard or Amos had a chance to get upstairs to kill John and Lee. It would have to be done with the precision of a professional military squad. And these two wouldn't qualify.

And even if they did, there was no guarantee they wouldn't kill her family themselves.

But sitting at the table with this man, Tracy knew he wasn't going to let her decide anything. She was his hostage now. From one enemy camp to another. Caught in a lethal hotbox; Javier's friends at second base, Richard Billie at third, her in between.

Tracy leaned forward and said, "If you promise me you'll kill him, I'll take you back."

"Yeah?" Miguel said. He was smiling now, amused at this woman's venom. He was becoming attracted to her.

"Yeah," Tracy said. "Give me the bag and we'll go."

Miguel cocked his head at her. He said, "That's a lot of money to be giving a lady I just met."

"You know you're getting it back."

Miguel studied her, looking for some sign that he was being played. Cute little lady with a little fire in her. Tracy maintained eye contact with him.

Miguel turned to Hector and said, "Okay. Give it to her."

Hector walked over and handed her the bag.

Tracy said, "We'll have to go in my car. If he sees you guys in your car, if he sees another vehicle, he'll be warned."

Miguel said, "I don't like that idea. Your car might be—"

"What," Tracy said, "wired? If that were the case, you'd've been arrested already and my family would be dead. You want to come or not?"

Miguel said, "I'll ride with you in your car. Hector'll follow us in ours."

Tracy started to say something, and Miguel said, "That's the way it's going to be. Let's go."

They walked out of the food court. Miguel walked with her, Hector behind, Hector keeping an eye on her. A couple with their bodyguard trailing them. Tracy thought that if she broke and ran, it would probably be Hector that would shoot her first. A bullet in her back followed by screams in the mall and then the killers would melt into the crowd and be on their way. John and Lee left alone to die.

Tracy kept walking. They walked back through the clothing store, past the perfumes and the notions and the ladies' lingerie, keeping their pace steady.

Tracy thought of the hairspray. She had left it in the car. What would she do with it? What would have been the point of having bought it? She knew that counselors would tell their patients that it was important to do something to solve your problems. That even doing small things would help you feel better. She had bought the hairspray as—what? A weapon? These men were armed with guns.

They passed a Zales jewelers and then walked past a Camille's Cafe, most of the tables taken. Muzak poured out a tune for the shoppers, a non-vocal version of *The End of the World*. They continued walking.

And Tracy thought, guns against a can of hairspray. It was ridiculous. *Draw, hombre.* A gun against a can of women's aerosol. They would laugh at her. She would have to be close to use the hairspray. And she didn't have it on her anyway. She had left it in the Jeep. And the smaller man, the leader, he had said he would ride with her and that Hector would follow them. Hector. Oh, Christ, he had used the man's name. Did that mean they were going to kill her too? That it didn't matter if she knew their names.

They walked past a shallow fountain pool, the bottom spotted with pennies. A woman in sweats pushed a stroller by.

And Tracy thought, it would be a start. Getting them separated would be a start. If she had the leader in the Jeep with her and Hector in the car behind, she would at least have only the leader to deal with. Maybe she could pick up the can of aerosol and spray the guy in the face when they were alone. And then he would cry out and she could push him out of the car. But, suppressing a cry, she thought that was ridiculous too because how could she do that while she was driving? Use one hand to pick up the can under the seat and flip the top off with the same hand and then spray him in the face and hope it made contact with his eyes? And would he allow her to reach under the seat? He would think she'd be reaching for a gun and he would stop her. Maybe shoot her. It would be a miracle if she could pull it off. And if she did, then what? The other guy would be in the car behind her. She'd have to outrun him. Outrun him in a Jeep fucking Cherokee. If he caught her, he'd most likely kill her. And if she didn't lose him, he would follow her back to the house and then Richard would kill John and Lee.

They passed a hut selling knock-off sunglasses, using brand names to draw you in, but upon examination the signs said Compare to Ray-Bans and so forth.

Near the sunglass hut there was a security guard, fat and white. Tracy looked at him and felt a piece of iron poking her in the back, Hector close to her saying, "Keep moving." And they passed the security guard too.

And Tracy thought, *I wasn't going to say anything.* The presence of the security guard had confused her more than anything. Say she had called out to him, what would he have done? At best, he would want to know what was going on. Tracy wouldn't be able to tell him without getting her son killed. Also, her time was limited. If she didn't return to the house within twenty-five minutes, they would kill her family whether or not she brought the money. Miguel didn't have to poke her in the back with a gun. She turned around and saw Miguel there, Hector right behind him. Miguel motioned with his head, telling her to keep moving.

They reached the up escalator and took their place in line.

They began to rise up, Tracy on one step, Miguel on the step behind her, Hector the step behind that.

And Tracy knew the hairspray shit wasn't going to work. Sure, it had made her feel a little better when she got it. Full of resource and grit, a contemporary pioneer woman, a vampire slayer, loaded with *grrrrl* power and all that crap. But now she knew it wouldn't do her any good. Not with these two. And she wanted to look behind again, maybe see if the security guard was still near the bottom of the escalator, but she decided against it, feeling Hector on her neck and back and if that wasn't enough to deal with, there was a huge fat man two steps above her, talking loudly on his cell phone, like it wasn't enough for the other person on the line to hear what he was saying but everyone else had to hear it too and Tracy thought, God he's big, at least three hundred pounds, and obnoxious too and now the fat man was saying, "You tell them they can kiss my ass," stressing and stretching out the last three words, and Tracy saw an opening between the man's right and the side of the escalator and she jumped forward and squeezed between them and just before Hector called out "Hey!" she was in front of the fat man and then she backed into him, putting a forceful shoulder into it and the fat man lost his balance and fell back, taking Hector and Miguel down with him.

The men bellowed and a woman cried out and Tracy ran up the escalator, taking the bag of money with her.

She reached the top and then she was running full speed.

Miguel and Hector fell most of the way down the escalator, the fat man still mostly on top of Hector, making even Hector look small. Miguel disentangled himself from the mess, got up and went after her.

FIFTY-SIX

Tracy kept running. People turned their heads as they watched her streak by, one or two of them thinking she might have been caught shoplifting. She ran all out, not thinking . . . just moving on instinct. Now she hoped she wouldn't be stopped by a security guard because there would be no explaining this. *What men? Who? What are you doing with all this money? Slow down and explain this again.* As minutes ticked away and her son's life hung in the balance. She ran and she ran and then there was the Dillard's store she had come through but she turned and saw, in the distance, the leader, the smaller Mexican, running towards her and she rounded a corner and knew that the Dillard's was too wide, too open and she saw the twin gray doors that said Authorized Access Only and she bolted to them and pushed the lever and ran through, hoping the pursuer hadn't seen her.

She ran down the corridor. She saw a break room and turned into it. Stopped and took a breath.

Miguel reached the corner and turned it. He saw the Dillard's department store in front of him. He stopped and did a slow pan, left to right. Women mostly, many of them dressed in black. He looked for the girl with the money. She could have run through the store and out to the parking lot. But she would have to be fast for that. Faster than he thought she was. She could be hiding behind a counter, behind a rack of clothing . . .

Hector caught up with him.

Miguel turned to him and said, "Get the car. See if she's in the parking lot. *Go.*"

Hector took off.

Miguel moved closer to the Dillard's storefront, did another pan.

Then he looked to the doors with the sign that said Authorized Access Only. Miguel moved towards them.

Tracy heard the doors open. Heard the doors close. Heard footsteps in the hall. She pressed herself against the wall.

Miguel moved down the hallway. It was long, dark, and empty. He saw a men's and women's bathroom, both of the doors on the right. On the left, he saw a door to a break room. The door to the break room was open. Miguel stood in the hall and looked through the door.

There was a small kitchen area. A countered sink and a refrigerator. There was a coffeepot on the counter. Taped to the refrigerator was a flyer from the Department of Labor. In front of the refrigerator was a table with four chairs around it. A newspaper was spread out on the table. He did not see the woman hiding behind the door, a few feet to his left.

Tracy remained still, holding her breath.

Miguel left the room. He moved across the hall and checked the women's room. No one. Then he checked the men's. No one there either.

He came back out into the corridor and moved toward the exit. Double doors leading outside. Miguel checked to see if they were fire doors. He did not want to set off an alarm. He didn't see any signs. He pushed open one of the doors.

Daylight. A little rain coming down. He looked at a section of parking lot that was sparsely covered. It would be the back lot, probably utilized during the shopping season. Miguel moved further out, keeping his foot against the door to keep it open.

He did not want to be locked out.

He took another look at the lot, listened to the traffic in the distance.

Then he turned his head, concentrated.

He heard something. A noise coming from the inside, coming from behind him. It was distant and muted, but he heard it.

A click, metal against metal. A latch . . . ?

Someone pulling a door open. The doors that led back into the mall.

Goddammit.

Tracy finished it, pulling the door and then stepping through it. Running after the door closed behind her.

Miguel stepped back inside the corridor, started running. He reached the doors to the mall and pulled them open. He dashed inside the mall and looked to his right. Looked past the salesgirls and the clothing, looked to the glass doors leading out to the parking lot . . .

There.

There was the girl, running out the doors.

Miguel ran after her.

Miguel reached the parking lot. He looked out, expecting to see her. But had no luck. She knew. She knew he was after her, knew he had been in the corridor. He had missed her back there, somehow. She had hidden from him and then doubled back. Now she was hiding again. Somewhere among these parked cars she was crouched down.

Miguel took his cell phone from his pocket.

Hector answered the call.

"Yeah?"

Miguel said, "Where are you?"

"Lot A."

"She's in Lot D. Get over here."

"Where?"

"It's by the Dillard's. Hurry up."

Tracy crouched along a minivan. She stayed and then she moved. Like a mouse in a maze. She went from the cover of one vehicle to another. She knew Miguel had seen her. She had seen him at the end of the hall, propping the door open and looking outside. She had doubled back through the mall, but the door made noise and he had to have heard it.

Now she was alongside a Chevy Suburban. She heard a vehicle approach. Should she stand up and ask for help?

Well, see who it is first, Tracy. Think. You must always think. She peered over a car and saw a Mercedes approach, a dark figure behind the wheel.

She dropped to her stomach and rolled under the Suburban. It was Hector. They knew she was in this lot.

It was bad because now they knew she was in this lot. One of them searching for her in the car, the other one on foot. She remained where she was until the Mercedes made another pass, this time from the other direction. And that was better because they would keep going through the other rows now. Hopefully going west to east because the Jeep was west from here.

Miguel motioned to Hector and Hector brought the car over to him. Miguel stood at the driver's window.

He said, "She's here somewhere."

Hector said, "How do we know she hasn't already left?"

"She hasn't had time. She's here."

"You want to get in?"

"No. I'll look for her on foot. Keep going through these rows."

The Jeep was parked on the western side of the lot. Hector had started his search on the western side and now was working his way east, driving the Mercedes up and down the rows.

Miguel, however, was in the middle of the lot, walking down a row, looking left and right. He had his gun in his pocket. He was angry at the woman. The weight of the fat man could have broken his arm and the woman would have caused that. He could have hit his head going down the escalator and the woman would have caused that too. Miguel didn't know if he would shoot the woman when he found her. He would need her alive to find out where Javier was. He knew he was going to hurt her, though. Make her regret what she had done to him.

Miguel looked to his left. Shit. Getting darker now, the rainy mist making it harder to see. He saw a car on the last row going south to north. The car slowed and stopped.

Miguel looked in front of the vehicle. It had stopped to let someone cross.

The woman.

Tracy allowed herself to turn around. She saw Miguel and he saw her. He was several rows over and the light was poor, but both of them were aware in that moment that they were making eye contact. Miguel shook his head, just, and then he was raising his arm and waving frantically to Hector in the Mercedes.

Tracy got in the Jeep and threw the bag on the passenger seat. She put the keys in the ignition as Hector pulled the Mercedes up to Miguel. Miguel got in and Hector hit the accelerator and drove the car south on the row, speeding the car up and then braking as they reached the edge of the lot and he made a wide right turn, driving past five rows before he swung back north again, the Jeep now in view as Tracy backed it out and then they saw the rear brake lights redden as she stopped the Jeep and put it in drive. Hector floored it, bringing them closer to the Jeep and Tracy reached the northern end of the row and turned right and stepped on the brakes, crying out.

A minivan was in her path. Tracy could see the soccer mom

behind the windshield. The woman looked at Tracy with a similar expression of fright and then the Mercedes was behind the Jeep, skidding to a halt.

Tracy put the gear in reverse and pushed the accelerator to the floor. The back of the Jeep smashed into the Mercedes and Tracy kept it up, pushing the Mercedes back now, wheels spinning on the wet pavement and the Mercedes continued its rearward path until it smashed into another parked car.

Tracy stopped the Jeep. She moved it forward a few feet. Then she put it in reverse again, floored it, and gave the Mercedes another smash. She put the Jeep in drive and moved the Jeep forward, toward the minivan at first and then a hard left over the curb and down the grass incline, pushing the Jeep as it angled down the hill, managing not to tip over and then she reached the bottom of the ditch and hurtled the Jeep back out the other side.

FIFTY-SEVEN

Karen Rudnick sat in the break room at St. John Medical Center reading a *People* magazine. Her EMT partner was in the break room with her, talking with a maintenance man about the Sooners' latest roster. They were having a mild argument that had something to do with Dean Blevins's knowledge of the program, and Karen didn't have the patience to listen to it. It was a slow shift, twelve hours, seven to seven, and Karen was thinking the time would go quicker if they were on a call.

She looked up when a man appeared in the doorway. He was a nice enough looking guy, with graying hair and one of those drooping mustaches you see on cops and cowboys. Karen examined him a little more, saw the gun and holster at his side and thought, *yeah, cop.*

He was looking at her.

"Ms. Rudnick?"

"Yes?" Karen said. "What can I do for you?"

He showed her his badge, doing it in a way that was not intended to intimidate. He said, "My name is Mike Prather. I'm an agent with the Kansas Bureau of Investigation. The admin nurse suggested I talk to you."

Karen said, "Why?"

"It has to do with a friend of yours. Tracy Coughlin. Do you mind if I sit down?"

"No."

Karen Rudnick examined the agent, her expression wary. She

said, "You're from Kansas?"

"Yes."

Karen said, "What is it?"

"Maybe nothing," the agent said. "You're a friend of Ms. Coughlin's?"

"A good friend."

"We have information that Tracy made a telephone call to a woman named Donna Wolfe in Dallas. Do you know who that is?"

Karen Rudnick said, "Never heard of her."

"Ever heard Ms. Coughlin speak of her?"

"No," Karen said. "I think she may be looking for a job in Texas. That may relate."

"What sort of job?"

"As a nurse. A scrub nurse."

"More money?" Prather said.

"No," Karen said. "It's not money. She—look, why do you want to know?"

"Well, Ms. Wolfe is a person known to be associated with Javier Sandoval. The night before last, Mr. Sandoval escaped from a penitentiary in Kansas."

"What does that have to do with Tracy?"

"Well, like I said, this man's friend received a call from Tracy."

"A woman who knows this criminal got a call from Tracy?"

"Yes. That's what our records show."

"But that doesn't make sense. . . . Unless. Oh, God."

"Yes, ma'am. And we're just—"

"Don't you see? He's got her phone. Oh, God."

"Hold on," Prather said. "Now don't jump to any conclusions. I understand she called in sick this morning. You're aware of that?"

"Yes. But I saw her yesterday, and she was fine. My God, where is she?"

"Her home has been checked. She's not home."

"You don't know, do you? Jesus Christ."

"All right," Prather said. "We don't know—"

"Listen to me," Karen said. "Listen to me. Tracy Coughlin is no more a criminal than me or you. That's not her. If this fucker has her phone, he has her. Don't you understand?"

Prather said, "Where would she be if she's not at home?"

"I don't know," Karen said. "Wait. Her sister-in-law, Katy . . . Katy Forgue. That's her married name. She's the one that usually babysits John."

Prather said, "You know her number?"

Four rings and then he got Devereaux's answering service. Prather swore—a rare thing for him. He dialed again and got the same thing. He left a message, saying at the end that Devereaux should call him as soon as possible.

His next call was to Katy Forgue. Another four rings and then he got another answering service. Prather sighed to himself, wondering if anything was going to go his way. He remembered that he was out of town, away from his resources. Away from people he could call that would give him a street address connected to a telephone number.

Prather walked back to the administrative desk. The nurse he had previously questioned acknowledged him and Prather asked her if she had a telephone book somewhere back there.

She gave him a shake of the head, like he was being a nuisance, but then got one out of a drawer and set it on the counter. She didn't say anything while she did it.

Prather looked through the residential listings and felt better when he saw a listing for Forgue, Mark and Katy. Fate wasn't out to screw him completely. The listed number was the same one Karen Rudnick had given him. Prather dialed the number on his cell phone again and again got no answer.

But the phone book listed an address. Prather took a pen and notebook out of his jacket pocket and copied it down.

He left the phone book on the counter, turned to go and there was Karen Rudnick standing behind him.

She said, "I want to go with you."

Prather said, "No."

"You don't know your way around town. You have Katy's address there?"

"Yeah," Prather said. "Some street called Toledo . . ."

Karen Rudnick said, "Do you know how to get there?"

"I'll find my way," Prather said.

Karen said, "Come on. I just cleared it with my supervisor. I can go with you. On the way, you can ask me more questions. And you'll get there quicker with me than without me."

"It's not allowed."

"I'm an EMT," she said. "I'm not exactly a civilian. And she's a friend."

Prather sighed. "All right. Let's go."

Five minutes later, he was glad he had allowed her to come. He drove out of the St. Jude parking lot and she told him to make a right and then the first left. Then they were going south on Utica Avenue, trees hanging over the road.

Karen said, "You couldn't get Katy on the phone?"

"No," Prather said. "I'm just hoping that someone will be home when we get there."

Karen said, "If I knew Katy's cell number . . . but I don't. She's a good lady, but a little airheaded."

"Tracy?"

"No, not Tracy. I was talking about Katy. Tracy's not scatterbrained. Not at all."

After a moment, Prather said, "That's good."

Karen said, "Her husband was killed in Iraq. Six months ago."

"I know."

"You know?" Karen said. "How did you know that?"

"The FBI checked her out after her number turned up on the Dallas woman's phone." Prather felt the woman's resentment. He said, "It's not an intrusion. They just accessed her tax records, that sort of thing."

Karen said, "Is she some sort of suspect?"

"No. I told you already."

"I know what you told me. Oh God, I'm scared. These are the guys that are on television, aren't they?"

After a moment, Prather said, "Yes." He thought about his words, then said, "Don't be scared. We don't really know anything yet."

But he was worrying himself now. The woman's panic was having an effect on him. She knew this Tracy Coughlin and he didn't. Before talking with Karen Rudnick, Prather had thought that any number of things could explain the phone call to Dallas. A friend of Donna Wolfe's. Maybe not connected to anything at all. As Devereaux had said, they didn't have anything solid. The Dallas feds had admitted they didn't have enough to persuade the prosecutors to file charges against Donna Wolfe.

But then Karen Rudnick changed things. She seemed like a stable woman, a solid witness. And to her, it seemed inconceivable that Tracy Coughlin would be connected to a drug dealer's girlfriend.

Well, that was a good character reference, to be sure. The woman had lost a husband in Iraq. But who was to say she didn't have secrets too? Didn't most people?

Ahead of them, a light went from green to yellow. Prather slowed the car.

He said, "How well do you know Tracy Coughlin?"

Karen Rudnick turned to him, her shoulders and expression registering some offense at his tone. She said, "She's a good friend."

"How long have you known her?"

"About four years."

"A solid character, would you say?"

"Yes. Very. She's not at all flighty. If she has a fault, it's that she tends to be a little too serious. But wouldn't you be?"

"What do you mean?"

"She lost her husband."

"I know that. Did that change her?"

"What do you mean?"

"What I mean is, did it get her to start drinking too much? Maybe something worse."

Karen Rudnick shook her head, mildly disgusted. She said, "No."

There was silence between them. At the next intersection, Karen pointed east and he made a right turn.

Prather said, "I'm not trying to cause offense."

Karen looked at him again. "No?" she said. "What are you doing?"

"I'm looking for an explanation of why she wouldn't come to work." It sounded weak when he said it, even to him.

Karen said, "Look, she doesn't tell me everything. I didn't say that she did. But if you're asking me questions about her character, I know her well enough to know that she wouldn't be into drugs or something worse. If she were a drunk, I'd know that too."

"But what she does, it's stressful. Isn't it?"

"Yes. And it's stressful to raise a kid alone too. And to bury a husband that she loved very much. She's pissed, yes, but she's not falling apart." Karen added, "She's too stubborn for that."

Agent Prather looked over at the woman, that last part sticking with him. He started to form a fuller picture of this Tracy Coughlin. And as he did, he became more nervous. He hoped they would find her at her sister-in-law's house. He hoped that the whole thing would be a misunderstanding. He hoped that he wouldn't have to call Captain Devereaux and tell him that they were closer to finding another victim.

When they got to the Forgue house, a Lexus sedan was pulling into the driveway. Prather saw the brake lights come on then go off as the vehicle shut off and a woman got out. She was helping two children out of the back when Prather pulled his vehicle in behind.

Karen Rudnick was out of the vehicle before he was.

She got to Katy Forgue and said, "Katy, have you seen Tracy?"

Katy Forgue looked to the unmarked KBI car and the man getting out. Then she said, "No. Not for a couple of days. What is it?"

Prather told the woman who he was and showed her his identification. He said, "There's nothing to be worried about. I just need to speak to her."

Karen Rudnick glared at him and he said, "Do you know where she is?"

Katy Forgue said, "She's at work, isn't she?"

"No," Karen said, irritated. "She called in sick. And she's not at home. Where's John?"

Then Katy Forgue looked alarmed. "What? I was supposed to pick him up at school yesterday, but I couldn't go."

"What?" Karen said.

"I was supposed to pick him up for Tracy and take him to soccer practice. But I couldn't, so I called Dad and asked him to do it. He said he would."

Prather said, "Do you know if he did?"

"Well, I guess he did."

Prather said, "What's your father's name?"

"Lee. Lee Coughlin. Do you want me to call him?"

FIFTY-EIGHT

Hector backed into another car when he tried to dislodge the Mercedes from the car the woman had punched him into. The car he backed into had an alarm on it, which started whooping, and Hector put the Mercedes in drive as Miguel started cursing at him and telling him to get them the hell out of there.

They exited the parking lot at a good rate, and Hector could hear the right front fender rubbing against the tire, a horrible sound. He made a series of turns, and after a few minutes, they put the mall about a mile behind them. While this was going on, Miguel had his silver Kimber .380 at his side, swearing he was going to shoot that fucking bitch the minute they found her.

But they couldn't see her anywhere. Her Jeep was out of the lot before they could get their bearings and get a shot at her. Gone with fifty thousand dollars.

Hector said, "Man, we got to stop. I have to look at that tire."

Miguel said, "We got to find that bitch."

"You see her?" Hector said. "You do, you let me know. But we got to stop or we're going to have a fucking blowout."

Miguel said, "All right." Like Hector was being a baby by insisting.

Hector pulled the Mercedes into the lot of a seedy-looking motel. He drove past the front and around to the back. Then he turned the engine off and got out to look at the damage.

Jesus Christ, she had done some damage. Two front panels

smashed in, one where the Jeep hit, the other where the car had been punched into the parked car. It was a wonder both front tires weren't rubbing. Hector began pulling the right panel out of the tire's path.

He looked up once at Miguel. Miguel was still holding the gun, like it was going to do them any good back here. He hoped Miguel wouldn't shoot at the car in frustration. Or shoot him.

Hector said, "Now what are we going to do?"

Miguel said, "We got to find her."

Hector was thinking more along the lines of how they were going to get back to Dallas. He figured they wouldn't get too far on the interstate before they got pulled over, driving a vehicle not safe for highway travel. Hector was thinking that it was Miguel's car that had been ruined and needed to be repaired. A nice car, shiny and black, and now they'd probably have to get rid of it and find some other way to get back home.

But Miguel didn't seem worried about his car. What he seemed worried about was the money and letting the girl get away. Though not in that order.

What they were both thinking about was Caesar. How the living fuck were they going to explain this to him? They lost the money and the woman and they had no fucking idea where Javier was. They were told expressly to bring Javier back. Caesar said it was up to Javier whether or not they would kill the gringos, letting them know Javier would be in charge.

Which didn't sit well with Miguel. But he would have never expressed his disappointment to Caesar. Caesar would not have tolerated it. Bring Javier back. It was an order. One of Caesar's favorite expressions was *Plato o plomo*. Silver or lead. Offer the policeman or judge or magistrate a bribe. He can take it and go along and be smart. If not, he can take a bullet. Silver or lead.

The men with Javier had demanded silver. And Caesar had agreed to it. He had agreed to pay fifty thousand dollars to retrieve Javier. It was that important to him. Who knew why. It didn't matter why.

Hector said, "I think we should go home."

"We can't go home," Miguel said.

"But we don't know where he *is*."

No, Miguel thought, they didn't. But how could they go back to Texas and tell them that? Tell them that they lost fifty thousand and they don't know where Javier is? Cross their fingers and hope for the best.

Christ Jesus, how had this happened?

The woman. The fucking woman had tricked him. A little thing with nice skin and a serious, scared face. She said she would take them to Javier and then got away from them. The little *zorra*. Who would believe it?

Hector said, "Miguel, what do we do?"

Miguel honestly did not know. He knew they couldn't leave. Not yet. They didn't know where the girl had gone or where she had come from. They didn't know her name. They would just have to wait and hope that Javier would get in touch with them.

Miguel took his cell phone out of his pocket. If he called, would it be Javier that answered? No. It would be the white guy. Richard Billie. And what would he say to him? That the fucking woman had outsmarted them?

Fuck it, Miguel thought. He dialed the number and waited for an answer.

But all he got was a recording of a girl saying her name was Tracy and to leave a message. Christ, the voice of the woman who had escaped from him. Miguel waited for the beep, then said, "I'm going to find you, lady."

Fifty-Nine

Mike Prather dialed Lee Coughlin's home and cell number. He got no answer from either. He stopped himself from leaving a message both times. He turned his cell phone off and said to Katy Forgue, "No answer at either number. Does he have an office?"

"Yes," she said. Then she gave him the number.

They were standing in her kitchen. The children had been sent into the next room to watch television.

Katy Forgue said, "Sometimes he works late."

Prather dialed the number, waited and got another answering service. He had hoped to speak to someone. He didn't leave a message.

Prather said, "No answer there. Doesn't he have a secretary or something?"

"Yes," Katy said. "But they close the office at six. Usually."

"But sometimes he works late?"

"Sometimes. Well," she said. "Often. But he's as likely to be in his truck when he's working as he is in his office. My mother died years ago. So . . . he works a lot."

Prather said, "Does he screen his calls at home? In case of telemarketers, things like that?"

"I don't know," Katy said. "It wouldn't surprise me if he did."

"Is it like him not to answer his cell phone?"

"No. Not really."

"He picked up your nephew from school yesterday?"

"Yes?"

"Do you know if the boy was in school today?"

"I don't," she said. "My kids don't go to the same school."

"Do you know someone who does?"

"Yes," Katy said. "A friend of mine has a boy in John's class. Do you want me to call her?"

"Please."

Karen Rudnick was looking at the agent now. She didn't seem at all reassured. "Something's wrong," she said.

Prather said, "Just hold on."

They did while Katy Forgue called her friend from the kitchen phone. The greetings passed quickly and they heard Katy ask the woman on the phone if her son Will had seen John at school today.

There was a pause and then they saw Katy's face break and they knew.

Katy said into the phone, "Are you sure?"

Then she hung up the receiver. She said, "He wasn't there today."

Prather looked at Katy Forgue and then back at Karen. He said, "Now you listen to me, both of you. We don't have any confirmation on anything right now. But I do not want either of you going to his house. Don't even think about doing that. Do you understand me?"

"I understand you," Karen said. "You think they may be over there right now. Your fugitives holding my friend hostage. Maybe her family too. Or . . ." She couldn't say it.

"It's a possibility," Prather said. "And we're going to check it out. But let us do it."

Karen said, "So we just let them sit there?"

"I didn't say that," Prather said. He picked up his phone and called Mal Devereaux.

This time, the man answered.

"Yeah?" Devereaux said.

"Mal," Prather said. "Where have you been?"

"I've been on the phone with everyone. What's up?"

"I might have something," Prather said.

He spent the next few minutes telling them about his leads. How one or two pieces that could have meant very little took on a significance when put together.

Prather walked out of the kitchen and onto the back patio, holding his cell phone. He shut the door behind him.

He said to Devereaux, "There's a good possibility that the fugitives are holed up at Lee Coughlin's residence. Or that they've been there and moved on. Maybe killed Coughlin and his daughter-in-law and the boy. But if they haven't killed them, that means they may all be in there with them."

Devereaux said, "A hostage situation."

"Yes. You send a patrol car up to the front door, you may get them all killed."

"I've got a homicide to deal with. And I've got a couple of goons from DEA hanging around here, chomping at the bit."

"What?"

"Yeah. They flew in from the Dallas section. Got here about an hour ago. And I have to warn you, they've got more pull with the feds than I do."

"Captain, listen to me," Prather said. "Don't bogey this thing. Don't let those men storm the house. I don't want any more innocent people killed."

"Well, what am I supposed to do?" Devereaux said. "You're the one that gave me this information."

"Just get them ready. But don't send them. Not yet. Mal, I'm asking you."

Devereaux sighed. Then he said, "All right. Let me contact the feds and we'll debrief. How soon can you be here?"

"I'm going to go by the house myself."

"You just said—"

"I'm not in uniform," Prather said. "I can be subtle."

"I don't like that," Devereaux said. "I don't like sending an officer without backup."

Prather said, "We're the ones that let them go."

"Oh, for God's sake," Devereaux said. "You want to take responsibility for this?"

"Just let me do a quick drive-by, and then I'll call you."

"What if you don't call? What if you get killed?"

Prather sighed, as if the notion were too unrealistic to consider. He said, "Give me twenty minutes. You can do that."

"All right," Devereaux said.

Prather clicked off his phone. He looked through the glass door into the kitchen. The women were looking back at him. He walked to the door and slid it open. He thought of his unmarked Ford Crown Victoria in the driveway. Dark blue and slick backed, but a police car to anyone who cared to examine it.

He said to Katy Forgue, "I'd like to borrow your vehicle."

SIXTY

They had been at a restaurant once when they ran into a girl Drew had dated in high school. The girl was a little heavy and loud and she was with a man who eyed Drew like they were still kids competing for a seat on the bus. Drew ignored him. The woman's name had been Missy or Melanie; Tracy couldn't quite remember it. Drew introduced her to the woman and her husband but didn't invite them to join them for dinner, and Tracy was relieved. Tracy could see that Missy/Melanie was still pretty gaga over Drew, making references to old times to get Tracy upset. Soon Drew said it was good to see her, and the girl and her husband drifted off.

Tracy said, "Prom queen?"

"No," Drew said. "She was on the drill team. That was a big deal back then."

"A big deal to date a drill-team girl?" Tracy said.

"And how," he said. Showing mock pride over it. Though maybe the pride was real too.

Tracy thought about saying that the girl must have been thinner back then, but decided not to. It would have been too easy.

Drew said, "She was a lot of fun. But God, she was hard on cars."

Tracy burst out laughing. "Hard on cars," she said. "What the hell does that mean?"

Drew. So wonderful and good, yet a hopeless Okie. A good-looking boy who drove fast cars and was a natural leader and dated pom-pom girls in high school. A boy without darkness or meanness or any sense of foreboding. A decent all-American.

Tracy had not known him when he was in high school. But she sensed that he had probably not changed much since. He had remained optimistic and generous and easygoing. A kind, simple man. A good man.

She was hard on cars.

Put that on her tombstone, Drew. The bitch was hard on cars.

It was coming back to Tracy now, that punch line. She was thinking of it now as she approached her father-in-law's house. About a mile away now. Hard on cars, eh? Had pom-pom Melly ever backed a car into a Mercedes and smashed it into another car? Ever run away from a scene of such an accident with fifty thousand dollars in her bag? Didn't think so. *You can't compete with me, pom-piddy-pom girl. You never could.*

For Drew was a prize. And Tracy had known it as well as the other girl. A man who took a certain pride in playing up the aw-shucks yokel bit, but was deeper than that. Bigger than that too. Tracy remembered the time she had heard Drew tell someone at a party, "Well, she's the smart one." Referring to her. And he had said it without any sort of resentment.

On the way home, she said to him, "Do you really believe that? That I'm smarter than you?"

"Sure."

"But I'm not."

"I'm okay with it."

"But I'm not smarter than you. I've just had a little more education."

She thought about it later. For the next couple of days, she watched him to see if this belief bothered him. It didn't. He had never lacked for confidence himself. And maybe it was that strength that allowed him to tell her this. He had always known who and what he was. A quality that she knew to be rare.

She would later wish that his belief in her intelligence would make him defer to her. But that didn't happen. Not when she wanted it to anyway. Lee was right; he could be stubborn.

She was thinking about Drew now. And in this moment, she could not be angry at him. She just couldn't. He had done what he thought was right. Maybe to impress Lee, maybe to impress her. Maybe he had done it because he had believed things had come too easily to him. Or maybe he had done it because he had thought it was right. Maybe it had been something he couldn't explain to her.

In this moment, she was afraid. For her own life, yes. And for the lives of her son and Lee, absolutely. These things terrified her. But she was afraid of something else too. She was afraid of letting Drew down.

It was something she had never worried about before. During their marriage, she had never been tempted by another man. Indeed, it had never occurred to her that anyone else could measure up. She had never lied to him, never given him cause to distrust her. She knew she had not been a saint, not always been easy to get along with. There had been times they may have angered each other, but never had they disappointed each other.

It was her son back in that house. But not just hers. His too. Drew's son. Drew's father. Drew wasn't here now.

She wished he could be. Wished that he could guide her now with some sort of Obi-Wan–like voice, telling her that Drew was with her. Telling her that she must not give up on John and Lee and herself. Telling her that she had to *think*.

When she got back to the house, what would they do?

Let them go.

They'd have their money now. They'd have their fifty thousand. They'd have what they came here for. Richard and

Amos were keeping Javier hostage as well. They were not going to allow him to leave the house until he paid his debt to them. Until he paid them the fifty thousand. That was why they had stopped in Tulsa, wasn't it? Once they had their money, they would have no reason to stay at the house anymore. Presuming they didn't want to hang around and rape her, leave her another nightmare she could remember. They would no longer need the house, no longer need a place to stay. So, yes, let them go.

Drew? Your thoughts?

But Drew wasn't here to bounce it off of. Maybe if he was, he'd say, "You're the smart one. You figure it out."

No. No, he wouldn't say that. It would be a little too nasty, out of character for him. He had never called her smart in a mean way. Never told her it must be nice to know everything. Because she didn't.

But he might say something more constructive. Something like: *do you really believe that? Do you, Tracy?*

Did she really believe they would let them go?

She wanted to believe it. She had never wanted to believe anything more in her life. Hope, hope, hope that Richard and Amos and Javier would say, wow, it's all here. Wow, we got the money. Well, kids, it's been nice. Thanks for your hospitality. Oh, can you give us a couple of hours' head start before you call the police? Just to be a good sport.

Well . . . no, they wouldn't do that. They wouldn't be able to do that.

So, what then? Maybe tie them up, put gags in their mouths and put them in the basement? That would buy them some time.

And Drew would say, *how likely is that?*

Tracy thought about things she didn't want to think about. Things she had forced herself not to think about in these last awful hours. She had put herself on a sort of emotional autopilot in order to cope. But she couldn't entirely shut out reality. She couldn't afford to avoid the truth. She couldn't forget that Richard Billie and his men had killed several people. Had murdered a girl. She couldn't forget that the three of them plotted to kill a man who had simply been unlucky enough to walk up to Lee's front door. And she had been part of that. She had picked Amos up after he killed the man. She had *helped* the scumbag get away. And in that whole time she had not seen a speck of remorse in him.

And even if she had not witnessed any of it, there was the last fifteen minutes to consider. She had, in effect, stolen fifty thousand dollars from Javier's partners. They had been determined to come with her and she had deprived them of that chance. Once they got in touch with Javier, they would tell him. They would tell him that they had intended to come and help him, but this bitch had tricked them out of the chance. Javier alone would make her answer for that.

She knew. She knew then that any belief that these men would allow her and her family to live was fantasy. They had allowed the hostages to live so far because they needed them. They needed her to run errands. Pick up Amos. Pick up the money. Do it or we'll kill your boy. Do it or we'll kill the old man. They enjoyed torturing the innocent, she could see. But there was a cold practicality in their actions too.

And now she had fulfilled her final mission. She was bringing back the money. The money that she had risked her life for. The money that she had been terrified *not* to bring back. For if she had returned without it, they would have killed John.

And now she was returning with it. And now she had no doubt they were still going to kill John. The money had been her savior. Now it was her death sentence. And not just hers.

It's not fair, she thought.

She had thought it before. Thought it when Drew went off to

297

war. Thought it when she opened the front door of her house to see two marine officers and she knew they were there to tell her that her husband had been killed. It wasn't fair.

. And for a while she had not been able to think about what Drew would have said. It was too painful to think about.

But now she imagined him saying very plainly: *No, it's not fair. But what are you going to do about it?*

No, not *but*. He wouldn't say *but*. That was a way of surrendering to the dark fate. That was a loser's answer. And Drew hadn't been a loser. The proper question was: *Now* what are you going to do about it?

Tracy turned the Jeep into the subdivision that would bring her to the house. Two blocks and then a left turn and then a right that would bring her to the end of a sparsely populated block and Lee's house at the end.

Tracy checked her watch. She had eleven minutes left to get back. She pulled the Jeep over to the side of the road. Then she looked in the bag and found the envelope Hector had put in there.

They had said it contained fifty thousand dollars. Had they been telling the truth?

Tracy counted it. Then counted it again.

They had. It was all there.

SIXTY-ONE

She had six minutes left when she pulled the Jeep into the driveway. She parked the Jeep and walked to the front door. She knocked twice and then Amos opened the door.

All of the fugitives were in the front room. Amos took her by the arm now and pulled her in. He closed the door and then Richard was moving toward her, trying to hide his anticipation, but not succeeding.

"Did you get it?" he said. "Did you get it?"

"I saw them," Tracy said. "Where's my family?"

"Is it in there?" Richard said, looking at her bag. Then he took the bag and started to examine it. But that was taking too much time and he hurried over to the dining room table and dumped the contents of the bag onto it.

Amos came to the table with Richard Billie. Javier moved with them, though not all the way. He looked at Tracy and she looked back at him.

And Tracy saw the question in his eyes. *Where are my men? Why did you come back here without them? Why did they allow you to come back here alone?*

It frightened Tracy, this scrutiny. But she saw, for the first time, that Javier himself was alarmed. Scared, but trying to hide it. Scared enough that he couldn't ask her his questions in front of Richard and Amos. Maybe Javier too felt that this money would be his death sentence. Or that he wasn't expecting money. He was expecting help.

She could say to him, *they're not coming.*

Bring him out of his cool shell. See what effect that had on him. See how he liked being frightened for his life.

But she didn't. She knew what was coming.

Richard had the envelope open now, dumping the money onto the table. Amos yelping out in delight.

Tracy said, "I want to see my family."

They ignored her. Richard was now counting the money out, putting twenties and fifties in stacks.

Tracy said, "I want to see my family."

Amos said, "Go upstairs then. They're fine."

Tracy started to go.

"Hold it," Richard said. "Hold it right there."

Richard gave Tracy a sharp look then looked back through his stacks on the table. He returned his attention to her.

Richard said, "I see eight, maybe nine thousand dollars here. Where's the rest of it?"

Tracy looked back at him, feeling the shakes in her chest and her hands.

"Huh?" Richard said. "Where's the fifty fucking thousand dollars?"

Tracy said, "I want to see my boy."

Richard threw her empty bag at her. *"Where is it?"* he screamed.

Tracy flinched, the bag hitting her in the body. Not hurting her, but frightening her. She was aware of all three men watching her now. Javier, confused. Richard, furious. Amos, not fully comprehending it.

Tracy said, "They told me—"

"What?" Richard said, his voice still raised.

And Tracy spoke up. "They told me," she said, "that they would give you the rest when you brought them Javier."

"What?"

"That's what they told me," Tracy said. "It's not my fault."

"You fucking lying whore," Richard said, his voice still raised. "You know what I think? I think you went to the bank and emptied out your own account. Because you were too chicken-shit to do what you were told."

"No—"

"No? Then where's the fifty thousand? Where the fuck is it?"

"I didn't go to my bank. Any savings I have are tied up in a 401K. I met with his friends." She gestured to Javier. "Two men. One about six feet tall, his hair slicked back. Fancy look-ing. The other was a big guy, built like a football player. His name is Hector. They have a Mercedes." She looked at Javier and said, "Am I lying? Tell them."

Javier looked back at her, some of the alarm having left him now. "No," he said. Javier turned to Richard Billie. "She's not lying."

Amos said, "Ah, shit."

Tracy said, "They're afraid that if they gave me all the money, you would—" She stopped, wanting to make it look like the no-tion horrified her.

"That I would what?" Richard said.

"That you would kill him," she said.

Amos was looking at the money still on the table. Eight or nine thousand was better than nothing. He wanted to take it and leave. He said, "Rich—"

"Shut up," Richard said. To Tracy he said, "You fucking idiot. Can't you do anything right?"

"Richard," Javier said. He wasn't going to call him Richie now. He wanted to get out of this situation. "Richard," he said. "She's on the level, man."

"You don't know that," Richard said.

Tracy said, "You sent me out there. I can't control what they do."

Amos said, "Well, now what?"

Before Richard could bark at him, Tracy said, "They want you to meet them. They want you to bring Javier to the Airport Inn. The parking lot at the Airport Inn. It's on Sheridan. They said if you bring him there, they'll give you the rest of the money."

"Or fucking shoot me," Richard said.

"No," she said. "They're not going to do that. Fifty thousand dollars is nothing to them. They just want him back."

"Bullshit."

"They picked the parking lot because it's populated. It's well lit. You bring him there and they'll give you the rest of the money."

"It's a trap," Richard said.

"No," Tracy said. "They wanted to do that, they could have followed me back here. I wouldn't have been able to stop them. They're acting in good faith."

For a moment, nobody said anything. Tracy thought of John and Lee and kept her eyes on Richard.

Then Javier said, "Man, it's another forty thousand dollars and change. You want it or not?"

It was with some effort that Tracy next spoke. It was a gamble, but she knew deep down she had to do it.

She said, "I can take him there, if it's okay."

Richard brought his eyes up, sharp and distrustful.

"No way," he said. "I'll take him."

"Rich," Amos said.

But Richard cut him off. "It's decided," he said. "You stay here with her. She steps out of line even once, shoot her."

"Rich," Amos said. "We're all over the television."

But Richard was moving back to the table, picking up the cash and putting it in his pockets. Amos's jaw dropped a little, not believing what he was seeing. He raised his gun and pointed it at Richard.

"Hey," Amos said. "What do you think you're doing?"

Richard stopped. His own gun was in his hand, but it was down at his side. He was afraid that if he left the eight thousand on the table, Amos would take it and leave. He still believed it now.

But that .38 was pointed at his belly, Amos's finger on the trigger.

Richard lifted his hands off the money. "Just taking a little for the road," Richard said.

"Yeah? Looks like you were taking it all, to me."

"I wasn't."

The men continued sizing each other up. Richard stepped back, his hands up in a conciliatory gesture.

"Okay, Amos. But you'll still be here when I get back, won't you?"

"Sure," Amos said. "We're partners, aren't we?"

Richard smiled, showing exasperation and fear. "Sure," Richard said. He turned to Tracy and said, "Give me your car keys."

Tracy handed Richard the keys to the Jeep. Her heart pounded as she watched him walk out the front door with Javier. It was working. It was actually working.

The front door closed behind them. Amos was still standing next to the dining room table.

Tracy said, "I'd like to go upstairs now."

"Go ahead," Amos said. His eyes were still on the money.

SIXTY-TWO

It was dark when they walked out to the Jeep. Richard handed the keys to Javier and said, "You drive." Javier took the order without comment, thinking, *It won't be long, brother.* He felt better knowing that his men were waiting for him. That they had been looking out for him. He still wondered, though, why they hadn't come back with the woman. Maybe it was because they didn't want Richard and Amos to have the advantage of the house. If so, that wouldn't be such a bad plan. Meeting in an open area, a neutral ground. It was not the way Javier would have played it. But it wasn't bad, either.

Richard was walking around to the passenger side. He stopped at the passenger door, peering at something.

Javier said, "What is it?"

Richard was looking at the damage to the back of the Jeep. Had that been there before? He hadn't seen the back of the Jeep before. Amos had . . .

"Come on," Javier said. "Let's go."

Richard got in the passenger side. He still held the Glock. Javier started the Jeep and backed it out of the driveway.

Mike Prather drove Katy Forgue's Lexus LS400 to the Coughlin house. It was a big, heavy car with a lot of unfamiliar gadgets. Much more luxurious than his Crown Vic, but a little too mushy in handling. Still, he felt better driving it than the police car. He had taken his handheld police radio with him. He would put it under the seat when he approached the house.

He was keyed up, tense as he got closer. Telling himself he didn't know for sure. He didn't know if the fugitives were there or had ever been there. If they had, he didn't know if the Coughlins would still be alive. He didn't know the Coughlins. He had met a close friend of the woman's and the sister-in-law and they both seemed like good people. He hoped very much that he wouldn't have to report the deaths of their loved ones. Adding to the list these men had made.

Prather made a turn off a heavily trafficked street and entered a neighborhood. As he progressed, he saw that the houses weren't as close together as he expected. It was probably a part of town that hadn't ever been fully developed, a pocket that was nice and pleasant to look at but had never become fashionable. A place that was almost secluded. He slowed for an intersection ahead that had four stop signs. There was a high streetlight illuminating the intersection, the sort you sometimes see in rural areas.

Prather came to a stop.

And watched another vehicle come to a stop on his left.

It was the damage to the rear of the vehicle that first caught his attention. It had been smashed in the rear, as if the driver had backed up full force into a garbage truck. The taillight was broken and inoperative. It would give a patrol officer probable cause to pull them over. A Jeep Cherokee. A suburban vehicle. An SUV. A woman's car . . .

Prather leaned forward and peered into the front seat of the Jeep. Two men in the front seat, one white, one Hispanic.

God Almighty.

The Jeep began to make its right turn, bringing it past the KBI agent in the Lexus. Prather looked out the driver's side window as it passed and saw the Hispanic man behind the wheel for an instant, and then they were past and moving behind him and that was all Prather needed. He recognized Javier Sandoval's photo from the file he had reviewed several times over.

Prather pressed the Lexus's accelerator and moved the car out into the intersection, lumbering right then swinging back left for the wide turn, not wanting to push it into a ditch, completing the arc and then bringing the car back around and when it was clear, he pressed the accelerator down hard and zoomed up behind the Jeep, then he was next to it, looking over into the cab of the Jeep, seeing Javier Sandoval turn to look at him, surprised, and Prather had no doubt anymore as he pushed the Lexus up ahead of the Jeep then swung it back in, closing, then making contact with it, metal crunching up against metal, and the Jeep went off the road and through a grass ditch, smashing into a fence and coming to a stop.

Prather stomped the brakes and brought the Lexus to a stop. Then he was out of the car and putting his pistol across the roof and shouting at the men in the car, *"Police. Step out of the vehicle with your hands above your head. Now."*

It was dark and he couldn't see that well and it was happening too quickly, maybe the driver was leaning forward with his head on the steering wheel. But then gunfire came back from the Jeep and Prather knew he hadn't made a rookie mistake, that his instincts had been correct. An eruption of gunfire and flashes came from the Jeep and Prather fired back once, then twice more, and heard windows shatter and then realized it was the window of the Lexus breaking now and he felt a sting hit him somewhere between his neck and his shoulder and he heard himself cry out involuntarily as he squeezed off two more shots and fell back in the damp grass.

SIXTY-THREE

When Tracy got to the bedroom, she saw John asleep next to Lee. Lee's eyes fluttered open.

"Are you all right?" Lee said.

"Yes," Tracy said. "You?"

"I don't know. John asked if he could lay here. He was afraid."

Tracy nodded. "Listen," she said. "We haven't got much time. Can you get up?"

"I don't think so," Lee said. "What's going on?"

"Javier and Richard left. But they'll be coming back. Pretty damn soon, I imagine."

Lee looked at Tracy and saw that she probably had some hand in this. He said, "What did you do?"

"I'll tell you later," she said. "Amos is still here."

Lee looked at his daughter-in-law and saw an intensity and determination that was new to him. She was in charge now. He said to her, "What do you want us to do?"

She said, "I'm going to help you get off the bed. And I want you and John to get underneath it."

"To hide?"

"Yeah. It's something. Okay?"

"Okay," he said. "Help me."

She woke up John and told him what she wanted him to do. She moved John out of the way and then pulled Lee off the bed. She saw his face contort with pain, but he held in any cries.

"I'm sorry," Tracy said.

"Don't be sorry," Lee said. He gasped again. Then said, "All right. I think I can scoot myself in . . . well, maybe you can give me a little push."

She got him under the bed. Then she directed John to get under there with him. She stood back and looked at the room. From the door, one might think they had escaped. It would take about a minute of searching to find them, only a couple of seconds to kick the locked door in. But it was better than nothing.

"Okay?" she said, her voice low.

"Okay, Mama," John said. He was scared, but holding it down. A brave boy, her son.

"Just stay there," Tracy said. "I'll be back."

She closed the bedroom door, locking it as she did so. Then she walked down the stairs. Amos was still at the dining room table. He looked back at her, suspicious. More afraid now than he had been.

Tracy said, "I need a drink."

"He doesn't want you going in the kitchen alone," Amos said.

"He's not here," Tracy said. Then she smiled at him. "Listen," she said. "I just went through a lot of shit, okay? If I were going to run away, don't you think I would have earlier? My kid's upstairs."

"I'm coming with you," he said.

"Fine," Tracy said.

He followed her into the kitchen. He took a seat at the kitchen table. And he seemed so relaxed, sitting there. Like he wanted to rest too. Wait for Richard to come back with the money and then he could be on his way. It tempted her, seeing him like that. Maybe she could rest too. But she knew that wasn't an option.

Then she saw him put the .38 on the table. His hands resting on his legs, like he was waiting to be served.

She could offer to cook for him. Make him some bacon and eggs in a heavy iron skillet. It would give her something to hit him with. But there wouldn't be time for that either.

Tracy opened the cabinet where she remembered seeing the liquor before. There it was, the big squarish bottle of Jack Daniel's. The one and three-quarters liter bottle. About three-quarters full. Drew had liked Jack Daniel's, had liked sharing it with Lee when he came over. Tracy took it down and set it on the counter.

Then she looked over at Amos.

She poured two fingers over a couple of cubes of ice. Then she took a liberal drink of it. Awful stuff, to her. She'd never formed a taste for it. But maybe the man was watching her.

She turned to observe him. His hands were still resting on his thighs. Getting sleepy maybe. Or hungry.

The gun. How could she get the gun away from him? She could try to snatch it and then shoot him with it. But Lee had said there was only one bullet left. And Lee had seemed sure about that. Besides, Amos was big and fat, but he could move quickly. She remembered that from when she picked him up near Southwest Avenue. She could try to snatch the gun but he'd pounce on her and probably beat her to death.

She thought, *You've got to do something. There isn't much time.*

Yes, she thought. *Do something. But it has to work.*

Tracy took a dish from the cupboard. Then she went to the refrigerator and took a piece of cold chicken out and put it on the dish. Maybe the food would distract him. He liked to eat. She could give him the chicken cold or microwave it. If it were her son, he'd want it warmed up in the microwave.

That was when Tracy thought of the hairspray can. She had left it in the Jeep. Her weapon of mass destruction. Christ. What would she do with it now? Spray Amos in the face? Or maybe use it to grease his bald head. Take *that* and *that*.

And Tracy looked at the microwave and thought, it doesn't have to be a can of hairspray. Any aerosol can should work. Hadn't she treated a patient in the emergency room who suffered injuries from such an incident? A couple of stoned kids who had been bored and looking for something to do. Who tried it to see what would happen, and found out the hard way what does.

Tracy opened the cupboard beneath the sink. She saw a can of wood furniture cleaner and took it out. An aerosol can.

She set the can of cleaner on the counter next to the Jack Daniel's bottle. She screwed the black top back on the bottle. She put the can of furniture cleaner in the microwave, put the heat setting on high and set the timer at ten minutes. Then, with the dish in one hand and the Jack Daniel's bottle in the other, she walked over to the table.

Amos looked up at her as she approached him. He placed one hand on the table, near the gun.

Tracy said, "I thought you might be hungry." Then she set the dish on the table in front of him.

He was still looking back at her, a little confused at her consideration, but then he looked at the chicken. He began to eat and Tracy sat in the chair nearest to him.

From the kitchen, she could hear the whir of the microwave oven.

Amos raised his eyes to look at her.

Tracy said, "I guess you're looking forward to getting out of here, huh?"

"You got that right."

He was looking at her still, his eyes twinkling in a way Tracy did not like.

He said, "But maybe we have time."

Oh God, Tracy thought. The fucking pig. Now he was grinning at her, chewing his food with his mouth open.

Tracy gave him a slow steady stare. Then she said, "I doubt it."

Boom! The microwave door exploded open, the gas in the aerosol can having expanded and heated beyond the container's limits.

Amos Denton hunched forward on the table, his chest and shoulders over his dish and Tracy jumped up and grabbed the Jack Daniel's bottle and bashed him over the head with it.

The big bottle didn't break with the first hit. Just made a sort of *thoonk* sound and his head fell forward onto the table and into the plate and then Tracy lifted the bottle again, still with two hands, and brought it down like a medieval executioner as hard as she could on his head and that time, the bottle did break.

Amos was out.

Tracy took the .38 off the table and stepped back.

Her breathing was hard now. He was out. He wasn't faking it. The shit. The fucking murderer. She knew she could kill him right now. An unconscious lump who wouldn't be able to stop her from doing it.

But . . . no. She walked out of the kitchen. And then rushed across the house to Lee's study. She would do that before she called the police, because the others could return at any moment. She went to Lee's desk and started opening drawers.

Which drawer? Which goddamn drawer? Did he say left or right? It was left, left, and she opened the left drawer and found the cigar box with the letters in it. *Please, Lee. Please be right.* And there were the letters. She pulled them up and found the bullets beneath them. She gave a short cry of relief.

There were about ten or so. She opened the cylinder of the .38 and emptied out four casings and one bullet. The fat ass had been telling the truth. There had only been one bullet left. Now there would be five.

Tracy started putting them in.

SIXTY-FOUR

Richard was pretty sure he'd hit the cop. He had gotten out of the Jeep as soon as it came to a stop, still wondering what the fuck was up, but then knew when he heard a man yell out that he was a cop and he knew the bitch had set him up. Richard crouched behind the hood of the Jeep and started firing the Glock at the voice and then shots came back and he knew one of them went through the window and took Javier in the head, slumping him over into the passenger seat. Richard fired some more shots and heard the cop cry out.

Richard decided to get the hell out of there.

Fucking cop. Fucking cop had been waiting for them. Driving a car that didn't look like a police car, but they were probably all around here now. Helicopters would be here any second, and if the spotlights didn't pick him up, the heat sensors would.

He started running back to Coughlin's house, which was about three blocks away. He would have a hostage if he got back there. Something to shield him against these pieces of shit.

But he knew as he made his way back that there would be no hostages. He wouldn't be able to stop himself from killing that bitch and her family. She had set him up, she had lied to him, made a fool of him. He couldn't allow her to live after that. Even if he did need a hostage. Fuck it, he'd take the old man's truck and the money and get on the road. There would be others.

He felt better as he got closer to the house. He saw no police cars, no suspicious-looking delivery trucks. He felt better.

But then when he walked up to the front of the house, he noticed the lights were off.

Christ.

He approached the front door. It was unlocked. He opened it and walked in.

He didn't see anybody. He walked over to the dining room and switched on the light.

The room illuminated. He saw the dining room table, the money taken off it now. Richard stared at the table for a moment. Then he walked to the kitchen door and opened it.

Christ. Amos was slumped over the table. Richard switched on the kitchen light. There was broken glass on the floor, along with whiskey. And if he felt anger before, it was nothing to the rage he felt now. The fucking whore. She'd planned this. Tricked him into leaving her alone with Amos, the stupid shit. Richard heard himself growl as he ran out of the kitchen and into the living room. He got to the stairs and was halfway up them when he heard a voice behind him.

"They're not up there," Tracy said.

Richard stopped. He was still holding the Glock at his side. He turned slowly to face the woman.

She was holding the .38 revolver with both hands, pointing it at him.

Richard took her in. Then he laughed.

He said, "Well, well. What do we have here?"

Tracy didn't respond to him. Richard noticed that her arms were shaking. *She doesn't know what to do,* he thought.

Richard said, "They're not up there, huh? What'd you do, spirit 'em out the back door?" He shook his head. "No," he said. "You're lying to me. Again."

Tracy didn't answer him.

He came down a step and said, "You fucked us over pretty

good, didn't you?"

Tracy said, "You had it coming."

"Oooh," Richard said. "Kinda feisty there, miss-miss, with your little gun." He came down a couple more steps, in the light now so he could intimidate her even further. He said, "Why don't you put it down, before you get hurt."

He was still holding the Glock at his side, thinking he would lift it and shoot her while she was still trying to get up the gumption. Maybe he would say something else to rattle her, keep her off balance. Look at her now. Trying to think of something to say to him, show him that she's a big girl. What would it be? *I mean it.* Or, *get out.* Or some other lame shit. The bitch.

What did she have anyway? A short-barreled gun with a limited range, which she'd probably never shot in her life. No match for a policeman's Glock. A gun Richard had grown very comfortable with in the last couple of days. Raise the pistol and add the little bitch to the list.

"Richard!"

The voice was coming from above. Richard Billie turned and raised the pistol in the direction of the sound. Christ, it was the old man, looking pale as a ghost and just about as dead, propping himself up against the corner at the top of the stairs.

Tracy pulled the trigger of the .38 twice, two shots booming out, one taking Richard Billie in the chest, the other in his torso, and he bucked and just before he began his tumble down the stairs, she shot him two more times.

Then he was conscious of lying on his back. His body and his head hurting . . . he must have hit his head when he went down the stairs. His gun . . . where was it? . . . the woman standing over him now . . . she had it. *She* was holding his gun. Christ . . . *Her?* . . .

Tracy threw the Glock to her side. She knew she still had one shot left in the .38. She suspected he was dying, but she needed to be sure. She crouched down and felt for a pulse. There was none. Richard Billie was dead.

Then she went and picked up the Glock. She decided she would keep it with her until the police arrived.

She ran up the stairs to Lee, who had now slumped to the ground.

"Mommy!"

John ran out of the bedroom. Tracy kneeled and hugged him and told him everything was okay. She clutched him as she never had before. Everything was okay now.

In time she released the boy and put her arms around Lee. She propped his head up. His face was gray and sweaty.

"Oh God, Dad," she said. "You were supposed to stay in there."

Lee said, "You complaining?"

"No." It made her smile, his trying to be funny at a time like this. He had some hard bark on him.

Lee lifted his head and strained to look at the man at the bottom of the stairs, crumpled and bloody. Richard Billie, the nightmare. The fiend who had invaded his home.

Lee said, "Is he dead?"

"Yes," Tracy said, her voice quiet as she was conscious of the boy.

Lee nodded with a grim satisfaction and then relaxed his body, his head falling back.

There was a tight smile on his face. He looked at Tracy and said, "He found out, didn't he?"

Tracy said, "Found out what?"

"That he chose the wrong house."

SIXTY-FIVE

By the time Tracy called the police, Mal Devereaux had already left his downtown command post. He was riding in the first car of four, the last two being FBI. The cars were followed by a Chevy Suburban loaded with DEA agents. They were about a mile away from the Coughlin residence when dispatch squawked and informed them of the 911 call from Lee Coughlin's house.

The report: Two of the escaped convicts were there. Richard Billie was dead. Amos Denton was unconscious. The Coughlin woman had knocked him out with a blunt object. The owner of the house was injured, a gunshot wound to his leg. The whereabouts of Javier Sandoval were presently unknown.

Devereaux's driver stopped at an intersection as an ambulance, lights flashing and siren blaring, went through.

The convoy of police vehicles followed. But Devereaux told his driver to stop when he saw the two vehicles off the side of the road and something else. A man lying on the ground. Devereaux had not heard back from the Kansas agent.

About a half-dozen law enforcement officers carefully approached the Lexus and the Jeep, their flashlights out and weapons drawn.

It was Devereaux who found Prather.

He crouched next to the agent and felt a pulse and demanded that someone call an ambulance.

"Prather. Prather."

The agent's eyes fluttered open. He was going into shock.

317

"Hey, Captain."

"Prather," Devereaux said. "You're hit."

"Yeah. My shoulder, I think. I think my collarbone's broken."

"What happened?"

"I never made it to the house. I saw . . . Sandoval and Billie
. . . in the Jeep . . . I went after them . . . cowboy'd it . . ."

Another officer was now in the agent's presence. Prather
recognized him. The young detective who had escorted him
into Devereaux's office.

"Mal," the detective said. "We found Sandoval in the other
vehicle. He's dead."

Prather said, ". . . the other two . . . they're probably at the
house . . . those people . . ."

"It's all right, Prather," Devereaux said. "They're all right.
Richard Billie's dead. Amos Denton's subdued. The civilians
are safe and alive. You didn't cowboy it. You did good."

Prather seemed to relax. Devereaux asked the detective where
that ambulance was.

Thirty minutes later, it was on television. Local newscasters
reported that all three of the Kansas escaped convicts had been
apprehended. One of them, Amos Denton, was in custody. The
other two—Richard Billie and Javier Sandoval—were dead. Billie
had been killed by Tracy Coughlin, a nurse and mother.
Sandoval had been fatally shot by a police officer.

There was a bar in south Tulsa with a punched-up Mercedes
parked outside of it. Inside the bar were two men watching the
Channel Six broadcast.

The Channel Six reporter said that DEA agents were on the
scene as Javier Sandoval had been a "high-ranking member of
the Tijeras Cartel."

Hector sighed and turned to the other and said, "We got to
get out of here."

"Yeah," Miguel said.

It would be a long drive back to Dallas. They would have time to work out what they were going to tell Caesar before they got back.

SIXTY-SIX

Captain Devereaux was not surprised to see the chief of police at the Coughlin residence. The chief got there after the television reporters, who'd picked it up on the scanners. It was a high-profile event that put the Tulsa Police Department in a mostly favorable light. The chief would not want to pass up that sort of camera time.

At the scene was the community of emergency vehicles and media trucks that is typically present in the aftermath of a significant local crime. Dozens of patrol officers, from county and city. A couple of patrol officers went around telling the people from the television stations to get their vehicles off Lee Coughlin's lawn.

Captain Devereaux had already briefed the assistant chief, but had to do it all over again for the chief, before the chief could talk to the reporters and somehow take credit for what happened.

The chief wasn't all brass and P.R. though. His first question to Devereaux involved the status of the KBI agent who'd taken a bullet from Richard Billie.

Devereaux said, "He's going to be okay. The bullet broke his collarbone and he's lost some blood. He's at Tulsa Regional now, in stable condition."

The chief said, "Why was he here alone?"

Well, that was not easy to explain. Devereaux said, "We were about ten minutes behind him. We weren't sure the fugitives were here. It was Agent Prather's hunch. It turned out he was right." Devereaux paused and then said, "He deserves the credit, really."

The chief said, "But it was the woman who killed Billie?"

"Yes, sir. She surely did."

"I like that," the chief said, a smile on his face. A not uncommon policeman's reaction to justified self-defense.

Devereaux said, "She told the detectives there's around forty thousand dollars in the back of her Jeep, by the spare tire."

The chief said, "What?"

"A couple of guys from Sandoval's outfit brought it here. She gave a pretty good description of them to the DEA. Apparently, Sandoval promised the other two fugitives money to break him out."

"But why would she have it in her car?"

"It's a long story," Devereaux said. "You'll have to hear it a couple of times before you believe it. There she is now."

A couple of paramedics were bringing Lee Coughlin out on a stretcher. Tracy walked alongside, holding her son's hand. The captain and the chief couldn't hear what she was saying to the old man, though they could see that she was speaking to him in a calm, steadying voice. The way a nurse would.

There was a moment of hesitation at the ambulance. One of the paramedics apparently trying to dissuade her of something, shaking his head; maybe telling her there were regulations prohibiting her from riding in the ambulance. The policemen saw the woman lean forward to the paramedic, saying something pointed and direct. The paramedic shrugged his shoulders and made a conciliatory gesture. He backed away and walked to the front and got in behind the wheel. Then the woman and the boy climbed into the back of the ambulance with the old man. The woman pulled the doors shut from the inside and the ambulance drove away.

ABOUT THE AUTHOR

James Patrick Hunt is the author of *Maitland, Maitland Under Siege, Maitland's Reply, Get Maitland, The Betrayers, Goodbye Sister Disco, The Assailant, The Silent Places, Bullet Beth, Reinhardt's Mark, Bridger, Police and Thieves* and *The Detective.* He lives in Tulsa, Oklahoma where he writes and practices law.